The Outcast of Spirit Ridge

The Outcast of Spirit Ridge

A Keystone Ranch Story

JAMES C. WORK

Five Star • Waterville, Maine

September, 2006
First Edition

Published in 2006 in conjunction with
Golden West Literary Agency.

Set in 11 pt. Plantin.

Printed in the United States on permanent paper.

Library of Congress Cataloging-in-Publication Data

Work, James C.
The outcast of Spirit Ridge : a Keystone Ranch story / by James C. Work.—1st ed.
p. cm.
"Five Star western"—T.p. verso.
ISBN 1-59414-398-6 (hc : alk. paper)
1. Indians of North America—Great Plains—Fiction.
2. Water supply—Fiction. I. Title.
PS3573.O6925O95 2006
813′.54—dc22 2006008406

The Outcast of Spirit Ridge

A Note from the Author

The Outcast of Spirit Ridge is the first book in the Keystone series not to take its plot from an Arthurian legend, even though the main character is modeled (somewhat) upon a secondary figure in *Owain and the Fountain*. After he appeared in my second Keystone novel, my favorite daughter-in-law asked me when I was going to write another book about him. So, because of Pamela, here he is again, the black creature with one eye who lurks in the forests along the mountain irrigation ditch in *Ride West to Dawn*.

Once again, I've made free use of archetypes and obscure legends, myths, and tribal lore such as the Blackfoot story of Napi, who insulted a monster stone which chased him, breaking into pieces as it went. In Norse legend I found the tale of an earth goddess who travels among tribes in a covered cart and vanishes beneath a sacred lake. The Roman historian Tacitus recorded that story in *Germanica*, 40. The idea of a one-eyed creature is common throughout mythology, from the Scandinavian Loki to the race of Cyclopes in Greek myth. And the Cyclopes, coincidentally, were blacksmiths.

I chose to include Arapaho people for several reasons, although there was no connection between them and the Rocky Mountain irrigation schemes of the 19th Century. But as I learned more and more about them, I discovered I had stumbled into a bit of historical irony. In 1874, just ten years after the Sand Creek Massacre of the Arapahos, the

Rocky Ford irrigation ditch was built to carry Arkansas River water to farms for the growing of onions, sugar beets, potatoes, and melons.

Prologue

"You'd be a Keystone rider," the voice said. "The second one!" It laughed.

Kyle turned, bringing the Winchester up. He would never doubt Brother again. The creature was just like Brother said: shaped like a toad and black as if he'd been burned, squatting on a boulder across the ditch. He wore a leather hunting shirt and leggings, and in one black hand he held an iron bar a good six feet long, like a man would hold a walking stick. His one eye was slightly to one side of his flattened nose; of his other eye there seemed no sign at all, not so much as a scar.

"That your question, what does the water do?"

"Yeah."

The black shape laughed again. "Cowboy, it follows the course made for it. Of course . . . hah! . . . some of it evaporates and escapes the ditch, but the clouds bring it back. It will water a acre of oats for your horse. Or drown your horse. Or you. Then it comes back on the wind to do it all over again."

"You said it goes to a lake."

"Ah! Once a beautiful valley of grass and flowers where the deer grazed. Living things, you understand. Now the grass and trees and flowers and bushes are dead muck drowned under water. Hah! But it could make life, if it would."

"That ain't much of an answer. Why don't you just tell me how to get this gate open, at least a little ways?"

"One answer a day, Mister Keystone, one a day. Tell you a secret, though. You'll never lift it because that isn't the way it

works. Hah!" And he rose and went off, clanking his bar on the rocks. "Not the way it works!" he called back, shaking his huge head as if he had just heard the best joke in all the world.

from Chapter Seven, *Ride West to Dawn*

Chapter One

BURIAL ON THE PLAINS

Excerpts taken from the 1845 Oregon Trail diary
of Mr. Titus Aspill,
with permission of the Aspill family,
Sacramento California

March 18, 1845:

I could not possibly imagine a less promising group than ours. With each passing day I find myself ever more cheered by the prospect of leaving this wagon train immediately upon our arrival at the base of the Rocky Mountains. Let them persevere to Oregon or California alone! They may follow Rev. Whitman's "Great Migration" clear to China, for all of me.

Having neither wife nor child, I informed the wagon company that I might "drop out" at any time, whenever some settlement along the way seems to present me with a business opportunity. The farther we travel, the more anxious I am for that opportunity to occur.

The daily grumblings increase. Every morning is witness to some kind of new setback or unforeseen delay, each of which is enough to make some member of the expedition express a half-hearted resolve to turn around and retrace his steps eastward. However, the plain truth is that the most of us have better reason for pressing ahead than for returning to what may await us in the rear. Two men that I know of—and presumably others I know not of—are fleeing from unhappy marriages or non-marital paternity suspicions. One and possibly two look to be gamblers seeking to escape their creditors. A young couple (whose legal union seems to be a matter of conjecture) appears to be on the run from either his family or hers, or both. Half a dozen of our wagons contain families whose only hope for better fortunes—or, indeed, any kind of fortunes at all—is to reach the Promised Land on the Western coast.

The Israelites had their Moses, whereas we have Mr. Webster. A veteran of two prairie crossings, he is an exemplar of meticulous preparation. His wagon carries only a few changes of clothing and provisions sufficient to "see him through," all tied in tight oilskin bales or else stored in lightweight trunks of rawhide leather.

"It's been put down in writing," Mr. Webster told me, "and I told each one of them two or three times, you can't bring along everything you can cram into a wagon. The animals are going to get tired out, there's mountains and streams to cross. The only way to get through to Oregon is to travel light as you can."

Three wagons behind Mr. Webster's is the stark contrast of Mr. Fevre and his brood, a man who could serve as a benchmark of backward thinking. A butcher by trade, he seems to have left Philadelphia with rather more money and with rather more alacrity than one would associate with a butcher.

One of Fevre's two wagons has a fault in one axle causing the nut to work its way off periodically and causing the entire train to stop at least once a day so that he may go back in search of it. His animals are clearly fading, which is hardly surprising since his wagons are carrying the weight of an iron stove and elaborate bedroom suite without which his wife would not leave Philadelphia.

The butcher's lady has brought all of her clothing, and also that of her pack of children, all of which is stored in heavy wooden trunks.

Behind the Fevre wagons is the wagon of a teacher who is departing the comforts of the Atlantic coast determined to change his occupation for that of farmer. His wagon is packed with books he has not read; atop this load he has arranged a heavy steel plow and the metal parts of what appears to be a cultivating machine, all of it packed 'round with bales and kegs of provisions.

Observe the carpenter in the next wagon, hauling his massive bench and cumbersome chests of tools across the almost treeless American Desert. In the past two weeks, we have not seen enough wood to build a milking stool. His wife remarked at camp one evening that he had better turn shipwright when they reach the coast, for it will be her principal objective to return to Pennsylvania, and she will not do it by crossing overland again.

Two ladies traveling together with a much lighter burden (thanks to the effects of poverty on the accumulation of worldly goods) say they are spinsters and milliners fleeing a cruel father and hoping to make their fortune in the new country. I do not know what kind of milliners they may be, nor what the market for millinery is in Oregon. In the end, they may find their true best asset to be their spinsterhood.

The government and land company agents have promised these people nearly 200 acres apiece for making this crossing, provided they will settle on the land prescribed and remain there a period of three years. For this they will endure months of crawling across this arid, blazing waste, floods at river crossings, numberless varieties of biting insects, snakes and vermin, dying draft animals, and marauding Indians.

Upon arrival in Oregon, I believe they will discover they are in no way prepared to make their living as farmers. Most have never set plow to soil. Some are hard-pressed to hitch a team correctly.

"I have all the government pamphlets on the subject of raising wheat," one man told me. "Written by professors at a leading university. It is a very straightforward process and a man can make a great deal of money at it."

If he does manage to raise a crop, he will find little market for it. Transportation in the new land is primitive; there is almost no currency for payment; very few mills for the wheat have been built, and there are no presses for the fruit. If he is careful what he plants and chary in drying and storing it, his family may be able to subsist upon it through the long Western winter and set about doing it all over again.

March 21

Today we remain "stalled." We are fortunate to be encamped near running water, and the wind and clouds have kept the weather mercifully cool. The train is nervous, anxious over being forced to remain motionless in this vastness of dry and treeless grass. Water is ever and always our primary concern. To follow a creek or river too closely is to risk quicksand, bogs, and arroyos. To remain on the high ground incurs the danger of dehydration of livestock. While this region is covered in grass, nonetheless it is called a "desert" for good reason, and will never be settled for civilization unless men can discover how to exist without water.

★ ★ ★ ★ ★

Scouts were sent out and have returned to report we are little more than a day from the hills overlooking the Platte River, where we will find a well-traveled path and the possibility of meeting up with other wagons. They also report seeing in the distance a band of Indians traveling on a course paralleling our own. Mr. Webster, who was outvoted by those who two weeks ago became infatuated with the idea of following these dim wagon tracks dubbed a "short cut", observes that the detour has cost us several days.

"You may thank God," he announced last evening, "that the main trail is less than a day away from us. Your so-called 'democratic' procedure could very easily have gotten us hopelessly lost on these prairies."

The core of the difficulty, the reason the wagon train has "stalled" is Mrs. Grimes. She is a young free African woman, who is a mother and now widow. Her husband, George Grimes, died shortly after the wagon train left the main trail to venture along this "short cut" when a river crossing was encountered. The man leaped from his seat on the wagon and splashed ahead to calm the off leader, which had stepped into an unseen hole. He became entangled in the lines and was held under water by the panicked horse. By the time the whole confusion was resolved and the body recovered and the crossing finished, Mrs. Grimes was unable to do anything but sit on the wagon seat rocking her little black infant in her arms and crooning, her eyes wide and fixed upon the featureless horizon.

"Oh, George!" she wailed over and over as the men carried the corpse away from the river. "What will I do? What will I do? Oh, George, the baby!"

★ ★ ★ ★ ★

But the black woman has but one option and that is to stay with the other wagons and go ahead to California or Oregon. Friendly hands turned to and dug a proper grave for her husband, and words from the Good Book were read over him as the dirt was shoveled onto the canvas tarp that served as his winding-sheet. The widow has little to look forward to now, and even less to go back for even if she could.

We have been delayed now for two days. Mrs. Grimes is unable to drive, indeed unable to fix her poor vacant mind upon anything other than to ride on a mattress in the back of the wagon while one of the young men from the other wagons drives for her. She alternately sits up and lies down, all the while moaning in grief. The young man rolled the wagon cover up and tied it off that she might have the benefit of air and light. Alas, his well-meant action has led to tragedy. The little black baby somehow rolled or perhaps crawled to the edge of the load and without the canvas to prevent it from toppling off the wagon, the child fell overboard and struck its head on the iron rim of a wheel. The horses of the following wagon shied at the little body lying in their path, a hoof of the near horse kicking it, further damaging the skull.

Tender and sympathetic hands cleansed the babe's poor head, now resembling a dark melon that has gone soft and sagging on one side. The eye could not be saved. Bandages have been wrapped tightly around the head, leaving the mouth free as well as the remaining eye. But Mrs. Grimes seems not to know the infant now. When it is given to her, she merely sets it aside and looks first at it and then at the far horizon.

"Oh, George, where you be?" is her only expression.

The tight bandages wrapped around the head have staunched the blood, but the breathing is so faint, and the woman in such a state of mindlessness, that no one knows what will happen or what to do. Shall we all remain camped here until death resolves all? Or shall we press on, and take this poor wretch and her pathetic little bundle on to Oregon?

March 22

Indians have resolved the issue. Indians, and the inhumanity some whites show toward our Negro brethren. Scouts returned yesterday to report the band of Indians has altered its course parallel with ours, and is now following our tracks. By all appearances, it is a village with ponies, drags, and dogs in evidence.

"I don't know about you people," Mr. Webster announced, "but I intend to hitch up and start at once to reach the Platte River road. You must decide immediately whether to stay here with the African woman's wagon or help her come along."

No one seems to doubt that the child's soul will shortly wing its way toward the angels. Some of the women asked Mrs. Grimes whether she had anything in which to bury the infant "if the worst should happen."

The question seemed to bring her back. She sat there holding the injured infant and looking around until her eye fell upon her husband's large tool chest. She asked them to empty it, and then, handing her precious bundle to one of the women, she lined the sturdy box with a baby quilt.

"Dat'll have to do," she said mournfully, "for he is shore gonna die."

The white woman holding the babe was casting anxious looks toward the horizon behind us. And at last, the baby drew a long shuddering breath and let it out again and lay still. After putting an ear to the little mouth for some moments, she pronounced that the infant was gone.

As gently as possible, she eased the body into its makeshift coffin. Some of the men came forward, one carrying a shovel. Out of consideration for the feelings of the bereaved, the men forbore to nail down the lid right there in front of the child's mother but rather carried the load to a rise of ground for a hasty burial.

Such are the wrenching tragedies of crossing the Great Plains, where the unfortunate dead must be buried quickly in graves forever unmarked.

Mrs. Grimes stopped the men with a little cry of alarm, and all of us supposed she would run after them and reclaim the little corpse, unable to let herself believe he was truly dead. Consternation ran through the group: the Indians had been seen only a few miles distant and everyone was anxious to be moving again. But instead digging among the bedding and clothes in her wagon, she brought forth a long, heavy steel bar of the sort they call a "rock bar" for digging post holes in stony ground. She carried it to the men and pressed it upon them, saying they could not make a grave "proper deep" in this hard prairie without it. With rock bar, shovel, and their sad burden they hurried toward the rise of ground, then one turned back.

"Mr. Webster," he said, "you must certainly start the wagons. There is not a moment to lose. We will bury the child and run to catch up with you."

"Very well," Webster said. "God be with you."

March 23

In reviewing my journal, I find I have omitted a most curious incident regarding that very same steel digging bar. I was not witness to the incident, but rather heard it from Mr. Webster.

Upon the second day of travel, a few days before I joined them, the train came to a good camping site with ample water and forage. Even more fortuitous, it was unoccupied except for a most singularly large, muscular man making his way west by wagon. His camp included a portable forge and blacksmithing tools, for he was a blacksmith by trade.

Mr. Webster told me the smith was assiduously forging an oval of steel, like a link of chain—only in size it was the length of a man's forearm. Forging this chain seemed to be his only occupation, but as members of our wagon party began to converse with him, it became known that he had all manner of metal items for sale. He had good hooks for hanging pots over campfires, together with rods and clever iron tripods for the same purpose. He offered axes, lengths of trace chain, wagon rods, nails and hoops for the making of kegs.

The free African—George Grimes—who was soon to perish in the river and whose child was also doomed—was particularly interested in the blacksmith.

"My people used to have skill with fire and steel," he said. "Long time ago in Africa they were the masters of the forge and anvil and hammer. But in my pappy's time they lost the art. In Africa tribes, when they needed to pick them a new chief, it was the blacksmith what chose. Like a medicine man or magic man, he."

Grimes somehow discovered the steel digging bar. It was five and a half feet long or more, its girth approximately that of a sturdy shovel handle, and looked to weigh twelve pounds or more.

The blacksmith had not put this tool out with the others he wished to sell. When Grimes brought it forth and said he wished to have it, the blacksmith took him aside. Mr. Webster said he seemed to question the black man closely.

"That evening," Mr. Webster said, "Grimes told me the blacksmith asked three times if he was certain he wanted the bar. Three times. The smith called it a 'heavy encumbrance' and said it could pose great danger to him."

Grimes thought he meant some child might drop it on himself, or it might attract lightning or some such thing. But he persisted in bartering for it.

"Damn' strange thing is," Mr. Webster said, "that the blacksmith didn't seem to have any choice but to let it go. You'd think he could just say no, but all the time he was arguing and bartering, it was like he had to give it up. You could see he was awful anxious about it."

Whatever the blacksmith knew, it was not the future. George Grimes's drowning was in no way connected with the steel bar, nor was the accident of the infant.

That steel bar is now with the infant's body, unless the Indians have stolen it. I heard the account of digging the little grave from one of the two men who volunteered. Only myself and these two know the real story, for to make it public among the others of the train, particularly the women, undoubtedly would cause undue anguish.

"Hard digging," one of them told me. "We barely had a hole deep enough to hide the box when we saw the Indians. We wanted to make a proper grave, but there was no time."

With the Indians coming across the horizon in large numbers, they hunted frantically for rocks to pile on the box, as a cairn against marauding wolves, but they found none. They also realized they had neglected to nail down the lid.

"Then Adolph, he had an idea. We put that heavy big steel bar across the top of the box, jammed it into the corners of the hole diagonally. It was the best we could do for a way to keep the top down and keep the wolves out. At least a little while. All we could do. Besides that, neither one of us wanted to try to outrun the Indians lugging that bar along."

And so, after hastily scooping earth back over the pathetic little grave, they ran for all they were worth to catch the wagons just vanishing over the rise to the west.

March 24

We have today glimpsed Indians again, mere tiny silhouettes on the southern horizon, apparently moving toward some destination of their own. It is possible they are the same ones who nearly caught the burial party, but there is no way of knowing.

According to our scouts there is another wagon company just ahead of us. We should catch up with them tomorrow or the next day, which will give all of us considerable relief.

Chapter Two

A FOUNDLING AND ANCIENT GODS

The box was dark, warm, and quiet. Bit by bit, cell by tiny cell, the infant brain awakened. Along thread-like pathways leading to toes and fingers, the miniature nervous system searched for the sensations that were its only proof of living. The awakening brain tried to process smells and sounds and temperature. The body lay on its back, slowly assimilating the warm ambient darkness. The little lungs took in air, expelled it again. The network of skin cells sensed a familiar softness of fabric folded beneath. The nervous system discovered the tightness around the head, like a giant hand was clamped over the skull. And there was numbness to one side; one side had either swollen or shrunken against the tightness and was without feeling as though the nerves went through half the head and were abruptly cut off.

He came to consciousness. The remaining eye not covered by the wrappings opened but saw only darkness. The mouth, distorted and twisted by the tight binding of the head, opened as if to cry or to receive the nipple, then closed again and no sound came forth.

He lived.

In the darkness, with pain his only contact to any kind of world, he endured.

All he sensed was that all must surely be the same as it always was, even with this strange feeling about his head. It was the same and would be the same. He had always known the deep darkness of sleep, and knew it always slipped away into a coming of light. When the light came back, so did the face that filled his vision, bending over him and making soft noises. Then came the lifting hands and the arms that cradled him, the warm safe holding, then the breast and the milk.

The tiny brain being fed impulses by a nervous system scarcely two months old could not formulate thoughts, nor had it any awareness at all of past or future. It could do nothing except sense its surroundings. Still, the baby knew that the warmth and the breast had always been there. It was as sure as the air filling the lungs.

It was true that there was a new confusion of sensations, a dull pain, an uncomfortable tightness around his head, but even though it was strange it did not take away from the certainty of the rhythm which was his life. The coming of the light, the coming of the breast. In all his experience, there was certainty in the return of the light and the return of the breast. Everything else that he might have known, the sudden frightening sounds, the cold, the sting of wind-driven sand, all else was transitory and made bearable by the unfailing return of the light and the breast.

His infant lungs drew in air and let it out. His little lips moved in anticipation of the breast. He drifted back into sleep.

The shallow little pit was another in the long line of forsaken graves stretching back across the continent. They were a people from Europe, a land where their ancestors had built holy places of wood and wattle and then of stone and mortar, all to pacify God and provide themselves with a sanctuary against His wrath. In the shadow of these temples they created sanctified ground in which to preserve the corpses of their dead. But these European races turned out to be an ever-westering people. Even when they reached America, they continued to feel the urge to move westward.

And so, just as they buried their dead in Europe and then abandoned the continent, now the newest Americans buried their dead on forested hillsides overlooking the Atlantic Ocean and left them. Soon, the dearly departed were no more than names listed in a Bible. The living Americans were pioneers, new people, newly born to a new life on a new continent. They were free of the dead generations, free to keep going on.

There was another change. In abandoning their ancestral graveyards, they left behind them a history that was only physical. Some earth, some bones, some stone markers. But they had abandoned something else, something more mysterious and far more troubling.

On their former continent there had always been forests. They lived among such dense forests that they took them for granted. But when they finally westered across the Missouri River, they found themselves embarked on a vast treeless expanse that some called the Great Plains and that others called The Great American Desert. And it was precisely there, at the entrance to the treeless land, where a dim, nameless apprehension seemed to set in. Their myths and legends were full of forest gods, dryads, goblins, druids, nymphs, brownies, faeries, all manner of animating spirits in the dense woods of Europe. Now, these supernatural beings were left behind, just as the dead ancestors had been.

Sometimes a full moon cast eerie light over endless miles of prairie grass that moved in the night like the waves of the ocean, even when there was no wind. Sometimes hard, sudden bolts of lightning slashed down from a cloudless sky to kill a team of oxen in its tracks. Sometimes on moonless nights the deep arroyos moaned in the dark. And at such times as these, some of the New People suspected that they had come into the presence of new and unknown forces. They no longer had churches or any kind of sanctuary, and these were invisible forces they did not know how to appease.

However ephemeral they were to the white people, the invisible powers of the Great Plains were well known to the Indians who the scouts had seen following the wagon train. The Indian band, traveling west, called themselves The People. They were The People in the Center of the World, who the Hidatsu called the "buffalo path people." Like the whites, they were making a sort of migration. Unlike the whites, who moved their lodges on great heavy wheels, pulled by animals they called "whoa-haws", The People moved their lodges on travois pulled by ponies and dogs.

Also unlike the whites, the Indians were not making a march into the future. Rather, it was a migration moving backwards in time, an unprecedented and very important journey toward the dark mountains where, according to legend, The People had originated. Those who undertook this trek were small in number, a group that had separated itself from the four main camps of the tribe. The occasion was so solemn and so important that their leader had given up his ordinary name and had submitted to a ceremony in which he was given the name of Standing Hollow Horn. It was done in order to honor an elder of one of the seven tribes of the First People. Long ago, before the memory of the great-great-great grandfather of the oldest person in the tribe, the elder named Standing Hollow Horn feared for his people. He sent young men to search for White Buffalo Calf Woman and beg her help for the tribe.

This is the story of the second Standing Hollow Horn, the man who led the people along the new wagon road toward the distant mountains.

For a longer time than many generations could remember, The People followed the buffalo path in the land where the sun was a god. Like the Kiowas and Lakotas, they performed sun dances and flourished under the protection of the buffalo. But always they listened to the stories of the elders who spoke of an earlier time, a First Time when their people had different gods. These gods lived a great distance away, back in the shadowy valleys of the mountains where The People first came out of the earth. The elders told of a time when there were no people. Then First Pipe Keeper fasted and prayed. Creator told First Pipe Keeper how to make the land and the people. It happened in those high mountains where the sun goes to sleep.

One elder was now worried. He worried about these changes in the land. These wagon people, these new animals, many new things. One day three hunters from another band came to The People and spoke of seeing a white buffalo calf. This had great meaning to the elder: in the old story, the birth of a white calf meant The People were entering an End Time. White Buffalo Calf Woman said so. He worried.

He took his worry with him to the shade of a small shelter built of sticks on a high hill away from camp. There he tied two eagle feathers to his long lance and thrust the point into the ground as a sign to others that he would fast and pray and did not wish to be disturbed. With uplifted arms he cast his worry into the sky, and then lay down under the shade to wait.

The eagle came on the morning of the third day, just a high speck in the dazzling sky.

"What do you see up there?" he called to the eagle.

The eagle circled downward and downward until it came to rest upon the shade shelter. It spoke a single word, gazing steadily toward the Direction-Where-Sun-Sleeps, The Yellow Way. Then it rose on great wings and disappeared.

"Mountains," was the only word the eagle had said.

The elder rose. He ate dried meat and pemmican from his pouch and drank from his water gourd. He took his long lance and walked among the tall lodges and spoke to everyone. He asked who would go with him to the mountains where The People first came out onto the earth. He said they needed to find the old gods of The People and ask them what was happening in the world. They would take gifts, tobacco and meat and the colored stones that made the Arikaras call them "the colored stone people" or "the blue stone people". After leaving their gifts and singing their sacred songs, they would pray for the mountain gods to tell them what The People must do. To show his commitment, he adopted the name Standing Hollow Horn. From that day on he would do nothing to bring shame upon that name.

Some argued against him, saying that The People in the Center had left those gods long ago and those gods would be angry to be disturbed by people who had forgotten them. Some argued against him by saying they were afraid of an attack by their enemies, the Utes or even the Pawnees or Crows, and they would need every warrior if that happened. But in the end, he found enough to go with him, enough families for six lodges, including six young men and four older men who were warriors. Crows Woman also said she would come with her lodge and her man, who was a white man.

The small band traveled steadily. One day they came to a village of lodges that looked like boxes being built on flat land where the grass was poor and where there were no buffalo paths. Another day, they stopped to trade at a new soldier village where the children laughed to see the white warriors sweating in heavy blue coats and practicing all walking the same way.

Farther on, they came to another soldier village, but it was burned. Brambles grew among the fallen and charred logs. After that they saw no more wooden walls or fences, no more square lodges. They saw only the tracks of wheels going in the yellow direction. They followed these tracks, but not because they were following the wagons and the whites. The tracks led toward the ancestors' mountains and followed the wide river. They stayed on the buffalo paths paralleling the wagon road, where there was no dust and better grass.

One day, The People came over a little hill and in the distance they saw some wagons also on the buffalo path. The wagons had stopped, but when the wagon people saw the Indians, they shouted at their whoa-haws and whipped them until the wagons began moving. There was much yelling and confusion.

Then two men jumped up out of the grass and went running after the wagons.

"They were sleeping and we surprised them!" Young Bear said.

"No," said Horse Boy. "They were squatting over their own droppings and we surprised them!"

The People stopped at the place and saw where the two men had been digging.

"What does it mean?" Young Bear asked.

"Those wagon people, they buried something here,"

Standing Hollow Horn said. "You boys go and bring Two Nose to me. He is not a wagon person, but he is a white person. He will probably know whether we should dig it up or leave it alone."

The white man's name was Two Nose Thomas. He was a trapper and a trader of fur and had taken Crows Woman as wife. Or she had taken him as her husband. No one really knew. Crows Woman said she would follow Standing Hollow Horn back to the mountains of the ancestors, and Two Nose Thomas said he would go along because it would be a good place to trap prime pelts. So the two of them packed their lodge and belongings onto two travois and went along.

Two Nose walked up and stood beside Standing Hollow Horn, looking down at the fresh dirt. He did not say anything at first, for he had been with the Indians long enough to know not to do things in haste. So, he stood with his long rifle cradled in his folded arms and regarded the mound.

Standing Hollow Horn pointed in the direction of the vanishing wagons and then at the mound and then grunted something about people who scatter things as they go along. It is typical, his gesture said.

"True," said Two Nose. "Wagon people leave plunder aplenty."

It *was* true. Alongside the wagon trails of the Great Plains there stretched a veritable refuse dump of discarded objects, ranging from stoves and bed frames and grindstones to kegs of spoiled flour and broken crockery.

Standing Hollow Horn looked at the mound and then at Two Nose, his question written on his face.

"No tellin'," Two Nose said in answer to that unspoken query. "Howsomever, it 'taint a dead body, I'm thinkin'.

Too small a hole. Might be they cached somethin', thinkin' to come back soon and git it."

He handed his rifle to Crows Woman and knelt at the mound. With bare hands he dug the dirt aside and discovered the steel bar wedged across the hole.

"Hmm."

He pulled the bar loose and handed it to the nearest man, who handed it to the next, who handed it to the next. Out of politeness, each man took it and examined it closely as if it were a present. It was finally handed to Standing Hollow Horn. He, too, looked it over carefully. He hefted it to feel its weight. He tried cradling it in his arm after the manner of holding a long peace pipe or rifle, but it was awkward. He took a few steps, holding the bar as he would hold a long lance, but again it felt clumsy. He thrust it, point first, into the ground and left it there. He did not want it.

Two Nose went back to brushing the dirt away from the box until they could lift it up. It was also heavy, like the steel bar.

"Tools, maybe," Two Nose muttered, opening the lid.

Two Nose and Standing Hollow Horn together looked into the box, then looked at each other, then stepped back and motioned for Crows Woman to approach. This was a woman's matter.

Crows Woman drew the small blanket aside and took up the infant. One eye opened and looked steadily at her. The other eye was covered by a bandage; indeed, the whole head except for the one eye and the mouth was tightly wrapped in blood-stained cloth.

Two Nose Thomas looked at the thing lying so quietly in his wife's arms. He touched one of the naked arms. "God Almighty," he said. "Skin's as black as th' inside of yore hat. This hoss has seen a right smart of Negras, rangin' from light t'dark, but never seed one so black as that. Never did see one buried alive, neither."

Crows Woman and another woman spread the blanket on the grass and put the baby on it to unwrap the bandages. There was some blood on the misshapen little head, and a dark purplish bruise discolored the whole side of the face like a hideously huge birthmark on the black skin. The head, once round and chubby, had been caved in on that same side as if some careless person had put his foot down on an overripe squash. The eye was gone entirely, the loose flap of bloody skin where the eyelid should be having already begun to congeal and stick fast over the eye cavity.

"God Almighty," Two Nose Thomas repeated, looking down at the pathetic bundle as Crows Woman set about rewrapping the damaged head. "Black ez coal t'start with, then bashed in so bad he lost a eye, wrapped up like some kinda sausage and *then* his people leave 'im in a shallow hole t'die. There's a Negra God Himself must 'a' had a grudge against."

Crows Woman cradled the infant in her arms. "Grudge?" she said. She had never heard the word before, but it sounded soft and at the same time firm in the mouth. It sounded like the language of her people, sweet and soft. "Grudge," she said. And looking down into the face, into the one eye that was fixed upon her, she said again: "Grudge."

So it became his name. Some of The People from the center, the Buffalo Path people, tried to suggest his name should be He Who Was Left, or Man Buried, or even Iron Stick because of the steel bar that seemed to be his only heritage. But Crows Woman liked the way her mouth moved when she said "Grudge," and after a time the baby learned to respond when she said it, and so he had a name.

The People did not know what the name meant, no more than they understood why the child had been buried in such a manner. How could the spirits find it, covered with earth like that?

It might be, they decided, that the wagon people had tried to return the child to the mothering earth in this way, by cutting open the earth and putting the child back. But it did not make sense. A shaman named Who Sees Far was with the band, and he said the whites had been afraid of the child because of the way it looked out from one eye. He could tell, even without performing any more of a ritual than fanning the infant with the eagle wing fan and blowing some tobacco smoke in its face, that the infant had powers. Perhaps the wagon people always buried such children.

Crows Woman's best friend brought a large cradleboard she no longer needed, and so Grudge was bound into soft furs and strapped onto the board where he would be safe. In this manner he could be carried on the travois, or hung from the saddle; when the band stopped to rest, he could be propped up against a tree. Twice each day Crows Woman unbound him and undressed and cleaned him, and she saw from his short, curved legs that he would never be a runner. He would be slow. But he was very strong. And there was something in the way he peered out from beneath his tight head-wrapping, his head bound to the cradleboard, that told her he did indeed have powers.

Standing Hollow Horn's small group continued to follow The Yellow Way toward where the sun sleeps until it led them into ancient places that they knew only from stories. It took them into the high, deeply shadowed mountain valleys where the First People, their ancestors, had emerged from the underground and had first walked on the earth. They discovered beautiful valleys with clear, cold streams and deep grass where the hunters killed deer for fresh, sweet meat. The young men caught fish in the crystal streams. The women found forests of tall, straight lodge poles. This was good; The People took pride in having the tallest, straightest lodges of all the Plains Indians.

Two Nose Thomas followed small streams up into other valleys and trapped many beaver for their pelts. He trapped otter and gave them to Crows Woman. She would keep them as gifts for her friends, who would make them into delicate strips for their men to bind their long braids.

Standing Hollow Horn and Who Sees Far went off to high places to fast and to pray. They made offerings of colored stones and meat to the gods, but they had no answer. Frustrated, Standing Hollow Horn starting talking to the gods of the First People even while he was walking or riding his pony, although he knew they were not listening. What way should we follow? he asked. What trail is best for The People? Some, like Bad Hand, are learning the talk of the white wagon people. Some say we should join with other tribes against these whites. Some say the buffalo will disappear and sickness will come. No one knows where the spirit lodge has gone or how to find it.

In the end, the band returned out of the mountains and traveled back along the path of the iron wheels beside the river and came again to the rest of their tribe with nothing to report and nothing to show for the journey except for some fine lodge poles, some soft otter skins, and a deformed black infant with one eye who had been found buried under an iron stick.

Five winters went by and life got no better. Then, after another fasting vigil, Standing Hollow Horn had a vision of another place in the mountains. Many of the same people who had gone with him the first time went with him again. Others joined them; the women wanted new lodge poles and the men wanted to hunt elk. Elk teeth were prized trade items.

This time, the black one with one eye, the one who the whites had thrown away, went with them, riding his own small pony. With his short, bowed legs he rode more like a Comanche. He was still as black as burned wood. The skin had grown over his eye socket and that same side of his head was flat from long binding in the cradleboard. Crows Woman watched him as he grew, knowing in her heart what it was like to be different. She herself was not one who had been born to The People. And she had taken a white man.

And there was more to it than that. Ever since she was a girl, Crows Woman had been aware that she had certain gifts, certain powers of seeing and of healing that every instinct told her to keep to herself. Now she began to see how Grudge had medicine, too.

One day he was sitting beside her, watching her sew trade beads on a moccasin. He had gathered two handfuls of tall grass from the streambank and was busy weaving them into the shape of a lodge.

"Look there," she said to him. "Look at your friends playing at their game. You should play, too, not sit here with an old woman doing nothing."

"I cannot speak with them. Let them play."

"You speak well," Crows Woman corrected him. "My friend, One Hawk Rising, said to me she has never known one so young to know so much of the words of The People. You speak with me. You also understand the strange talk of Two Nose. What is this medicine that teaches you the language of so many others?"

"Mother," he said politely, "these children, they speak

as babies. They do not know many words. All they talk about is play and eating. I would rather be with the older boys who are learning to ride and hunt, but I am too small for them."

Crows Woman was right. Grudge spoke in adult words. Two Nose claimed that the boy had only to hear a word once and he could repeat it. He knew things no one had taught him, such as how to weave long grass into shapes of lodges and even of animals. When he did play with the others of his age, Grudge soon had them on their knees in the dirt, or in the mud beside the river, making miniature villages or drawing animals with sticks. The most remarkable thing was his strength, many times that of any other child of his years.

One day Two Nose went looking for Grudge and found him in a grove of trees with some of the other children. Grudge had managed to lift a long log, a small cottonwood, over another fallen tree to make a kind of see-saw for them to play on.

"Right smart lad," Two Nose said as he took Grudge home. "Tomarra we'll fetch the axe an' I'll show 'ee how t'notch thet log so's it won't be slippin' off t'other 'un."

The shaman Who Sees Far and Standing Hollow Horn also took notice of Grudge's precocious development. However, it meant a great deal more than Two Nose or any white person could even suspect. The black boy with the deformed head and missing eye showed signs of becoming a water dreamer. He was weaned at three—not uncommon—and shortly afterward he was found beside a small stream running among the prairie grass, talking to it. Twice in the year that followed, it was he who told his mother, who told Two Nose, who told Standing Hollow Horn, when the tribe would find running water. He would not throw sticks at the water striders as the other boys did, nor would he go with them to spear the fish. One boy even told his mother how he had seen the little black one cause a small creek to stop and back up, but this was the same boy who said he had seen a burning man rise out of the cooking fire.

Who Sees Far was himself a cloud dreamer who drew his prophetic and divinatory powers from clouds, as had been his vision when a young man. Standing Hollow Horn was a buffalo dreamer, one of the most important and elusive kinds of power to have. Both men, however, could only see their visions after several days of fasting and prayer. The one Crows Woman called Grudge seemed able simply to walk to a high place and point into the distance and that is where a good stream would be. They had heard of water dreamers among various tribes, but never thought they lived among the whites of the wagon road. Perhaps, Who Sees Far said, it explained why the white wagon people had thrown him away. Perhaps they thought that, by giving the child back to the earth, they could make the rain come. But they seemed to be lost and looking for the wagon road beside the big river, Standing Hollow Horn replied. Why throw away a water dreamer who could point the way? And Who Sees Far said, remember he was newly born at that time. It may be that there was a witch among those humans who resented his power and wanted to be rid of him.

The second trek into the far mountains ended as had the first, with many good lodge poles and skins for trade and for decoration. But Standing Hollow Horn found no sign of the ancient gods. He prayed and fasted. He climbed up to high places to study all the surrounding peaks and ridges for some sign that the Old Ones lived there. The summer gave way to colder nights and shorter days, and with reluctance he led his small band back down to the plains to rejoin the tribe. On the return trip, they seemed to see even more of the white people on the wagon road, and they saw fewer signs of buffalo.

Four more winters passed and Standing Hollow Horn decided to set out once again for the ancestral mountains although he was becoming too old for long days of riding and especially for long days of fasting on the snow-patched passes among the peaks.

Grudge by now was so strong that he carried burdens his mother could not lift. He stopped wrestling with other boys because he saw they were afraid of him. As a game he would wrap his thick arms around two boys his age and lift them both at the same time. It was a game they did not much care for, but they still liked to play with him. He was very clever with his hands. If the children wanted to catch insects or small animals or birds, it was Grudge who could build an ingenious trap or a snare. He showed them how to throw stones with a long forked stick.

Standing Hollow Horn wanted to enter the mountains at the place where they had earlier built a medicine circle. "Perhaps the old gods found it after we left," he told Two Nose Thomas, "and have left us some sign there. It would be good to stop and pray."

The circle of stones lay in the first range of mountains on a high tableland from which both the tall mountains and the flat plains could be seen. Standing Hollow Horn's band lingered there for several days, adding large stones to the outside circle and smaller stones to the lines running through it, each person praying in his own way.

Two Nose Thomas went looking for Grudge and found him on a rock in the middle of a stream a long way from the medicine circle. The boy was squatting there, looking like a large dark toad dressed in deer skins. He was facing up-stream, his steel bar resting on the rock beside him. Unaware of Two Nose's presence, he spoke loudly against the rumbling of the fast-moving water.

"You!" he said in English. "You water! Here's Grudge, *waugh!* I know you! Why, ye're hyar all the way from the shinin' mountains. Traveler, you are. Fresher'n mare's milk, an' sweet. We palaver, you and me. Say whar we find the gods for Standing Hollow Horn. It's Grudge askin' it, in the name of The People From the Center. Tell me!"

Two Nose watched as Grudge repeated this four times. It was a mite strange to hear the young one making white talk, but Two Nose knew how Grudge spoke white when he wanted to sound powerful. The boy took dry sage from a pouch on his belt and sprinkled it. Then he sat and listened. Finally, discouraged, he slid down off the rock, picked up his steel bar, and waded through the current to the shore where Two Nose stood.

"Water palaver with ye?" Two Nose asked.

The boy looked up into his face, concern and sympathy showing in his one eye. "*Waugh,*" Grudge said. "This water don't know. This hyar water wonders if mebbe the gods went under, passed over t'the other place. It says maybe when The People left 'em, the gods ciphered they'd been throwed away. And so they left."

"Waal," Two Nose said, putting his arm around the boy's thick shoulders, "mebbe so. Might happen thet ye're the hoss what's gonna find them ol' gods again, one day. Tomarra we'll hunt beaver acrost the mountain. Y'kin mebbe larn somethin' from that crick thet's over thar."

"All the water runs away," Grudge said, jabbing a hole in the ground with his stick.

" 'Course it does," Two Nose said. "Runs downhill, don't it."

"Not that," Grudge said, now using his mother's language. "Away from The People in the Center. All the water. It will stay in the sky or go to Spirit Lake until the gods come back. The land where the buffalo eat grass will be dry."

Two Nose spoke in Indian. "Does water tell where Spirit Lake is found?"

"No. Far over the mountains. On the other side of the snow."

Chapter Three

OUTSIDERS

Over the prairie, winter's freezing wind went howling as if they were in pain. When it came from the south, it seized up pellets of hard snow and slung it like miniature hail against The People's tall lodges. The north wind drifted dry snow into coulées and gullies, leaving the brown grass as brittle and bare as before. Then the west wind soughed down off the mountains with its warm breath to suck up all moisture until only a few patches of mud were left to show where the snow had been.

This procession of changing winds went on all winter, like a circle dance. The buffalo herds drifted with it, wandering this way and that way, forcing The People to move the entire camp many more times than was usual. The hunters rode farther and stayed out days longer than anyone could remember.

Spring brought a few rains, but for the most part the water did exactly what it had told Grudge it would do. It stayed in the sky in the high white clouds that went flying west over the mountains. No one had ever seen clouds do that before. Clouds often blew from the mountains, and sometimes clouds came off the prairie to strike the mountain range. But no one remembered a time when so many high clouds went over the mountains. Who Sees Far went to a high hill and tried to talk to the clouds, but they were too far away to hear him. A young hunter became frustrated because the watering places of the buffalo and antelope were drying up, so he shot an arrow at a cloud. But he missed and the arrow fell back and tore a hole in the lodge of Red Pipe, who went shouting and chasing after the young man until he had to sit down to catch his breath.

There came another ominous sign. One day, the clouds gathered into vast-reaching herds, turning the sky into greenish-looking darkness. A group of The People who were searching for berries saw the clouds boiling and colliding with one another until one mass put forth an angry-looking finger, a curved finger like a long talon, and touched the earth. They heard the terrifying roar and saw bushes and trees lifted into the air. The wind blew them down and they crawled into a ravine so they would not be blown away. After the wind stopped, they went to the place it had been and saw the deep wound in the earth and the broken cottonwoods. The earth's wound was a deep gully running with thick red water and foaming with froth.

Sky and earth were angry, even with each other. Many wondered if they had done something to anger the grandfather spirits, but no one could think what it might be.

The dry summer turned to an autumn that was even drier, and too soon the winter winds returned to howl around the lodges. There were meetings almost every day now, the elders coming together in one lodge to sit in their somber circle, sharing food and deliberating the meaning of the drought. They were a nomadic people and a religious people; it was their way, as it was the way of their ancestors, to put their faith in movement. They should move the camp, make a long migration if necessary, but first they would need a sign. Perhaps something would tell them where the buffalo were going. Then they could follow.

Young men volunteered to ride out in search of the herds. The elders talked and waited.

But there were no buffalo to be found.

There came a day, early in the spring, when things seemed ready to change. There was a good rainstorm, after which there were new shoots of grass and some flowers in bloom. The People had been moving for many, many days and now they had come to a running stream where there was good grass for the horses. Hunters shot antelope and rabbits. It was the best camp they had seen in a long, long time. Old people rested in the sun. Young couples walked long walks together. Little children shouted and laughed and chased the dogs.

Among the group of older boys, which now included Grudge, there were hunting games and war games. They practiced with bow and lance and bragged about the brave deeds they would do when the great herds of buffalo were found. Or when the enemy came. One day a young warrior who had traveled among many tribes showed the boys the way of the dog soldier. Taking a long strip of leather, he tied it around his waist like a sash, leaving the end to trail on the ground. With an arrow he pinned the end of the sash to the earth. He nocked another arrow to his bowstring and stood in a defiant stance, ready to do battle.

"The dog soldier will not pull his arrow from his sash. Here he will fight and will not be moved until he or the enemy is dead."

The older boys were very impressed by this and soon could be seen sporting long sashes and playing a game in which one would pin his sash to the ground and the others would try to frighten him away from that spot with feints of their lances and even blows across his back. This was good bravery, they said. This is the way to intimidate an enemy.

The most wondrous, most miraculous thing to happen that spring was when the first of the outsiders came to the village. He was the one they called Black Robe, and with him he brought the buffalo.

He came riding up over the horizon one morning, leading a pack horse. He had visited The People before, this thin, earnest-looking man with the long black robe and wide black hat. They had seen him Where The Water Turns on the big river. They had seen him near the place where pipestone is found. He never asked for anything. He spoke in two languages, Two Nose said, and all he wanted was for The People to listen while he told stories about his holy man. They listened, but no one knew his words.

Several elders raised their hands in greeting and walked out to meet him. He, in turn, rode toward them, holding aloft the metal cross he wore on a chain around his neck. He paused on a rise of ground at a respectful distance from the lodges, knowing it was impolite to ride closer without invitation. He called out to them in the few words of their language he knew, but his pronunciation was bad and he spoke too loudly. The elders walked nearer so they could invite him into the village.

And then they saw the buffalo.

As they approached Black Robe, ascending the little rise of ground, they saw the buffalo in the prairie beyond.

The animals were no more than small specks on the distant skyline, specks that moved down into the wide and grassy flat plain between hills and began to graze, but there was no doubt what they were. There were hundreds and hundreds of them. There could be no doubt. Black Robe had led the buffalo back to The People.

After three days of hunting came three days of feasting. The feet of the dancers pounded the joy of The People against the mothering earth while the smoke of all the cooking fires carried prayers of thanks skyward. Black Robe became guest of honor in any lodge he approached, women offering him food and warm robes to sleep on and everyone trying to talk to him at once. Speaking through Two Nose Thomas, he told how his own chiefs in the big lodge of the black robes had given permission for him to baptize The People and make them know the will of God and the power of Jesus.

The elders took this information into council, sitting in Three Eagles's lodge and patting stomachs that had not been so full of buffalo meat in many seasons. There could be no harm in what Black Robe wanted. Two Nose was summoned for his advice and the elders questioned him closely.

Did Black Robe say where he found the buffalo?

No. They seemed to follow him.

Black Robe asks for nothing?

No. He is harmless.

He carries no weapon? Is he a shaman, then?

No. He speaks for the shaman.

He speaks in a strange tongue and worships a foreign god.

Why hold that against him? Because he led the buffalo to us, and on the word of Two Nose, we will allow this baptism. It is done with water?

Yes.

Good. Perhaps a water ceremony will bring the rain back.

Black Robe had taken notice of Grudge. It was hard not to notice the round black figure who was always sitting with his long steel bar. He belonged to the lodge of Crows Woman and Mr. Thomas.

"What shall be his Christian name?" he asked Two Nose.

"Christian name? Waal, Reverend, he never said. He be a cast off, that 'un. Fur ez enybody knows, he never had a name. Funnin' around, y'understan', this here hoss lets slip thet thar was a Negra chile' the gods had a grudge ag'in' and I'll be a pork-eater iffen Crows Woman don't take a shine t'th' sound of it. So Grudge we calls him."

"Grüdj," repeated Black Robe, mispronouncing it in his thick Norwegian accent.

"Somethin' like that," Two Nose said.

"In Norway we might call him Loki."

"Loki?" Two Nose said.

"Yah. Because of his one eye, you know. In some of the stories he only has the one eye, Loki. Oh, he had a bad time. Loki, he was a hero, but he fought with the gods. The old gods, I mean. You know how they punished him?"

"Can't say as I do," Two Nose admitted.

"Chained him to three boulders, rocks! Then they put a serpent, a snake, to drip venom on him. But his wife . . . she's named Sigyn . . . she protects him by catching that venom in her wooden bowl, you know. Problem is she has to go empty the bowl sometimes."

"It figgers," Two Nose said.

"Yah. And when she's gone to empty the bowl, that poison venom? It falls on Loki's face. That pain, it makes Loki twist and struggle and moan, and that's what makes the earthquakes happen. Norway kids, they hear of an earthquake or even thunderstorms and they say . . . 'Ah, there's old Loki again, twisting in his pain.' It doesn't pay to fight with the gods."

"Waal, Reverend, yore story shines, so it does. I'm figgerin' the name Grudge sorta kivvers th' same ground."

* * * * *

The itinerant evangelist took particular interest in the younger Indian people, those who might learn some English or Norwegian and someday spread the word of the Bible through the tribes. He took special pains to come up with an appropriate Christian name for each one and to teach it to them. He took it a step further: on his last visit to his home church—the Big Lodge, as Mr. Thomas called it—he acquired a supply of cheap brass disks, punched to hang on a cord of sinew. One side was stamped with a cross, and under the cross was stamped the word **JESUS**. Each time he baptized someone, he gave them a name he chose from the Bible. Then, each evening, Black Robe sat at the fire with his disks and a pointed tool, inscribing the names of those he had baptized. Before long, every youth in camp was wearing a brass disk with a Christian name on it.

All but Grudge.

Black Robe prayed for enlightenment and read his Bible fervently, but for the life of him he could not come up with a proper-sounding name for this very black, almost shapeless, one-eyed being. He was not a John, or an Isaiah, or even a Moses. He was strong as Samson or even Goliath, but so ugly. It seemed sacrilegious to name such a creature after any of the Biblical people, especially any of the saints or prophets, and so in the end he took his pointed tool and one of the brass disks and engraved the creature's name as well as he could: **Grüdj**

The black, one-eyed boy stood quietly while Black Robe prayed over him. He remained still while the fingers dipped water and dripped it onto his head. And afterward he allowed the loop of sinew with the brass disk to be draped around his neck. When it was over, the others who had been through the ceremony that day sat politely listening to

Black Robe as he talked in his strange tongue and pointed toward the skies and talked some more. Grüdj did not stay to listen. Instead, he walked upstream along the creek and prodded the water with his steel bar, trying to make the water talk to him. This creek had drawn The People to it and now many buffalo had returned. Grüdj found it strange. What did it mean?

He came to a place where the creekbed narrowed and the water flowed over a rock into a deep pool. The falling water seemed to say his name with the accent of Black Robe: "Grr-ooo-dj." He lay down on the grassy bank with his head out over the narrow dark place and put his steel stick down into it.

"What water are you?" he said in Crows Woman's tongue. "Do you come from the mountains where the old gods live?"

At first the water only went on burbling and moaning into its deep pool and making the sound "Grr-ooo-dj." Then suddenly it seized hold of his stick and nearly succeeded in wrenching it out of his hand. At the same time the water lunged up at the brass disk, splashing in Grüdj's face and blinding him, ripping at the sinew around his neck. He pulled back and rolled away and the water had to let go of his steel bar because it had never felt so much strength in one person before. The water became quiet and went on flowing and did not talk to him again.

Summer saw more feasting and good deep grass. Black Robe's visit gradually faded until it was just one of many stories told around the lodge fires. The brass disks became headdress ornaments, or were sewn onto special shirts. Some were heated and pounded into more decorative things such as rings and ear hoops, while a few young men experimented by making them into arrow points. Time passed pleasantly. Only the memory of the drought was a worry to The People. This summer the water was good in most of the streams and the hunters had enough buffalo. But none of the elders knew what to do if the dry time should return.

Late summer found The People camped near yet another river, this one called Broken Grass, when the runners made their visit.

There were two of them. One was a Cheyenne, a very fast runner and exceptionally handsome even by Cheyenne standards. No one could say for certain what tribe the other young man was from, but he, too, was handsome and a fast runner. Some of The People looked at his moccasins and his arm band and said he might be Nez Percé, but others said no. Some said he might be Pawnee, although the Pawnees had not been seen in that country for many years. Nor, for that matter, had any runners been seen.

The two young men were welcomed with solemn cordiality. People nodded to them and offered them food and water, but no one spoke. They accepted the bowls of meat and the water skin, then walked through the camp, followed by a crowd of people until they came to the lodge of Standing Hollow Horn, where they stopped. There they sat down, cross-legged, and set the food bowls and water skin before them and waited. A murmur went among the people. These were indeed very polite young men.

The flap of the lodge moved and Standing Hollow Horn came out. It was a signal for six other elders to step forth. They sat down in a semicircle, facing the strangers, and meat bowls were brought for them. When everyone had meat, the handsome Cheyenne runner raised his bowl to the sky, then lowered it, and took a piece in his fingers, putting it to his mouth gracefully.

The others ate. While they were eating, The People spoke in excited tones so that it made a murmur like bees in a hollow tree. What message have the runners brought? Has anyone ever seen them? One old woman remembered a time when runners came to The People. Afterward, many young men went away with their bows and lances and never returned. Then, too, her mother had told her of a time when the buffalo had vanished and runners brought word where antelope were to be found. The hunters went there and saw more antelope than anyone had ever seen in one place before.

Suddenly those who were standing nearest heard the Cheyenne speak The People's language as perfectly as if he had been born to it. His words were passed back through the crowd, and then the crowd was silent.

The medicine lodge was coming. The spirit lodge.

For now, that was all that needed to be said. Having eaten, the Cheyenne said they were tired from running all the way from the camps of the Blue Bead People and would rest. The one who might be Nez Percé or Pawnee had a thorn in his foot that needed attention. So the elders rose respectfully and the runners were shown into the lodge of Standing Hollow Horn. Tomorrow there would be more talk.

The news was so important, so stunning, that even the old woman who gossiped would not talk about it unless a shaman was present. She would tell what she knew, she said, but only if a shaman was there to verify her story and say what was true if she happened to remember things wrongly.

So they gathered, the people, the old woman, and Who Sees Far. Beside the waters of the Broken Grass the old one told what she knew of the medicine lodge. Often she stopped to shake her head, worrying her memory as a camp dog might worry a piece of old deer hide.

"It all began," she said, "when The People left the northern mountains. It was a coming-out for them. They would never more return to the country of deep valleys and cold peaks. There were powerful spirits, powerful gods in the mountains, but The People turned away and forgot them. Everyone remembers this story. They became people of the open plain, people of the place where the sun ruled. The sun became one of their gods. Here they forgot how to live in lodges made of brush, because there was no brush. They learned to live in lodges made of buffalo hide stretched over long poles they brought from the mountains. A lodge gave them shade in summer, warmth in winter, and protection from wind. Someone once came to The People and showed them how to make these lodges, how to make them tall so the fire smoke could get out, how to make the bottom snug against the wind."

This person, the person who taught about the lodges, who was it? The old woman did not know. Who Sees Far shook his head. It was a shame that such a memory would be lost.

The woman continued: "The People realized they had changed. Now they lived in the land of the sun. Three young men were chosen to travel toward the sun's resting place and offer him presents and tell him they wished to live in his hunting grounds. This was when The People began to collect and polish the colored stones, especially the blue ones.

"The young men watched where the sun awoke each day and they traveled in that direction until they finally found the sun just emerging from the dark doorway of his great lodge. He was so impressive in his fine clothes, so powerful with his fine weapons that they began to worship him. He showed them a dance they might do in his honor, and, when they returned, they taught it to The People."

"This story is going to be too long," Who Sees Far said.

The old one blinked once and went on.

"For a long time after that, The People worshipped the sun alone. They forgot to respect the earth and water. They forgot how to speak with animals. All they thought about was the sun. Everything they did was for the sun.

"Sometimes, when they dug in the earth for roots to eat, they left the holes unfilled so the water got in and made deep wounds. Sometimes they killed more animals than they needed, and the meat spoiled and the skins and bones sent a stink flowing across the grass for many lengths. But some humans still went out to greet the sun as he was rising from his red and orange blankets. One day, one man who had gone to greet the sun's awakening had to pee. He was too lazy and impolite to remove himself to a correct place and so he made water in the river.

"The animals were offended. The earth was offended. The People found it hard to hunt buffalo. The antelope shunned them. Small rivers dried up as they came to them, and large ones turned bitter and clouded with silt. Who would pee in a river that way?"

Who Sees Far nodded. "Those were hard times. My grandfather said his grandfather said it."

"But what of the medicine lodge?" asked one of the more impulsive youngsters in the crowd. The old woman deferred to Who Sees Far.

The shaman spoke: "It is a great mystery. But here is how it worked. One day a small party of people would arrive with some pony drags and a sacred lodge would be erected. This was the medicine lodge, or the spirit lodge.

People would be selected to take offerings to the doorway. These were handed in, but no one saw who was in the lodge and no one spoke. If all the correct ceremonies were observed, the lodge and its keepers would vanish as quickly as they came and there would be an abundance of grass and good hunting for many years."

"But who remembers the correct ceremonies? What if something goes wrong?"

The old woman and Who Sees Far exchanged worried glances.

"No doubt," the shaman said at last, "these runners are here to tell us what to do."

His words were true, for the Cheyenne runner began to tell the story the next day.

"One morning," he said, "just after the grass had turned green, my village awakened to the sound of drums. Going out, we found a painted lodge standing at the edge of the encampment, a lodge no one had ever seen before. Six men were there, also painted with mysterious symbols, sitting around two drums which they played with curved sticks."

He told them that when the Cheyennes heard the drums, they knew something important was about to take place. Women went back into their lodges and came out wearing their finest dresses decorated with shells and elk teeth. Men went into lodges and came out in their good moccasins and wearing feathers in their hair. When everyone was assembled, they started to dance to the slow rhythm of the drums. Other people came bringing gifts and sat down respectfully to wait.

After a long time had passed, the flap of the medicine lodge moved and out stepped a tall figure dressed in dazzling white clothes of the finest deerskin. One by one he took the gifts and handed them in under the flap to some person who stayed in the lodge and who the people never saw. There were beautifully painted gourds. Beaded white moccasins. Tortoise shell rattles. Necklaces of colored stone and elk teeth. Sometimes this tall stranger would summon a person to him and whisper and that person would go away and return with something special. A painted arrow. A hawk feather fan. He seemed to know everything everyone owned, and asked for what he wanted.

"Finally," the Cheyenne said, "the stranger asked that a runner be brought to him. This one who is speaking to you now was the one chosen. I was brought before them and told what I must do. I was to go find five villages and announce the coming of the medicine lodge. When I said I did not know how to find these villages, did not know where they were, the man in white buckskins told me to take a certain trail. At a place where the trail divided, I would find another runner who knew where to find these five villages.

"The one who speaks was given extra moccasins and a water gourd and a blessing ceremony. Then I set out on my mission. After I had run for two days, I came to where the trail divided. There I found another runner . . . this man you see here . . . who spoke in a strange tongue and whose tribe was unknown."

Somehow, the Cheyenne runner continued, they were able to speak together in perfect understanding. And so they went running and after several days found the second village, for the Cheyenne village had been the first. The first of six. While they were running, the other had told the Cheyenne what to say, so they rested and ate among the Blue Bead clan and in three days told them what was needed.

"No one must speak to those who bring the medicine lodge. If anyone sees it arriving or sees the men who bring it, or if they should see she-who-sits-within, they must say nothing. It must be as if the lodge appears without anyone seeing it, and it must go away in the same manner. This is the way of it.

"No one is to go apart from your village as a sentinel, saying . . . 'I will watch for it to come,' and no one must follow the tracks when it disappears and say . . . 'I know where it goes.' If any person is out of camp afterward, perhaps hunting roots or searching for game or for rocks to chip into arrow points, and sees the tracks of the pony drags, they must not say anything. They must not wonder where the tracks go. Instead, they should take branches of sage and wipe out the tracks and say they have not seen them."

The elders nodded. This was good wisdom. The People needed to remember such ceremonies. It is a good reminder to the young ones to show more respect for what is sacred. They could even learn to be as polite as this young Cheyenne.

"Gifts should be brought to the medicine lodge, but only such as are made of things of the earth. They are given to the shaman, who will hand them in. No one must touch the lodge or try to lift the flap or try in any way to peer under the edge or find out what is inside. Do not act like curious children. Do not ask what the painted symbols mean.

"No one is to speak to the six warriors, or to the guardian unless he speaks first. The horses that draw the travois will need to be fed and watered, but your horse guards who take them to the stream are not to ask those animals their names or where they came from. It is better if they do not speak to those horses at all. They will not wander off as long as the medicine lodge is here."

The runner paused to take a drink of water.

Ah. The elders looked at each other in mutual understanding. Medicine horses. They had seen such animals. It was not unknown for a horse, especially of white or light tan color, to wander into a village and go about the lodges. No one ever tried to catch such a horse. No one asked who owned it. And good things often followed such a visit by one of these horses.

The runner set down the drinking bowl and folded his hands. He had come to something very important. Something meaningful.

"Weapons. Metal."

The elders exchanged glances again.

"Are there to be offerings of metal? Offerings of weapons?"

"No. All weapons, even flint knives and stone clubs, are to be put away while the medicine lodge is here. Out of sight. All things made of white man's metal, even as small as a fish hook or amulet, even spoons if any have them, are to be put away. I have seen those decorations which Black Robe gives to hang around the neck. These, too, are to be put away."

One elder spoke. "We will hold council about this."

They rose and went into a lodge to talk among themselves. They had heard of such tricks before, of some visitor asking that all weapons be put away as a sign of peace, then, in the night, making an attack on the unarmed people. It could be a trick. One said it was only a gesture of trust. Another replied: "If everyone trusted, no one need put away his weapons."

They went back to the Cheyenne runner and told him this. They said they did not understand.

"My companion spoke his thoughts to me about this. He says the medicine lodge is a spirit dwelling that began before The People were born, before the coming-out time. The medicine lodge can only appear where everything is as it used to be, before humans needed metal, needed these guns and knives. It is from a time when spears and clubs were only used for hunting. A time when humans did not know war. All such things must be put away."

The youngest member of the elders, who was many times a father and a vigorous warrior, spoke next. "I would put my weapons in my lodge, beneath the robes where I sleep."

Others nodded in agreement.

The runner said: "In the village of the Cheyennes, many warriors slept on their weapons. Nothing happened. It seemed acceptable to the medicine lodge as long as no metal or weapon was seen outside. That is all I know."

The elders thanked him for coming all that way and for his information, which was very helpful and which he presented with admirable respect and politeness. They would now withdraw to smoke and discuss what it all meant.

Seeing the elders walking away, several women rushed to conduct the handsome young Cheyenne to a lodge that had been cleaned and made fragrant with sage for him and his companion. There they almost overwhelmed them with tender bits of meat, wild plums and cherries, and other treats. Two women gently tended to the injured foot while the others tried to pry more information from their visitors. The Cheyenne spoke of things he had seen during his run, of herds of antelope and rattlesnakes and thickets of plum and chokecherry. He answered questions about the women of other villages, what they wore and how they made their hair look.

But of the medicine lodge he said nothing more.

Chapter Four

THE OUTCAST

The sound began softly, just as the Cheyenne runner said it would.

At first it was only the sound of one stick lightly tapping a drum in the early dawn, waking them as they lay in their robes. The People woke and remained still, listening, gazing up into the tall lodges where the coming light on the lodge skins was just beginning to reveal the long pole shadows.

Another drumming stick joined the first, the two of them making the same rhythm together. As the sun's first rays struck the tips of the lodges, a second drum took up the beat. People rose in the lodges and took care to dress themselves for company. Metal utensils, knives, guns, medallions—all were scrupulously gathered and thrust beneath the robes. When the drum rhythm increased and hardened into a summons, The People stepped out of their lodges in unison, as if they had practiced for this occasion. All eyes turned toward the edge of the village. The new lodge was taller than any lodge they had ever seen. Six horses grazed near it. Six men sat in a line before it, drumming on two drums.

Such a thing had never happened in their village, yet, when the people heard the drums, they knew what was to be done. Standing Hollow Horn and his wife, now bent with age, hobbled into the center of the circle of lodges.

They began to dance, slowly and with dignity. Who Sees Far followed next, and then two elder women. As more people joined them, it became a moving circle. Children came and took their parents' hands and moved their small feet in the rhythm. Crows Woman danced, graceful in her best white deerskin dress, but Two Nose Thomas sat apart and watched. He felt uncomfortable without his Green River knife. He felt undressed without his elk skin bandolier, the one decorated with dozens of gee-gaws and pewter trade tokens—beaver, crosses, hoops, bison heads. Several times he reached automatically for his patch knife, which he carried in a small pocket of his bandoleer, to trim a callus while watching the dance. But even the patch knife was in the lodge, under the skins with his Hawken rifle. He looked around for Grüdj, for the youth was not dancing, but Grüdj was not to be seen. Probably still in the lodge, talking to his water bowl.

The People danced to the beat of the two drums. When they saw someone moving with special grace and respect, that person was tapped on the shoulder. It meant they should dance nearer to the center. Someone else would tap that person again, meaning they should again move toward the center. After a time, there were two dancers in the very middle of the circle, Crows Woman and She Who Hides, the wife of Elk Runner. They had been selected as the two who showed the greatest dignity and respect for the sacred rhythm of the drums. They would be ones to carry gifts to the medicine lodge.

The drumbeats slowed, and then stopped altogether. The People waited silently. The flap on the medicine lodge moved and there emerged a tall man dressed in white deerskin and carrying a medicine bundle cradled in one arm. In a loud voice he began to speak. First he talked of the other villages, then of the strangers who came with wagons and built villages out of logs and mud, then of the buffalo and the grass. Times were hard, he said, but The People of the six villages were keeping the old ways. It was a great responsibility. The tall man pointed his medicine bundle at Standing Hollow Horn and recounted the trips Standing Hollow Horn had led into the mountains in search of the first gods. He praised Standing Hollow Horn for that, and told people there still might be time to find those old gods and talk to them. It would be a good thing if someone could tell the old gods that The People were facing difficult days.

Resting his medicine bundle in the crook of his arm, the tall man began to walk around the circle of dancers. He placed each foot very deliberately, walking in the sacred manner, in the manner of a blessing. So respectful of the earth were his steps that he seemed to be floating upon a layer of air. He spoke to some people and amazed them by saying their names, this man they had never seen before. Once, twice he made the circuit, speaking the names of people, stretching his bundle toward the sky, and then pointing it toward the earth, saying prayers for individuals.

This was a powerful blessing. An invisible but almost palpable energy spread through The People until they felt bonded into a single spirit. Beginning his third circuit of the village, the shaman began to describe the kinds of offerings The People might bring to the medicine lodge.

Then abruptly he stopped. He scowled with anger. His arm trembled as he stretched out his medicine bundle to point in the direction of the lodge and drums.

The spirit of the ceremony was broken. Everyone turned to look where he was pointing.

It was Grüdj, shambling toward the medicine lodge, carrying his metal stick. He was also wearing the brass medallion around his neck. He had heard the drums when he awoke. He saw Two Nose putting his weapons under the sleeping robes while Crows Woman put on her best dress and plaited her hair. He sat up. Crows Woman brought him a bowl of meat and dried cherries, and then she made her mistake. She brought him a bowl of water that he might drink, and then she left the lodge. Grüdj bent over the water, staring at his reflection until he went into one of his dream times. He began to talk with the water. That was when Two Nose went outside.

This medicine lodge, the water said to Grüdj, it has great meaning. It brings powerful words from the Old Ones, from the gods of the first water. The holy man with the medicine bundle, the one who speaks, will not tell The People this, but the one who sits within the medicine lodge is the water spirit. She knows where the Old Ones live.

Grüdj set the bowl on the ground before him and stared into the tiny ripples as they danced to the pounding of the drums and the rhythm of The People's feet. The waves began in the center and spread outward. Grüdj saw himself in the water, his one eye staring back at him out of his dark face, but his image seemed surrounded by mountains. The mountains were white, buried in snow, frozen. He put forth a finger to touch and see whether the water was frozen, too, and in that instant the trance was broken. Once again it was only a bowl of water. Once again he was sitting in the lodge.

Grüdj got to his feet, took his metal stick, and went out. No one noticed him. He did not join the people. Instead, he made his away around the village, behind the lodges, until he came near the place where the tall new lodge sat. He would watch by himself and find out what it meant, what it was for. These mountains that had been shown to him in the water vision—the vision had meaning. The one who sits within might be able to tell him.

As soon as she saw Grüdj approaching the dance circle, Crows Woman uttered a cry and ran to intercept him, three elders hurrying along behind her. Grüdj was taken by the shoulders and pushed and shoved until he was behind the lodges and out of sight, but it was too late. The ceremony had been corrupted. The tall holy man made an angry speech in a language The People did not understand. He gestured to the six guardian warriors, waving his hand as if wiping something away. Four warriors picked up the two drums. Two took hold of the ropes of the six horses and all of them vanished into the medicine lodge, horses and men and everything. The flap was then tied down tightly from within and utter silence descended upon the village. The People sat down where they were and waited, but nothing happened. The sun went all the way up the sky and nothing happened.

The sun reached its midday point and seemed to hang there a while, then began its descent toward the place it sleeps.

At last, one of the elders stood up and addressed the others. Someone must go to the medicine lodge and ask what to do. The council agreed. They chose Three Eagles, the one who was most courteous of all The People and the one who, it was said, was the oldest person of the tribe. And so Three Eagles stood and carefully arranged his robe about him and walked with great solemnity to stand before the door of the medicine lodge. The People heard him ask his question, then saw him stand respectfully, listening. When he returned to the group, some thought they could see the beginnings of tears in his pale old eyes.

"Nothing," he said. "One thing only was asked of The

People, and the black youth was allowed to show contempt for it. There is nothing that can be done now. Perhaps the spirit lodge will return after many more seasons have passed. The People will have a hard time finding the buffalo. They will not find sweet water. The sun will dry up the grass and rivers. There is nothing to be done about this. That is what the voice said, the voice within the spirit lodge. I have no more words," Three Eagles said. "Perhaps it is the end of everything."

The other elders rose and went into the lodge of Crows Woman to take council with her, since she was the one who had adopted the child. They talked until the shadows grew long, discussing what was to be done. But no one knew. The only thing anyone knew for certain was that Grüdj had offended the medicine lodge and he must go away. If any kind of appeasement could be made, it had to be done immediately. Perhaps if they showed the elder of the medicine lodge that it was the fault of the one with the iron stick and not theirs—if they sent him away? This might be the thing to do, said another. And there is this: Crows Woman and others had already noticed things about Grüdj, certain indications that he was approaching the time when he should undertake a vision journey. He could leave on that journey now, even though it would mean there would be no time for a shaman to make him ready for the quest, not even time for Crows Woman to prepare food and weapons and extra clothing and moccasins for him as she did when they went to the mountains with Standing Hollow Horn.

Perhaps Grüdj would return with a healing vision. Perhaps with Grüdj gone, the keepers of the medicine lodge would forget their anger and counsel The People how to purify the village and stave off the drought and starvation. Telling Grüdj to leave would certainly not cause more trouble. It might make up for the trouble he had caused. And so discussion went back and forth until at last the elders of The People were in agreement—the black one and his iron stick must be gone by morning.

By the time the sun left its blankets and stepped up onto the edge of the world again, Grüdj was nowhere to be found in the village. And neither was the medicine lodge. No one had heard the keepers taking it down; no one heard the horses being loaded. It was as if it had vanished like the morning mist lifting silently off the river. For a long time, after daylight came, The People stayed inside their lodges, fearful lest they anger the keepers of the medicine lodge by coming out before the drums began. Then gradually one person at a time peered out through the lodge flaps to discover that the medicine lodge was no longer there. There was only a circle of flattened grass where it had been and the tracks of the pony drags leading away.

Two Nose and Crows Woman and her friends searched here and there among the lodges, over by the running water, everywhere, and did not find Grüdj.

As instructed, some of The People went out and cut fresh cedar boughs and swept away the tracks of the horses and travois until there was no sign of where it went. Some stood around near the place where the lodge had been, not daring even to stand on the same ground. No one knew why the medicine lodge had come, no one knew what it meant, but all seemed to know its sudden departure meant a dark time was coming.

Grüdj had knelt in the gloom to put dried meat and pemmican into a leather bag. He had felt around for his other pair of moccasins and his good knife and put them with an extra shirt onto his trade blanket, which he rolled into a bundle and tied around his shoulders as Two Nose had shown him. He untied the flap of the lodge and had gone out into the pre-dawn stillness, quiet as a spirit and dark as the shadows themselves. He went away from the village far enough not to be seen, and then found a high place on which to sit and watch. He did not have to wait long before he saw the six horses moving away from the village, the six warriors walking beside them. There were three travois carrying unusually tall burdens. Grüdj felt his spirit fill with a conviction more overwhelming than any he had ever known; he knew beyond any doubt that those travois held more than the lodge and sacred bundles and the unseen person who The People called She Who Cannot Be Seen. They held the answer to the uncertain future. They held the secret of how to find the old gods who could help The People.

Grüdj knew he could not return to the village. Nor could he set out on a vision quest because he was unprepared for it. But there was one thing he *could* do. He could follow this medicine lodge and try to discover its secret.

Grüdj let the procession pass out of sight before walking down the hill to see if they had left a trail. He expected to find heavy tracks of the horses and deep ruts from the poles they dragged. But the trail of the three travois was very dim. In places he could not see it at all. The horses' hoofs left no tracks whatever. Nonetheless, Grüdj followed, picking up the trail where he could. He made an odd figure there in the dawn, a shapeless dark blob moving hunched over, using a heavy steel rod as a walking stick. The bundle strapped to his back made him look even more like a giant humpback toad moving across the grass and sage.

Two days he followed the medicine lodge. On the

morning of the third day the tracks turned and followed a small, clear stream into a steep-walled cleft through a ridge. Fearing they had somehow detected him and were going into the ravine to make a trap for him, he found shelter among some rocks and trees and waited. No one came back. Grüdj went to the stream and cupped water in his hand and drank. It was so pure as to be invisible in his palm, and on his tongue it had no taste and was neither cold nor warm. He went to his knees to listen to what it was saying, but the stream spoke a strange language he could not understand.

Grüdj got up and followed the faint tracks into the shadowy gorge and after a time he saw that it opened out onto a wide valley surrounded by forested slopes. At the center of the valley was a lake with a wooded island in its midst. The six horses and six warriors had stopped at the edge of the water. Grüdj crept forward and looked around until he found himself a niche in a rock outcropping. Hidden behind bushes, it was small enough and secret enough that he could squeeze into and be hidden. From there he could see everything without getting any closer. There he could eat his dried meat and sleep.

As Grüdj sat in his shadowy crevice and watched, the six warriors unloaded one of the travois and erected a small lodge of just three poles. They built a fire in a circle of rocks before taking out their drums, and, as they sat down and began drumming, the tall shaman with the medicine bundle appeared in the door of the lodge. Until the dark fell and the moon rose high, they drummed. The elder pointed his medicine bundle at the darkening sky, praying. Grüdj chewed on his meat and his eye grew heavier and heavier with fatigue. He slept.

In the morning, the warriors were still there, sitting in a

line by their fire. Sometimes one would rise and go to the trees and bring more wood, but Grüdj could not see that they were eating or resting or doing anything except sitting. As the sun started down behind the mountain, they began drumming again. Again Grüdj slept.

And so it went for three days, this strange, lonely ceremonial. The warriors of the medicine lodge and the tall elder fasted and drummed and stood vigil, staring into the forest. Grüdj felt stiffness and pain all through his body, but he remained where he was, watching. At sundown on the third day the elder put tobacco in a pipe and offered smoke to the six directions. Grüdj caught the scent of it.

The next morning when Grüdj lifted his head from his dreams and looked toward the lake, there was another person with them, a small figure like a girl or small woman. The six warriors were taking this new person to the edge of the water. As he watched, they took her blanket and put it aside, then undid her sash and let her dress slide to the ground. She stood naked and motionless while the warriors stripped off their leggings and breechclouts. They walked her into the water and took water into their cupped hands, lifting it toward the sky before pouring it upon her. Afterward, they poured water in the same manner onto each other.

While the six warriors and the woman were performing their bathing ritual, the shaman touched his medicine bundle to the small lodge, and the skins and poles fell down immediately into the shape of a pack upon a travois, which the shaman then hitched to the back of one of the horses. He held his medicine bundle out over the fire and the fire stopped burning. Then he went to the shore and extended his medicine bundle out over the water.

Grüdj had to rub at his eye to be sure he was seeing what

he thought he saw. The lake was shrinking. Down and down the surface went. He could not see where the water was going, but it was going somewhere quickly. Before long, the seven unclothed figures were standing on a long, narrow strip of dry land that led to the island. The shaman stepped onto this causeway, leading the first horse and travois. The other horses followed. The warriors waited until the horses had passed, then turned and followed. The girl went last, and then the entire procession vanished into the trees of the island.

He was about to leave his hiding place, although he was not sure where he would go. It seemed very dangerous to follow them to the island. Then something moved in the trees and he shrank back into the shadow of the rock. The six warrior guardians were returning, but without the shaman or the girl. They were now clothed in pure white deerskin from head to foot. The bows slung on their backs and the lances in their hands gleamed as if made from freshly stripped aspen wood. Grüdj feared they had seen him and were coming for him, but if they knew he was there, they were ignoring him. The six stopped on the causeway and turned to face the lake. They stood shoulder to shoulder in a sacred manner, arms crossed, faces straight ahead, remaining motionless. The water began to come back. The lake rose again, coming up rapidly, climbing to their waists and then to their shoulders and necks and finally swallowing them entirely.

And they were gone.

All that remained was the lake, shining smoothly, reflecting the sky and the trees.

Grüdj could not move for a long time. The deep silence engulfed him. When at last he walked cautiously to the edge of the lake, he saw no tracks, no discarded clothing, no sign at all that anyone had ever been there. Feeling dizzy, he gripped his steel stick for support and stared into the lake. There were words in his gut that would not come into his throat. The spirit within the medicine lodge had returned to her home to be purified, leaving no more trace than when rain vanishes into the earth or into the sky to return to the mountains, returning on cloud horses after spending the winter locked in ice.

Grüdj slumped down and sat, cross-legged, beside the lake. He bowed his head and shut his eye and gave himself up to the spirit of this place, for the water dreamer in him told him there was much he needed to know. But his dream mind was closed and the trance would not come. This water was not good medicine for him. He could not tell what it was saying. Sitting there like a fat old bear squatted on its haunches and wagging its head, Grüdj took counsel with himself. He mumbled questions, mumbled answers in reply. Finally he came to a decision: he must go somewhere else, must find other water, somewhere to fast until his vision returned.

The *clatter* of hoofs on rocks brought him to himself. It was the sound of horses walking up behind him. Grüdj could only sit motionless; there was nothing else he might do. He could not get up and run because he had the lake in front of him. He was not a slender, strong warrior who could leap to his feet and whirl around with his knife ready to strike the enemy approaching. The hoof beats came up closer until they stopped. He heard the grunt and plop of someone dismounting.

"*Waugh!* I took 'ee fer a fat beaver, hunkerin' thar like that."

Grüdj turned. It was Two Nose. He had three horses, two carrying big packs.

"Ol' Two Nose thought he teched ye better, Negra. Ye left a trail a blind man could foller. Kain't say sich fer y'r medicine lodge folk, however. Scarce a pony track t'see. Whar be they?"

Grüdj pointed at the lake.

"Ah," Two Nose said. "Gone acrost thet lake? Mebbe so. Skunked ye proper, did they. Waal, I seen ye and was feered they'd lodge-poled ye an' left ye fer a varmit feast." There was long silence. Two Nose spoke again. "Soon's I'd ciphered out thet you was follerin' the medicine lodge, I held high palaver with Hollow Horn. Him and Crows Woman. Seems thet crafty ol' Horn knowed more about this lash-up than he says. Tells me I'd find 'ee at a lake like this 'un, with a island. A spirit lake. Not the big 'un thet's over yon mountains, but another."

"We will go back now?" Grüdj asked, preferring the talk of The People to Two Nose's speech.

"No," Two Nose said. "Hollow Horn, he says not. Thet savvy ol' coon, he's been t'places. Me, I suspicions thet he larned some white talk. Dunno. Enyway, Hollow Horn figgers ye t'help The People best by sumpin' ye're t'do all on yore own. Sumpin' doin' with white folk."

"You? You are white tribe."

"Naw. Gove'ment, he figgers. Not this dog, no. Horn, he had medicine oncet. Figgers you got it now."

"Why does Two Nose follow Grüdj? If not to bring him back to The People?"

Two Nose laughed a huge laugh that echoed over the glassy lake and vanished into the trees.

"Hah!" he said. "Fer one thing, Crows Woman, she'd break th' stick an' split th' blanket with me iffen I never set out fer ye. Hollow Horn, he says ye're bound t'high country north o' the big medicine wheel. So, this hoss figgers he'll tag along an' get enuf plew t'be rich. Thar's beaver up there, boy. Ye got the med'cin t'git the rivers t'tell ye whar the critters be, and ol Two Nose, he's got the med'cin t'make 'em come, so he has. Plew aplenty! *Waugh!* Figger one, two winters an' we'll have us more skins than ol' Sublette an' Jed Smith iver dreamt of. Shinin' times, boy, shinin' times ahead!"

Two Nose and Grüdj withdrew from the spirit lake. They traveled three more days and crossed two ridges of mountains before they found their own secluded spot in the forest, a spot sheltered by trees and rich in grass for the horses. Two Nose unloaded his bales and opened them up to show Grüdj all the things he had brought with him. He had good things, like coffee and sugar, and a frying pan and axe. It would be like old times again, Two Nose told him, the old days when he and a brigade of other young eager mountain men went into the northern Rockies to hunt beaver plews. They would build a weather-tight shelter, chop a winter's supply of firewood, hunt deer and jerk the meat, then settle in for winter trapping "jes' like when me an' the boys was true hibernauts, *waugh!*"

Grüdj was content. He liked the thought of returning to the faraway high mountains where Standing Hollow Horn had searched for the old gods. And if he was to have a powerful vision, like that of Hollow Horn, he would need some companion to stand watch and bring him food when it was over. Two Nose could do that. As for this thing Standing Hollow Horn said he was to do for The People, it would be revealed in time.

Two Nose Thomas came out of the trees guiding the pack horse, dragging two good-size logs for the lean-to. He expected to find Grüdj at work on the logs he had already hauled in, shaping the ends and smoothing off the knots. Instead, he found Grüdj sitting on a log, holding a piece of bark in his hand and staring at it.

"What ails 'ee?" Two Nose asked, unhitching the logs and coiling the rope for another trip into the woods. "Yore dream time come on 'ee, has it?"

"No."

"Sumpin' peculiar in thet bark chunk?"

"These have tracks," Grüdj said, pointing at the meandering grooves that grubs had excavated along the underside of the tree bark.

Two Nose looked. He picked one of the white grubs and popped it in his mouth. "Food fer ba'r, mostly. This hoss favors venison, he does. Yore mountain griz, now, he'll toothpick a whole tree t'get himself a mouthful of them grubs."

Grüdj traced the worm channels with his finger, obviously lost in thought.

"She's diggin' at yer brain pan, ain't she?" Two Nose said sympathetically. "Cain't find where t'have yore vision time. Bothers ye some, not knowin' whar yore stick's s'pposed t'float."

"These are food for the great bear."

"Shore. The gods give 'em a part in all this," Two Nose said, waving his hand to take in most of the northern mountains. "Them gods, they'll palaver with ye, jus' wait. Ye're like thet iron bar, shore t'be needed, somewheres. Let's git these logs up."

Two Nose should have been used to the idea of Grüdj's great strength after all this time, but every once in a while it still took him by surprise. There would be a log so heavy that Two Nose couldn't lift more than one end of it, and only a little way off the ground at that, but Grüdj would hoist it easily to his shoulder and from there to the top of the unfinished wall. When it came to a tree that needed dragging or a log that needed lifting, there seemed no limit to the boy's strength. He wasn't much of a hand with an axe when it came to notching the ends or trimming a log to fit snugly, mostly because his thick arms and squat body made it hard for him to strike accurate blows, but he was learning fast. And he was clever at figuring ways to build shelves on the log walls and ways to cut logs so as to lock into one another.

One day, when Two Nose and Grüdj were scouting for beaver sign, they came upon a rock outcropping where the stone had fractured in straight lines, creating squarish-looking blocks.

"*Waugh!*" Two Nose said. "Hyar's sumpin'!" He pushed at some of the rocks without any effect, since each one was the size of a grub box or immigrant's trunk. "This Negra *do* wisht he'd set sights on this y'ar clearin' afore buildin' whar he did, by thunder. Lookee, Grüdj! Why, iffen we'd lever three, four o' them square rocks onta one 'nother, then put the lean-to just hyar . . ."—he scratched a line in the dirt with the butt of his rifle—"we'd have us some fine fixin' fer a fire, so we would. Just like a honest-t'-God fireplace t'shine th' heat back on us."

The following day Two Nose set out alone to "git a gawk 'n' gander" over yet another ridge into yet another valley. He was gone two nights, and, when he returned, he found six of the heavy square stones set in a semicircle before the log lean-to's open side, piled two stones high. He again shoved at one of the rocks and found he couldn't begin to budge it.

"Boy," he said to Grüdj, "how d'ye manage thet?"

Grüdj's eye seemed to sparkle, just a little, and the white teeth showed against his black face. He pointed at the steel rod propped up against the lean-to.

"Lever'd 'em, did 'ee? Waal, a man oughtn't call 'nother man no liar, not when they set t'winter togither, no. But iffen you pry-barred all them rocks all thet ways, waal . . . come the thaw, we jus' might take us t'rendezvous an' mark ye down f'r the tall tale tellin', yes, sir. Ye'd win hands down."

Two Nose dug in his possibles poke for a bit of char cloth and tinder, then took his flint striker and got a fire going up against the rocks. Just as he had predicted, the blazing pine sent heat and light aplenty into the lean-to.

Lying on their robes that night, eating good venison and tossing chunks of wood into the fire from time to time, Two Nose and Grüdj made talk in the language of The People.

"Whites build houses with such stones," Two Nose told him. "Grüdj might find his place where the stones are made." Two Nose had no word for "quarry" or even "cut stones" except for the term for chipping arrowheads from flint.

"Grüdj could. . . ." Again the language lacked words for "find his purpose".

"Whites would pay Grüdj to move rocks, I say this."

Grüdj held out one black hand to the firelight and pointed to it with the other hand. He pointed at his face. His quick signing gesture for "no" was so abrupt that it was almost rude.

"Ah," Two Nose said. "Reckon so."

"Those grubs," Grüdj said. "Food for the great bear. Food for the bird who picks."

"Hah?" Two Nose said. "Ye wonder what four-legged would eat you?"

It was the nearest thing to a joke that could be managed in The People's language. Grüdj dismissed it with the same negative hand gesture as before.

"This one knows," Two Nose said. "Knows a long time, many seasons. Four-legged, the air people, all know what to do. This 'un knows t'run. That 'un knows t'fly. Some eat grass. They jus' natcherly know what to do. But a two-legs, he needs a vision to tell him."

"The one who is now with you," Two Nose said, politely referring to himself, "came out to the buffalo prairies to catch beaver, marten, lynx. He found Crows Woman. Found the good pipe, the full belly, the warm lodge. Found The People to be good. He would do this for all his days."

Grüdj tossed a pine knot into the blaze and looked at Two Nose. In his single eye there seemed a dark sadness, a question too deep for utterance.

"Waugh," said Two Nose, "ye're carryin' heavy in yore innards, jus' like all o' ye. Pore Grüdj. This hyar hoss knows, he does. He savvies. Cain't be goin' back t'the lodges, not after that spirit lodge bizness. Cain't cipher fur trappin with ol' Two Nose, neither. Tain't whar yore stick floats."

Grüdj pulled his robe more tightly around himself and rolled to his side.

"Aye," Two Nose said. "Thet's best. Sleep. Better day comin' tomarra."

The fire burned low, glowed red a while in the midst of its own ashes, and finally surrendered to the darkness. In the warmth still emanating from the rocks, two figures slept, one white and one black, tiny specks of human life engulfed in a vast wilderness, roofed by a night sky of infinite stars. To the one there came a dream in which he heard the sounds of hundreds of beaver tails slapping water and of fat venison sizzling over a fire. To the other came only the unending sound of falling water, water that was forever leaving the mountains and returning again.

Chapter Five

THE POWER OF THE STICK

Grüdj halted.

It seemed many days since he and Two Nose Thomas separated, the trapper to return to the prairies and Grüdj to go up into the mountains. Since leaving Two Nose, he had traversed two more ridges, followed animal paths beside creeks, backtracked and gone around cliffs, and finally labored up the highest mountains of all, where he discovered a clear trail leading westward. He first encountered it at a place where the trees became shorter and the mountains touched the sky. Here even the stunted, twisted trees could no longer grow. A chill blew over this rocky, treeless land, stirring the short grass that grew between the outcroppings of cracked granite worn slick by ice and wind. Low bushes struggled to survive in the shelter of boulders. Below him in the valley were gigantic scars running downward through the forest and enormous piles of rock that looked as if some huge force had been scraping away at the mountains.

Looking toward the ridgeline ahead, Grüdj saw the whole horizon of the mountain and no mountains beyond, and by this he knew he was nearly at the top of the earth. Breathing was hard, made even harder by the dry wind. The sunlight was dazzling. He leaned on his iron stick a while to rest. Spirit Lake must be somewhere down below him in the direction where the sun sleeps. The rest of this day he would climb up and over the ridge, and then would sleep in the trees down on the other side. Maybe in another day or two he would reach Spirit Lake.

The stone cairns marking the trail were like the ones he had seen during the treks with Standing Hollow Horn. Standing Hollow Horn had never been in these mountains, but knew about the trail over the great mountains to Spirit Lake. The piles of rock marking that twisting route over the top of earth were made by others, others who were often enemies of The People. In old times crossing here could mean capture and death.

Grüdj turned to look back down the long forested valley, back the way he had come, back across the many mountains folded like dark robes tossed carelessly. He saw a silver line where a big river ran. Two Nose would be at that river by now. Maybe he would be farther if he had not stopped to trap more beaver, out onto the flat country where The People would be in village. Winter trapping had not been good. Grüdj tried to help by asking the rivers where the beaver were, but the waters would not speak except to taunt and chide him for violating the medicine lodge. The beaver would not come to him. Twice, while he and Two Nose were wading across icy streams, the water had tried to snatch his iron bar from him.

"Figger t'pint m'moccasins back to'ard Crows Woman, come the thaw," Two Nose had said. "This hyar coon, he forgot what work it is, winter trappin'. It don't shine, *waugh!* Two Nose, he's fair fash'd fer a warm lodge an' nothin' t'do. Ye kin have all th' gold and plew ye crave, so ye kin. Yes, sir, rendezvous be hanged. Hyar's a Negra what's turned inta a village Injun fer fair! Fixin' t'spend m'days with a pipe o' good 'baccy and a full belly, somebody warm under the robes at night. No more wadin' froze-up cricks fer beaver, no."

Grüdj knew he could not go back with Two Nose, not until he had some kind of vision, some kind of sign. And Two Nose knew that Grüdj "had his stick pointed" at Spirit Lake on the other side of the big Rockies, over where the Green and the Grand rivers married up to start their long flow toward Mexico. Spirit Lake. Enemy territory, but plenty of medicine power there. Grüdj, he'd be all right. Two Nose had spent far too many years as a free trapper, often wandering for months alone in the country of the Blackfeet and Crows and Utes, to worry about the chances of a single man surviving. It was just a way of life, something a man did.

Grüdj looked around. Just below him, he saw a small herd of elk slowly moving into a meadow between gigantic earth scars to graze. Above the herd, on a rugged cliff, he saw moving specks of white where a family of mountain goats foraged for fresh moss and lichen. And not far from Grüdj a marmot stood beside its hole, studying this intruder that looked like itself only of giant proportions. A pika squeaked out a warning as a hawk with silent wings rode a rising thermal overhead.

Grüdj set his eye on the next cairn and resumed walking. The patches and valleys of old snow seemed to chill the breeze and it made him shiver despite the hot sun on his back. This was where the clouds brought the water and rain. Here the snow imprisoned the water for long winter months and here the winds blew it into deep drifts filling all the valleys and cañons. Grüdj saw why the water would want to run away from this country. Everything up here was cold, lifeless, and forbidding. There were no tall trees, no deep grass, no thick warm mud, no beaver, and no fish. For the stream's bed there was only cold rock. The mountains might hold the water all winter, but at the first touch of summer sun, in the moon of calving elk, the water would gleefully run away on its journey down toward the prairie once again.

He did not know what his vision would be when it came, or what it would tell him to do. He did not know why he had been drawn to this high, cold country. Maybe his vision would show him how to release the water so it could go to The People. Maybe if he brought water, made it "come" in the talk of Two Nose, the spirit lodge would return to help The People.

As Grüdj followed the trail of cairns, he began to hear sounds. He stopped. They were the sounds of men shouting. He heard a gunshot, then another and another. He looked around for some place to hide, some crevice in the rocks or some thicket of low-growing willows where his large body could be concealed, but there was no time; six riderless horses came galloping over the ridge. They wore saddles such as The People used, but they also wore the painted signs of The Enemy. The animals were in panicked flight, their eyes wide and frightened and their nostrils flaring. Three, then four, then six warriors broke into sight, shouting as they ran after their horses. When they saw Grüdj standing there, four of The Enemy ran on, but two stopped. One carried a long gun like that of Two Nose. The other had a lance and his bow was slung across his back with a quiver of arrows.

"Hai-eeyah hehy!" the one with the gun shouted. Both of them were very angry and out of breath. Their eyes glared and the muscles of their bare chests were knotted hard. The one with the gun took out his knife as they came toward Grüdj.

At first Grüdj stood frozen where he was. He had never fought with anyone, except in play. He had never been on a raiding party or acted as horse guard in the village. He and the other boys had only pretended to be warriors. What does a man do when he faces a real enemy? It was easy for small boys to pretend, to put on poses of imaginary warriors. He remembered the young man who had told them about dog soldiers. He did not know exactly what it was that a dog soldier *did* after taking his brave stance, but he could think of nothing else to do. And so Grüdj faced the two angry warriors of The Enemy and raised his iron bar. When they got a little closer, he would thrust it into the ground as if to say: "Here will I die before I will move." But he saw the glint of sunlight on the warrior's naked blade and the gun pointed at him and he knew he was about to die. Grüdj lifted his iron bar with both hands and brought it down onto the rock.

What happened next was an event The Enemy warriors would carry back to their people, where it would be told around the lodge fires for many years to come. Some would say it was just another hunting story, while others said the men had made up a story to explain why it took them so long to catch their runaway horses. Still others would say: "I once tried to run, tried to chase an animal like a deer except smaller, and it was near the high place these men describe. I became dizzy and saw brightness behind my eyes. I could not breathe and I fell down. Perhaps the thin air made these warriors see something that was not there." But whether it was believed or not, it was a story such as their tribe had never heard.

As the two warriors ran up across the top of the bare ridge, they spotted the squat black one-eyed creature. They thought he was with the white men they had been attacking, and so they should attack him before he could take shelter with them in the rocks. But as they moved toward him with their weapons ready, they saw him raise up his heavy stick and ram it, point first, down into the granite. One said that lightning flashed from it. Both swore they heard thunder. The ground beneath the creature began to rise as if it was going to bear him up into the sky, and in the next instant the rising and swelling of the earth came rushing toward them and knocked them off their feet. Before they knew what was happening, they were lying on their backs with the rock heaving and throwing them about like children being thrown into the air. Big standing stones at the edge of the stunted forest swayed and toppled over and went rolling down through the trees. As soon as the thunder noise stopped and the ground stopped rising and falling, they got up and ran in terror after their companions.

The three white men who had cached in a stony outcrop, prepared to fight for their lives, were witnesses to the same bizarre event. Just as things looked hopeless for them, something spooked the Indians' ponies and caused them to stampede. When they saw the Indians running after their horses, the white men realized that they had been given a reprieve, however momentary. They seized the advantage by following the running warriors and shooting their guns in hopes of causing even more panic in the horses. Thus they, too, crossed the top of the ridge in time to see what happened. There was some kind of strange dark creature with a long bar. Then came a heaving, rolling earthquake through the granite that knocked them off their feet. Before they could get up again, the Indians were already running in a panic down the mountain slope. The surveyors hurried to gather up their instruments and make a dash for the relative safety of their own camp, below timberline on the other side of the ridge.

Not knowing what else to do, Grüdj trundled after them. They regarded him warily at first, but, seeing that he was alone and unarmed and obviously not an Indian, they motioned for him to follow them into camp. Grüdj found a rock to sit on and watched while the white men made sure their pack horses were secured. Finally satisfied that the Indians had retreated and that their camp was defensible, they tried to make sense out of what they had seen.

"Clear blue sky," one said.

"Yes," said another, "but I've seen lightning come out of a cloudless sky before. God was just looking out for us, that's all."

"Well," Robert Green said, "since I was 'way out in the lead ahead of you fellows, I think I got a better look than you did. There I was, running and firing at the same time, when I looked off to my left and saw this strange-looking Negro with a long stick raised over his head. Two of the Indians headed for him like they were going to shoot him. But then I'd swear he brought that stick down and just hit the rock with it. He just hit the rock and they both fell down. It looked like they had been *thrown* down!"

Green paused for breath and no one else said anything. "So in a couple of seconds, I felt the rock swell up like the whole top of the ridge was going to erupt, just like an earthquake, and lost my balance. By the time I got my feet under me again, those Indians were almost out of sight down the slope. There was only that black man standing on the rocks, holding his stick."

Green looked at Grüdj a few times as he told the story to his two companions, but, although he acknowledged his presence, he spoke almost as if Grüdj were only a camp dog sitting there, an object rather than one of them. He had said nothing so far, only making a grunting sound when asked a question. He was dressed like an Indian, but obviously was not one. Grüdj merely listened. These men had a strange way of talking. It was not like the speech of Two Nose at all.

The surveyors agreed on one thing: what they had felt had been some kind of strange earthquake. One of them said he had experienced a tremor in Yellowstone, where the ground rose up like an ocean swell and the swell went moving along like a wave, knocking animals off their feet. But this incident. . . .

"It sounded more like the rock was being shattered," William Marinas said.

"Not shattered so much as just fractured," said Sanford Thatcher.

"There was a sound like rocks breaking," Green suggested.

"Whatever it was, it sure put the fear of God into those Indians!"

"If they know about God."

"You know what I mean. Still, I don't think we should stay here any longer than necessary. They might be back," Marinas said.

"Another two days, maybe, and we'll have enough measurements," Green said. "But we still need to get to the tops of at least two more ranges to the north and record the altitude."

Thatcher looked at Grüdj and pointed at the pot of beans and loaf of bread near the fire circle. Grüdj accepted a plate and spoon and ate.

"You look like you might be a trapper," Thatcher suggested, indicating Grüdj's leather pants and hunting shirt.

"No," Grüdj said.

"Looking for your people, maybe," Marinas offered.

"Get separated from your folks, did you?"

"No," Grüdj said.

The three resumed discussing Grüdj as if he could not hear them.

"Well, he isn't a runaway or else he'd've hightailed it when he saw us."

"Nah," Thatcher said. "He's no runaway. I think he's been a trapper of some kind, but he's cached his traps and pelts somewhere while he goes for pack animals."

"Maybe he's headed for Oregon," Marinas said. "Or with that digging bar, he might be prospecting for gold."

The others laughed, because gold had become a joke among them. Wherever they traveled while making their grid survey for the government, every white man they ran into would invariably ask the same question: "Find any sign of gold in those mountains?"

Grüdj put out a foot and prodded one of the wooden boxes.

"Trade goods?" he asked. Two Nose's "companyeros" once came to the village with similar crates containing geegaws, bits of cloth, glass beads, and such.

"Instruments," said Thatcher. He opened the box to show Grüdj a brass bound barometer and a theodolite. He took the top off of a leather tube and removed a roll of paper, which he flattened out on the ground by the fire. Grüdj saw lines drawn all over it.

"We're surveying this trail over the mountains," the man said proudly. "Making a map for others who want to come this way."

Grüdj was not interested. He spooned up his beans and gazed into the fire.

"And we're also mapping some possibilities for irrigation canals."

Grüdj looked at him. He did not know this word.

"Eh-rah-gashun," he repeated.

"You know," the man continued, "ditches for water. To take the water where it's needed."

The man named Robert Green snorted and let out a laugh.

"Thatcher, you never get over being the teacher, do you? This fellow doesn't look like he can read or write, and he certainly can't read maps, and here you are getting set to explain to him all about 'er-ra-gashun'. You're a case for the books, you are."

"Rivers," Grüdj said.

"What?" Thatcher replied, ignoring his comrade's scorn.

"Whar the waters go," Grüdj said.

"Oh, rivers take the water to the plains. No, not always to the right place. There's lots of land, where the rivers don't go. But if a company can dig a ditch, make the water come to that land, everyone can get rich. Maybe you don't know about the irrigation law that Washington passed."

"Law," Grüdj stated.

"Oh, God!" Green guffawed. "Now he's explaining law to him! Give me strength!"

"Land law," Thatcher went on. "Irrigation law. Out east of the mountains . . . in that direction there . . . if you bring water to dry land, you get to claim the land as your own. Keep it."

"Keep it?"

"Yeah, keep it," Robert Green interrupted. "You savvy 'town'? Take for instance a bunch of black people like yourself wanted your own town." He grinned mischievously at the third man, now that he was mimicking Thatcher's teacher-like tone. "You lay out a township, establish homesteads, build roads, and so on. You do know what township means, of course. Some of your people already done just that, out in Kansas. Place called Aspiration. Say you and a bunch of other blacks were to go up to the mountains and find a watershed that hasn't been claimed, see?"

"Water. . . ." Grüdj looked puzzled. He had never heard this word watershed.

"Watershed. A place where creeks and rivers run down into one . . . well, into one valley or into one river. You dig a ditch and you divert some of that water."

"D'ver?"

"Make it go some place else," Thatcher put in. "Some place it doesn't go. Look here."

Green took his spoon and scraped a shallow trench in the dirt. He scraped the outline of a rectangle at the end of it.

"This is your ditch, see? It brings water from the mountain. Now, the government says you can have this land . . . that's the rectangle here . . . because you brought water to it. Got it? Your ditch takes it from the mountain out onto the flat land. Then you can use it to grow your food, hay for horses and livestock, things such as that. The government gives you that land."

"Thatcher," Green said, "you're dumb as that there stump, thinking this nigger understands anything about it. Save your breath."

"Keep it," Grüdj said.

"That's right!" Thatcher said. "You and all your people, you keep whatever land you bring water to. This map here, you see, it shows how somebody might make a ditch from here to 'way out that direction where there's free land."

Grüdj looked at the crooked lines on the paper. Despite what Robert Green believed, Grüdj had grasped the concept almost immediately, just as his medicine helped him see the meaning of the strange language these men used. He wanted to know more.

"Thet might shine, some," Grüdj said, using Two Nose's tongue to speak with these whites. "*Eny* country hereabouts? A Negra what makes water come, he puts his mark enywheres hereabouts?"

The three surveyors laughed.

"No, not hardly. All this territory around here, it's been pretty well mapped and marked out. Those Indians, those hunters we ran into, they think they still own it, but they don't know the government has already opened it up and promised most of it. You'd need to go quite some ways north to find unclaimed watersheds. Quite some ways."

Grüdj's face wore a puzzled look.

"That way," the surveyor pointed. "That direction. North."

But Grüdj already knew the word and the direction from Two Nose Thomas. What had puzzled him was a sudden realization. He had been thinking about it just before The Enemy came running up over the ridge. Spirit Lake did not seem to be pulling at him, did not seem to call to him as it should. He had been considering turning his tracks in a different direction in search of a vision. North, to be exact.

Grüdj slept near the warmth of the surveyor's fire. In the morning they gave him food but did not speak to him. They had to make plans for the day and look at their maps and notebooks and had no time to talk to him. But he was not concerned. Grüdj listened intently, often repeating phrases under his breath. He watched how their gestures went with their words. Many words were familiar from Two Nose's language, words like rifle, walk, horse, and so on. Others, like "tangent" and "barometer" had no meaning, at least no meaning that he could figure out.

Grüdj followed after Thatcher, helping to carry the leather cases. They trudged up one summit and then another, Thatcher looking through his instruments and making notes while Grüdj sat on the rocks and looked off into the immense distances. That evening everyone was too tired to do much in the way of talking, and in the morning they all went to still another summit, Grüdj carrying his iron stick and a heavy tripod for the theodolite. He watched them as they took measurements and drew lines on their maps, which they rolled up and stored in the leather tubes.

"These will tell people where to go," Thatcher told him. "How to find their way through the mountains."

Grüdj did not reply, but wondered how Standing Hollow Horn—and Two Nose Thomas, for that matter—could find their way through the mountains without tubes of maps.

That evening they were lounging by the fire, eating beans and boiled venison. Sanford Thatcher pointed to the brass medal Grüdj wore around his neck.

"Where'd you get that?" he asked.

"Black Robe." Grüdj held the medallion so the surveyor could see the cross stamped on it.

"Oh. Got a Christian cross on it. So, a missionary fellow, was he? Now you mention it, I think I've seen one of those disks before. What's on the back of it, some scripture or other?"

Grüdj turned it over.

Thatcher read the name. "Grüdj?" Thatcher carefully pronounced it twice. "What does 'Grüdj' mean?"

"This hoss, him." Grüdj slapped his chest in the manner of sign language.

"You? Your name is Grüdj?"

"Waugh."

The surveyor laughed. He was a man with some learning, an educated man who saw the ironic appropriateness of giving the name Grudge to a boy who was misshapen, black as your hat, had only one eye, and who was apparently all alone in the wilderness. The gods *must* have had a grudge against him.

"I'd have guessed you to have the name of one of the Cyclopes," he said. "Or even Polyphemus. Let's see . . . one Cyclopes was named Arges. Can't remember the other two."

Grüdj only looked at him.

"Greek stories. The Cyclopes were one-eyed and were blacksmiths. Polyphemus, he was one-eyed, too. And he could make earthquakes and lightning happen!"

"Damn," Robert Green said. "There you are *again*, giving college lectures to a black Negro! Thatcher, you missed your calling. Should've been a grade school teacher!"

Grüdj had no idea what either man was talking about, although the tongue he spoke seemed related to that of Two Nose Thomas. This one liked to talk, though, and Grüdj's instinct told him the man would say things of value. Instinct also told him that this talk of owning water and keeping land the water ran to, it was important. He would stay with these men and learn what they knew, learn their talk. Somehow, he felt, the old gods of Standing Hollow Horn had drawn him to this strange treeless place. It was they who meant for him to find these whites.

The idea of going to Spirit Lake faded from his mind. Instead, he would learn from these white men. And then he would go north for his vision. Everything was beginning to have meaning, if he would have the patience to wait.

★ ★ ★ ★ ★

During the days that followed, it was the surveyors who asked question after question of Grüdj, never seeming to grasp the fact that he had never been in this part of the mountain ranges before. "What is that mountain called?" they would ask, consulting their charts, or—"Do you know where this place is?"—or—"That trail of rock cairns where we met you, where does it lead?"

He knew the answer to the last question. The trail of piled stones was made by the others during their yearly trips across the mountains to Spirit Lake. Everyone—Crows, Shosones, Cheyennes, Arapahos—knew about it. Grüdj watched closely, fascinated, as the surveyors squinted through their instruments and drew lines on their paper to show where the trail went. The line went this way and that way, like the trail. Other lines showed the deep cañons and the high places of the mountain peaks. He saw how it worked.

While they peered through their shiny tubes and made marks on their bits of paper, Grüdj listened and learned. What Two Nose called "firestick" or "thunderstick" or "ol' bull bringer", they always called a gun, a rifle. A "Green River" was a knife. "Mokksins" were shoes or boots. "White billy" were mountain goats, and "ol' Ephraim" was the grizzly bear. They called their paper "maps" and gave numbers to the four directions. This place called Oregon was somewhere the whites were always trying to get to with their lodges on wheels. They said some "blacks" were trying to get to Oregon, too, but the distinction was lost on Grüdj. He knew his skin was black, but he was one of The People. Two Nose was a white. The distinction was lost on him, but somehow all their talk about wagons and people who were known as "blacks" crept into his dream thoughts and stayed there many days.

The Enemy warriors never returned to harass the surveyors. Grüdj did not strike his iron stick against the rocks again, at least not when any of them could see him. When he was not walking with the surveyors or sitting with them around the fire, he went to the water and tried to talk to it. He found a small lake of very still, very quiet water—the surveyor called it such places "tarns"—and impulsively thrust his stick into it. The metal struck a stone beneath the surface, whereupon there was a shaking underfoot and the water moved and sighed and sloshed out of its basin. Then it flowed back again, but like all the other water it had nothing to say to him. He saw no moss in this water, no fish, nothing. He cupped his palm and drank of it, and it was only cold and had no taste.

Below camp, farther down where the trees became a forest again and grew to their normal height, he did find a small trickle of a stream with life in it. Moss was living on the rocks. Tiny fish darted away at his approach. The stream could not talk, but, when Grüdj put the point of the iron stick into the current, the water heaved up and seemed about to boil. It leapt from its banks as if it were afraid, then it ran a long way between tree roots and under the thick carpet of leaves and pine needles before dropping back into its bed once more. The stick spoke a message to Grüdj's hand, a message about fear and the unknown. He tapped the iron stick on a rock, lightly as he could, and felt the ground tremble a little.

"Hey, Grüdj!" he heard Robert Green's voice calling. "Come give a hand with these boxes! We're getting ready to leave! Hurry it up!"

Sanford Thatcher, Chief Survey Agent
Continental Pass Survey Party
Denver City, Colorado Territory

TO: F.V. Hayden, M.D.
United States Geological Survey
c/o Fort Fielding, Nebraska

My dear Dr. Hayden:

I trust this letter finds you in good health and spirits and enjoying a productive season of survey. I anticipate being able to report to you in person and show you our findings this coming spring. We plan to complete our measurements within the month and then repair to Denver City to compile results, make charts, etc.

Knowing your interest in seismic activity in and around the Yellowstone region, I hurry to inform you of a phenomenon my colleagues and I observed on the Continental Divide in the Rocky Mountains east of the headwaters of the South Platte River. My notes, as well as those of Mr. Robert Green and Mr. William Marinas, with whom I am traveling, are attached. In abstract, what happened was this: a moving or rolling seismic wave passed under rocks upon which we were standing, a smooth upward heaving followed by an equally smooth subsidence with no fresh evidence of surface fracturing. The force wave traveled roughly north to south which surprised us somewhat in view of the fact that the predominant anticlines and synclines in this region lie on an east/west axis. Also surprising is that the *extent* of these shocks is so limited and seem to center around a pivot or pinpoint, much like the ripples formed when one throws a pebble into water.

We have since felt two lighter but similar shocks, but unfortunately did not witness them. They were witnessed by a person who we found wandering the tundra, but he is unqualified to give any useful description. Please see the accompanying map and notes for further information.

This person I mention, I must say, is almost as much an oddity as are the earth tremors. He appeared the day we were beset by hostile Indians—in fact, seemed himself to be a target of the same war party. The savages were frightened by the earth movement, which threw two of them off their feet, and we saw no more of them. The creature was baptized "Grüdj" at some point in time and has lived among fur trappers and Indians. He is dark black, nearly ebony, and has but a single eye located very near the center of his face above the nose. His back features a hump or else he has a misshapen spine, and he is quite heavy and very strong. To assist in his walking he employs a bar of steel, a tool of perhaps five and a half feet in length and weighing more than ten pounds.

"Grüdj" spends much of his time alone, although he likes to accompany me as I go about my work of setting out points for the theodolite. Whenever possible, I take time to teach "Grüdj" the names for things, and the black has an amazing capacity for learning not only terms but language in general. When we first encountered him, he spoke in that odd hodge-podge dialect of the mountain men, a mixture of corrupted French and Spanish words mixed with ungrammatical English. We could barely understand him. But after only two weeks we find he has adapted to our manner of speech with great alacrity.

This is being written at the top of the world, the Continental Divide, where we see the first indications of approaching autumn. We will soon return to Denver City where I shall post this letter and settle down to the drudgery of re-ordering and interpreting our notes. The Negro, "Grüdj", has let us know his intent is to proceed northward on foot and alone. He is quite interested in the possibilities of gaining land through irrigation. While he has said nothing about it, we privately are of the opinion that he envisions a whole community of free blacks homesteading somewhere on the high plains along the northern Front Range.

Our Respects and Best Wishes, Etc,

Sanford Thatcher for the Continental Divide Survey

Chapter Six

ON THE RIVER OF THE MOUNTAINS

His night dreams were always vague and troubled, moving across his mind as if they were thin clouds pushed about by invisible winds. Insubstantial, they drew Grüdj farther and farther north along the crest of the mountain range. He knew he was in search of something . . . but what? His best hope was to find a vision telling him what he should do. Failing that, perhaps he would find a lake or river that would give him important messages to carry back to The People. Each day the sun beat down upon him and each night brought freezing cold. Here, on the top of the world, he was a witness to the unending struggle between earth and sky. The one seemed to have no relationship to the other except some kind of hostile, enemy force to be endured. The earth tried to send up small plants, only to have the sun dry them out and beat them down again. The sky sent down its moisture, but the earth either drank it up or froze it into ice and snow.

Grüdj hiked on, crossing ridge after ridge. Between the mountains he stumbled and slid down into deep valleys only to climb up the other side again.

One day, he left the grove of gnarled, misshapen trees in which he had slept and labored up a slope of dangerously loose rock. The rock yielded fruit to him, small sweet berries and berries hanging from prickly bushes, and searching for the fruit kept him moving ever upward. Eventually he came to a more stable, grassier slope, which led to the rounded summit of the mountain.

Rather than suddenly shooting down into another deeply shadowed valley, the way most of the mountains did, this one presented a flat ridge lying out to the north. The walking was easy, and he continued to find berries along the way. All day long, the sun was warm and the breeze was light and he could see enormous distances as he walked, the prairies stretching out forever on one side, the mountains rising on the other side as if there were no end to them anywhere.

"The night will be cold," he said aloud, using Crows Woman's language. "It is time to be drawing nearer the village."

The village had been much on his mind, probably because he could see so much of the prairie so far away. Grüdj began to look for shelter, and, as he came over an easy rise of tundra, he found it waiting for him, a tiny mirror of a lake backed up by a low rock cliff. The cliff protected a thicket of twisted, wind-tortured evergreens. Here he would make his sleeping-nest.

He collected chunks of wood, old dry wood polished smooth by the wind, and piled it under the evergreens. He crawled into the thicket and cleaned off a place to lie down. And then he crawled out again, took up his iron bar, and went to the edge of the little pond. The water was cold and pure. He knelt and drank, twice, being careful not to let his bar touch the water, and, when he had finished, he stood up again.

"Thank you for the water," he said.

There was no reply except for a low, almost inaudible sigh.

"It is the wind blowing across rocks," Grüdj said.

Except that there was no wind.

The pond was nothing more than a dip in the tundra, filled with dead water. It had been imprisoned here at the top of the world, after the clouds were captured by the mountains. This place was so high and cold that nothing would grow in water here, not even moss. For a long time, Grüdj stood contemplating the tarn and its rocky basin on the ridge. In his mind, he began to see pictures of the water receding, shrinking and shrinking like the lake where he had seen the spirit lodge disappear. The images in his head showed the tarn becoming smaller and smaller until the six warriors and the naked woman reappeared.

A fantasy, nothing else.

"I dream awake," he said to the empty air.

Then an idea came to Grüdj. He began to study the ground. He walked to the opposite edge of the tarn, the edge nearest the place where the ridge dropped off into the valley. The ground fell away in a long humped curve toward the dark forest far below. A thread-thin wisp of river coursed along the bottom of the cañon. Using his bar, Grüdj scratched a line that would lead from the drop-off and back across the tundra to the water.

Grüdj then struck the ground with his bar, lightly at first, carefully experimenting. By being very careful, just allowing the weight of the iron bar to drive the point, he could crack the rocks without making the ground heave up. *Crack! Crack! Crack!* There in the late afternoon light, high on a long and lonely ridge of the great mountains, a shapeless figure hunched along, shuffling along the line he had scratched, tapping and breaking the rocks. Using the flat end of the bar as a digging stick, he next moved the loosened rocks and soil to one side and then went back along the scar he had made, fracturing more rocks. Again he pried out the broken rocks and set them to one side, then again he hit the ground with his stick. Grüdj smiled. For the first time since he helped Two Nose Thomas build the winter shelter, he was enjoying what he was doing.

During that day and the next, Grüdj went back and forth along his line until he was satisfied that he had created a river way deep enough and wide enough to lead the water to the edge of the basin and down to the river below. It was what Sanford Thatcher called a "ditch". Years later, a team of white men surveying for the establishment of a national park would look at it curiously, asking each other why Anasazis would hike all the way up to the Continental Divide to dig a ditch leading nowhere, a ditch fifty yards long and two or three feet wide. Elsewhere along the Divide the same men would find circular windbreaks made of stone and write in their reports that the Anasazis evidently covered these with brush for the purpose of using them as blinds from which to seize eagles for ceremonial purposes.

With a few final blows of the bar Grüdj broke into the shallow tarn. The water did not wait for him to lift the rocks and set them aside, but rushed from its prison and down the channel he had made, eager to be free. He smiled again; seeing the water run brought back memories of boy play. He and his young friends had sometimes dug trenches in the soft sand next to a river simply so they could watch the water go where they wanted it to. To Grüdj it seemed forever since he had been a boy at play.

He listened to the water burbling and chuckling as it ran away from the cold mountain. It would find itself a river and forget the nights of icy rocks and the days of burning sunlight.

"You can go," Grüdj said. "May the rivers lead you to my village, to my people."

The water did not respond, did not thank Grüdj. But he heard it making noises to itself, and that was enough for him. He waded into the basin, careful not to slip on the slick mud, and finished trenching a channel to drain nearly all of the water. He was satisfied with what he had done. He had made a good ditch. It would last many seasons, so it would be a long time before this shoulder of the mountain would be able to trap and keep the cloud water. He had freed the water.

Feeling defiant and proud, Grüdj walked toward the nearby summit of the mountain. His wet moccasins left dark stains on the rock as he went. This was a good thing to do, he thought as he walked. He would make ditches for many such places, using his power for the waters. This was why his dreams had pulled him to such a remote place so far from his people. He had been called to set the mountain water free.

His mood quickly changed to discouragement when he stood on top of the mountain surrounded by a blue sky afternoon and looked out all around him. In all directions and everywhere, he could see shining disks of sparkling mirrors and each one was a miniature lake. Some glimmered in the thick forest. Some winked reflections from high and treeless basins like the one behind him. They were as many as a herd of buffalo spread out across a prairie. To get to them and set them all free would take a lifetime. Perhaps many lifetimes. And who knew how many more such water places would be found in the mountains? It was too much of a task.

Grüdj's shoulders slumped as he walked down from the summit, dragging his iron bar behind. It made a clanging noise as it bumped from rock to rock.

Later, sitting in his nest beneath the bushes, he stared into his small fire and thought about what he had seen and what he had realized. He sat there so long and was so tired from his day's work that sleep toppled him over even before the darkness came. Grüdj curled up and slept on, dreaming he had set all the water free with his iron stick. He dreamed that old Three Eagles was standing in the village circle. Black Robe stood on one side of him; Grüdj stood on the other side. "Black Robe brought the buffalo," Three Eagles told The People, "but Grüdj has freed the water and brought it to us. Without water there can be no buffalo, no People, nothing. His vision has been powerful and good."

When the dream faded, he was content. He slept in peace until the morning sun found him under the bushes and poked him awake, and then the memory of seeing lakes more numerous than buffalo put a crease across his brow. He sat up, his one eye staring into the cold ashes of the fire. Surely this could not be his vision.

He took up his leather bag and iron stick and went on, the path of the highest ridgelines taking him ever farther north and west.

One morning, above timberline, Grüdj woke to snow.

He crawled out from under the sheltering tangle of stunted willows to find the whole world transformed into an unbroken expanse of white lying under a dull gray sky. He was not surprised by it, nor was he particularly troubled. It was a natural thing. But what was *not* natural was the disappearance of his iron bar. He had gone to sleep with it lying beside him, as he always did, and awoke to find it gone. Then he saw that it was not gone at all. Somehow, during the night, it had moved. It was over at the edge of the ridge, standing upright with its point stuck in the snow where the ground dropped away toward the distant valley.

Still on his knees in front of his shelter, Grüdj took a piece of jerky from his leather bag and chewed it while he contemplated this thing. How could the iron bar move itself? If someone had come in the night and taken it, why did they leave it standing there? He did not know what it meant. He found that it did not surprise him any more than waking to find the world covered in snow surprised him. He just did not know how it happened or what it meant. He thought he saw small footprints, but he could not be sure whether they were human or animal. The glare of sun on snow made it hard to see. Maybe there had been footprints and they had filled in with more snow.

Grüdj finished his jerky and slung the bag across his back, then rose to his feet and waded through the snow toward where the bar was standing. The snow was not too wet, but still clung to his leggings almost up to his knees. More snow would come soon, so it was time he looked for better shelter farther down the mountains, a winter camp. He thought about Two Nose Thomas. Together they could build a fine winter camp. He thought about the lodge of Crows Woman, which would be warm on such a morning as this. In the village there would be the sounds of people talking in other lodges, the odor of wood smoke on winter air, meat boiling in a pot on the fire.

"I will take the iron stick and go down the mountain, in the direction where the sun wakes up."

But when he reached his bar, Grüdj knew it had been placed there for a reason. There was something he was supposed to see.

Except for the iron bar being moved, he would not have walked that way, out onto that edge of the ridge. The best place for a winter camp was on the other side of the mountain. It was in that direction, where the sun first wakes, that the country was friendlier, more familiar. But, as he put his hand out to grasp his bar, he saw there was a river below him. Not just another mountain stream, but a river as big as the River of Twisting Ribbons out on the buffalo prairie. It came from mountains to the north and stretched broad and silvery out of sight to the south.

He studied the course of it, straining to see as far into the south as he could. Standing Hollow Horn had spoken of a great river that took water to Spirit Lake. This must be that river. On it he would find his dreaming place. Grüdj was seized by a certainty such as he had never known. His vision would come to him somewhere along this gleaming water, but not in the direction of Spirit Lake. Upstream, where the mountains held the rain.

Slipping on rocks, falling over logs hidden under the snow, and getting slapped by tree branches, Grüdj went down the mountain. By mid-afternoon he had descended far enough to be out of the snow and he was tired. He began looking for a place to sleep, maybe a cave or a tree whose branches touched the ground and made a lodge. He saw hiding places everywhere, for these forests were tangled and dark with shadows, but each rock overhang and every bent bush he looked into was ominous and threatening. He would rather stay awake and keep moving all night than sleep in such places. The sun went away and the forest was dark and cold. The thickly interlaced tree branches kept him from seeing very far ahead and all he could do was to keep moving downhill. A deep layer of needles and moss cushioned his steps, so that, except for the rasp of his own breathing, there seemed to be no sound anywhere in the forest. Finally exhausted, Grüdj found a cavity between the roots of a huge tree with drooping branches. He wedged himself into it and went to sleep.

His dream that night was of Who Sees Far. The old man's hair was white. His clothing was all white. Even the beads decorating his shirt were white.

"Where are you?" Who Sees Far asked him. "What was your vision?"

"This one had no vision," Grüdj answered, remembering to speak politely in the third person. "He traveled to the great mountain where piles of stone show the path to Spirit Lake. He talked with whites. He has found a great river."

Who Sees Far seemed not to hear him.

"The People have no water. There has been no rain," the old man's apparition said. "For food there are only a few antelope and a few deer. No buffalo. Where are you?"

"Who Sees Far, this one has found the river of Spirit Lake. The People might bring their lodges here, their ponies."

"Where are you?" the vision repeated.

"I do not know," Grüdj admitted, twisting painfully in his sleep and muttering.

"Crows Woman worries. Two Nose worries. Standing Hollow Horn worries. Where are you? The People are moving their lodges. They will go toward where you are always facing. Perhaps they go as far as the Sand Creek country."

"Wait!" Grüdj tried to shout, but the vision of Who Sees Far was already fading. "Here is one who will find the old gods for Standing Hollow Horn. He will find water for The People. Wait!"

The dream passed. The night, too, passed. In the morning, there was blue sky to be seen through the tops of the trees, but no sunlight penetrated the forest where Grüdj struggled out of his hole between the roots to stand upright again. He stood slumped over and staring at the ground. He knew his dream meant that Who Sees Far had passed to be with the grandfathers and the ancestors of The People. The others were so hungry they were moving their lodges south in late winter, not even waiting for the spring grass to become green. He had never been where they were going, and, if he wanted to find them, he would not know where to look. He did not know where Sand Creek might be.

There was no water and he had no more jerky in his leather bag. There was nothing for Grüdj to do but go on struggling through the gloomy shadows of the forest. The ground under his feet was soft and difficult, with tendrils of plants to trip him. Tree branches grabbed at him. At times, he did not know which way to go because the forest floor was flat and the sun was hidden by the trees. He knew he was wandering back and forth too much, but he saw no way to go in a straight line. He half expected to come upon his sleeping spot again and discover he had been going in circles.

Much of the day passed and the forest ahead of him seemed to have more light in it. The trees were farther apart. There were bushes now, the willow and the rose bush. He found a rose bush still bearing the dried hips of last summer and collected as many as he could find to stuff into his mouth and into his bag. They were dry and full of many tiny seeds but still tasted good. He saw sunlight ahead and heard the sound of much water running, and, when he emerged from the forest at the foot of the mountain, he found himself standing at the edge of a grassy meadow bordering the mighty river.

He had made it to the river at last, and a dead deer lay at his feet. The deer had been killed by a single slender arrow and was lying where he would come out of the forest as if it had been placed there as a gift. The body was still soft and yielding to the touch, so he knew it had been killed very recently. The meat would be good. He stood thinking. If it was meant for him, he needed to act in a very polite manner in accepting it. If it was some hunter's quarry and the hunter was still looking for it, he needed to acknowledge that he did not assume it was his.

In a respectful way, Grüdj gently withdrew the arrow that had killed the deer. It had been an accurate shot, just behind the shoulder and straight into the heart. But the arrow was like none he had ever seen. The shaft was polished white and had no markings on it. The tip was tiny and delicately chipped from red flint. The feathers were airy and fragile like those of a mountain grouse, only white. He stood up and held the arrow in both hands above his head, calling out in the tongue of The People.

"Hunter! Your arrow has killed this deer! I say it . . . Grüdj of The People! Hunter! Come claim your kill!"

There was no answer.

"Hunter! Your aim was good. This is your meat. I honor your skill."

Again there was no answer, only the sound of the river.

This was the tradition of The People. During a buffalo chase, a hunter might shoot his arrow or throw a lance at a running buffalo and keep on riding after another. Later on, when the meat was being collected, whoever found a dead animal made such an announcement as Grüdj had just made. That person could claim a portion of the meat. Sometimes the hunter wanted some widow or old person to have the meat, so he would not answer their announcement and would let them have it.

"Hunter! Grüdj hungers for meat! I would eat from your kill!"

There was still no reply, only the sound of the big river pounding over rocks. From the corner of his eye he caught a quick flash of white as if some small person had been running between the trees, but no one appeared to claim either the arrow or the deer.

"Hunter!"

Still no reply. Grüdj took out his knife and went to work.

Grüdj decided to remain there in the meadow alongside the river. After he had made a fire and cooked meat to relieve his hunger, he used his great strength to break thick branches from the trees to build a crib in which to dry the venison into jerky. While he was looking for suitable branches, he found more rose hips and old dry chokecherries that he collected. Later, he would pound them into strips of the venison. He dragged logs from the forest and built a windbreak for his fire, then rested and cooked the liver of the deer.

For many days, he was almost content, almost at peace with the river and the valley and his own spirit. The sun had warmth in it. The snow did not reach down to the river. He had a good place to sleep, with his fire in front of him and logs behind him. He would have considered building a winter lean-to in this place, were it not for the unanswered question of who had killed the deer and for the feeling he was being watched.

Out collecting sticks for the fire one day, he saw the sudden flash of white again as if there was someone running through the dense forest. Eyes seemed to follow him as he set snares for rabbits and speared fish with a sharpened willow stick. He asked the river who it was, but the spirit of the water only laughed at him in a rude way. The river was angry about something. Some days it would not talk to

Grüdj at all. It was a fast river, very busy pounding at the rocks, whirling sand and gravel in its eddies and rolling boulders along the riverbed beneath its icy water. The sound of the boulders rolling was like far-off thunder.

Another day, he walked down the stream farther than he had ever gone, following animal trails in and out of the trees, sometimes walking on the very edge of the stream and sometimes forced to clamber up over a shoulder of the mountain. Even from high places he could not see where the river went, but he did find a place where a beaver dam had caused one part of the stream to be diverted into a separate channel. Here there was just a little of the water and it was flowing calmly. He could talk to it. He got down on his stomach in the cold grass at the edge of the bank and asked the river about its dreams. He asked about its parents.

The running water murmured of having once been trapped in ice and locked into frozen rocks. It remembered being divided, a dim memory of sisters and brothers taken away to a place they were not supposed to go. It was a bigger river, before this happened. There was more of it, running from stone to stone and dropping over ledges.

"Speak of your before time," Grüdj said. "Where were you before the ice and snow?"

The water had no memory of before, but only quick fragments of sensations and feeling. Some sense of bitterness. Very hot sun. Endless strange water and strange creatures moving in it. Salty water. Beyond this the water could tell Grüdj nothing of its past, but it had told him enough.

"You, river," Grüdj said. "You have not been where The People live. That is not where you go."

The waters of the big prairie did not know the kinds of limitless lake this water spoke of, nor did prairie waters ever see such giant creatures as this water had known. This river went somewhere else. Perhaps that was what made it angry.

Grüdj returned to his camp that evening to find the arrow missing. He had set it carefully on a flat stone just outside his windbreak and it was gone. The one who watched him must have taken it back. Grüdj ate and sat by his fire thinking about the arrow and the river. He awoke in the morning thinking he had heard something, a sound like a soft long whistling, and, when he rose and went around the windbreak, he found that another deer had been left for him. Like the first deer, this one had the slender white arrow sticking out just behind the shoulder. The flesh was still warm. As before, Grüdj withdrew the arrow and held it aloft in the traditional manner, calling to the hunter.

"Hunter! Your aim is true. Here is your kill. Come!"

As before, there was no reply.

Good days followed one upon the other, days of warm winter sun and good meat. He explored the meadow and the fringe of the dark forest carefully, but he found no sign of fire pits, no stone circles showing where people had pitched lodges, nothing but the faint thin trails left by animals coming to the stream. He did not try to cross the stream nor did he try to talk to it. It did not talk to him, either, but went on crashing and roaring among its rocks. Grüdj soaked the two deer skins and staked them out to scrape away the flesh, but he had little skill when it came to such work. He had watched women scrape buffalo hide many, many times, so he knew that the clinging bits of dried flesh had to be chipped and pried and scratched at until they came off the skin. He banged rocks together until had some sharp pieces suitable for scrapers and labored on his knees until the hides were clean. But they still remained stiff.

A third deer was left for him. In the same manner he

claimed it, laid the arrow aside with care and respect, and cut up the meat. Some meat he hung in his makeshift crib of logs to dry. Some he cooked. And it was while he was scraping the hide clean that the idea came upon him. He would make a medicine lodge with these hides. And *in* that lodge he would find his vision. It would be like the spirit lodge whose warrior guardians he had offended, and in such a lodge his vision would come to him. He had no companion, no elder to watch over him and bring him water as he made his journey along the vision path, but he did have a spirit hunter bringing him meat. He had warm sun with no wind. He had the sound of the river. This place must have been intended for his dream.

Grüdj selected four long, straight poles in the forest and remembered to ask the trees' permission as he cut away the limbs and peeled off the bark. He soaked the deer skins and lashed them to the poles, using sinew thrust through holes made with his knife. And when he finally pushed his lodge upright and spread the poles, it was nothing like the spirit lodge. It was small and crooked and ugly. The deer skins did not reach the ground. He made trips to the forest for tree branches which he leaned against the lodge until it looked more like a pile of brush. All that could be said for it was that it would keep out the wind and some of the snow, if the snow came. Grüdj crawled inside and sat cross-legged, looking west toward the river. It was very small, but it would do.

Grüdj emerged from his medicine lodge and went back to his log windbreak where he discovered a plump rabbit, freshly killed, waiting for him. It is a sign, he thought. It is a sign that the spirit of the place approves of his medicine lodge. The spirit wanted him to eat, then have his vision time. He wasted little time skinning the rabbit and putting it on a willow skewer over the fire, for rabbit was one of Grüdj's favorite things to eat. But something nagged at his mind while he was sitting there watching the meat cook. Something was not right. But the smell of roasting rabbit seduced his mind away from wariness and all he could think of was how fine it would taste.

It was after he tasted it, after it had cooled and he had used his teeth to strip the meat from a leg, that Grüdj realized what was wrong.

The iron bar was missing.

Suddenly the rabbit did not matter. He got to his feet, his eye staring at the place where the bar had been lying on the ground just inside the windbreak. He turned and looked over the logs. He went to the medicine lodge and looked inside. He searched the place where he had staked out the deer skins, went to the tree under whose low-hanging branches he stacked his firewood. Grüdj went everywhere in the river meadow without finding the bar, and the he went to the edge of the river itself. Far out in the water he could see a long dark shape lying on the bottom in a deep part of the current. It was the bar. The river had taken it. The river had taken his iron bar and was keeping it in a place he could not reach.

He stood staring out into the river for a long time, muttering at the water. But the water did not answer except to go on rumbling against its rocks. Grüdj finally shambled to his medicine lodge and crawled inside to sit with slumped shoulders and glare out at the river with his one eye. The winter sun continued across the sky over the valley. From time to time his nostrils caught the scent of his cooking fire. The little lodge was warm. His anger and frustration seemed to seep away from him and left him drowsy with half sleep. He did not know whether he was awake or was sleeping when the voice came to him. It was a light, whispering kind of voice, a voice somewhere outside the tiny lodge. It was so small a voice that it could barely be heard above the constant rumble of the river.

"Black One," hissed the small voice. "Black One."

Grüdj's head lifted slightly. His eye remained closed.

"Black One, it is time to go back to your people. Soon it will be the moon of new grass. You have come far and you have far to return."

"No," Grüdj muttered. "The time of snow is here."

"You stay longer than you know. You have forgotten the seasons. You have forgotten The People."

It was not true. Grüdj remembered The People. He remembered Standing Hollow Horn and Two Nose Thomas and Crows Woman. He had come far. He would like to return. But he had not found the way to repair what he had caused. He had found no water that would go and help the buffalo and the prairie and The People. The voice knew his thoughts and spoke to him once more.

"Return. There is no water here for The People. The way is guarded by The Enemy. The snow is deep in the forest. Go, tell them. Go back."

He thought about Two Nose Thomas. Two Nose. The small whispering spirit voice ceased and Grüdj drowsed again until his round body was heaving with deep and regular breathing. The dream that came to him then was not a dream of the river or of the open prairies or the spirit lodge. It was only a dream memory of the time he had helped Two Nose trap beaver.

"Hyar's how t'make 'em come," Two Nose told him, dipping a twig in a leathern bottle and sticking the twig in the mud next to where the beaver had climbed out of the pond.

"Mister Beaver, he smells thet med'cin clear out'n his pond."

The stuff did smell strong. Two Nose made it from the glands of other beaver, mixed with bear fat. Two Nose took a steel trap from his pack and cocked it and laid it under the water just where the beaver would be sure to step in it. The chain from the trap went to a stick driven into the mud.

"Yes, sir," Two Nose said as he worked. "Ol' Man Beaver, he cain't never resist thet smell! Figgers he's just gotta git him a closer sniff on't. Comes swimmin' over hyar, and snap! *Thar's a gone beaver an' a good plew,* waugh!*"*

The dream lingered, the dream of fooling beaver into the trap. Grüdj dreamed of Two Nose showing him how to fool fish, too, with willow traps. And antelope, who would see a bit of antelope tail atop a stick that Two Nose waved and would follow their curiosity within range of his long gun. But these dreams meant nothing to Grüdj. They were not visions. The spirit voice was right; it was time for him to return to The People again. Perhaps on the other side of the mountains he would find beaver and catch them and take the plews back for Crows Woman. He would leave the very next day.

But the next day found him sitting on the edge of the fast-flowing river staring at where his iron stick lay. He would not return without it. After a long time of looking into the water, he finally rose and went to his wood cache for an armload of firewood. He built a big, hot fire inside the windbreak, banking it with the thickest pieces of wood so it would last a long time. One strong stick of wood he set aside to use for support when he entered the river.

Satisfied that the fire was burning well, he returned to the riverbank and removed his clothing. For an instant he paused, not because he was afraid of the icy water but because he had a memory vision of the warriors who guarded the spirit lodge and how they had vanished into the strange lake.

Grüdj plunged into the current well upstream of where his iron bar lay, using the wooden stick and flailing his thick short arm to keep his balance. His toes gripped the slippery rocks and the strength in his bowed legs served him well, keeping him upright. Each time he raised a foot to take a step forward the power of the river started to spin him around, making him fight with his arms, but step by step and inch by inch he moved against the current, his feet feeling for a way along the slick rocks. The water came up to his hips, then above his belly, and by the time he reached the place where the stick was, the water was up to his armpits, and each time he took a step the current threatened to float him away.

Then his foot touched the metal. Once he had the bar he would be all right. It would give him weight and something to balance with. Letting go of the wooden stick, he filled his chest with all the air it could hold and dove beneath the surface. The instant his hand touched the bar the current shoved him downstream until he felt the end of the bar slip through his fingers. He was being floated away, just as he had feared he would be. Thrashing and coughing for air, Grüdj bobbed to the surface and fought with all the strength in his arms to get back upstream. The river seemed to curl waves over his head like giant hands, forcing him under, but he used his feet to thrust himself forward along the bottom and used his arms as paddles. He got to the shallows by the bank and shivered violently while he stepped from stone to stone upriver. When he had gone far enough, he waded out into the swift current to fight his way to the iron bar once more.

His foot touched it and he could tell exactly where it was, so Grüdj thrashed his way farther up the current and dove beneath the surface. His fingers felt the metal and grasped the bar in a desperate grip. He got his feet under him and pushed off from the bottom. Again the river carried him like a cork bobbing through the rapids, the bar dragging behind. At times, it was all he could do to keep his head above the water. It slapped at him, knocked him this way and that, tried to rip the bar from his hands, tried to knock his legs out from under him so he would sink. But Grüdj held on. He kicked against the bottom whenever one of his feet touched a stone. Each time he bobbed underneath the water, he hurled himself backward toward the shore. Little by little, gasping for breath and fighting the icy chill that cramped his muscles, he managed to come nearer and nearer the shore. Just within arm's reach of the bank, though, the river tried one more trick—it washed him into a bottomless swirling eddy right against the bank, a place where the bank was a sheer wall of soggy dirt. Grüdj let go of his bar with one hand and clawed at the dirt with his stubby fingers but the half-frozen mud only crumbled and came loose. The river current swept him into the corner and held him prisoner.

Grüdj saw that he could not stay afloat in this place for long. With the last of his strength he gripped the bar in both hands, let himself sink and twist in the cold black whirlpool until his feet touched bottom. He struck out as hard as he could with the bar, jabbing it into the bank the way a hunter would lance a buffalo.

There was a rumble and the sound of earth splitting in pain. The river drew back. The high muddy bank cracked open, then slumped and slid into the water. Mud flowed under Grüdj's feet until he was able to crawl up it on his hands and knees and onto the solid ground of the riverbank. He was nearly exhausted, but he knew he could not rest here or he would die of the cold. He lurched to his feet.

With his iron bar as his staff, he forced his legs into an awkward half-running gait and, shivering, hurried back up along the river to his windbreak and his fire.

Chapter Seven

TOWARD THE SOURCE

Grüdj ripped up handfuls of dry grass to rub the mud from his knees and belly before putting on his clothes and warming himself at the fire. After he stopped shivering and his teeth had stopped chattering, he devoured the remainder of the rabbit meat and slumped, exhausted, against the logs. A long time went by before he felt like moving, and then it was only to build up the fire again. With the iron bar clutched in his arms, he curled up in the warmth of the windbreak and fell into exhausted sleep.

A dream came upon him.

"Waugh!" *The smiling face of Two Nose Thomas was complete in every detail, from his yellow teeth and stubble of beard to his pale eyes.*

"Two Nose," Grüdj said, running the words together as he always had. "Where are you?"

"With The People, pointin' our tracks south," the voice of Two Nose replied. "Buncha grubbin' gold miners done fer the last ev the buffler, so they has. The People move south now. No water yit, nossir. How be ye, Grüdj?"

"I have no vision," Grüdj said.

" 'Course you ain't," said the voice. "Ye're not gittin' a vision 'cause ye be gittin' yore meat on th' peraira and ye're all warm an' comfortable ez a fat cow. This here whole consarn o'

yourn t'aint nuthin' but a winter camp an' a cozy 'un at thet. Ol' Standing Horn, he'd tell 'ee thar never wuz no vision come like thet. Starvin' is what brings it, Negra. Fastin' an' bein' still."

"This place, it brings me food," Grüdj protested. "There is a spirit being here who wants me to have it."

"Ye're thinkin' this *hyar cañon's friendly t'ye? Way out* hyar? Waugh! *'Tain't likely so. You better cipher on it some more. This hyar hos, he never turned down nuthin' what was give t'him free on the peraira, whether she be fat fleece, poor bull, or Taos lightnin', but he allus wanted t'make blame' certain sure he knowed whar it come from. Nuthin' comes fer nuthin', hos, not in th' mountains. Iffen thet spirit bein's bringin' ye meat, ye'd better figger why. Mebbe it don't want Grüdj t'hev a vision dream. Hah?"*

Grüdj started to answer, but the face of Two Nose began to shrink and shrink until it was far away and finally no more than a point of light.

Grüdj woke without moving and without opening his eye. Someone was in the windbreak with him. Whoever it was had put more wood on the fire; he could tell by the warmth. Wanted to keep him warm so he wouldn't wake up. And now the person had hold of one end of his bar and was trying to slide it out from under him without waking him. Grüdj gripped it hard and suddenly rolled up into sitting position. The thin female recoiled in surprise, losing her balance and toppling over. She came to rest against the logs, facing Grüdj across the fire.

She was a young woman. She wore a capote like the ones the fur trappers made out of Hudson Bay blankets, except that hers was as pale as aspen bark. When she tumbled back against the logs, the hood of the capote was pulled back to reveal that her hair was the color of autumn leaves. But what Grüdj could not stop staring at was the hue of her skin. He had never seen anyone so white. Nor anyone so thin. Even though she wore high deerskin boots with long wrappings and skirt of pale yellow leather, and, in spite of the fur shirt she wore beneath her capote, he could tell she was as thin as a willow stick. Her bare hands and her face told it all. Across her back she wore a quiver of arrows and he saw her bow leaning against the windbreak.

For a time they only sat there, this incongruous pair. On one side of the fire sat Grüdj, round as a well-fed bear and just as dark. On the other sat the thin girl, white as alabaster.

Grüdj began to speak, but then stopped. Did she speak the tongue of the whites or the language of Two Nose? Or even the language of The People? Seeing his hesitation, she spoke first. He knew instantly that her voice was the one he had heard whispering to him when he was in his crude medicine lodge.

"I came to see to you," she said. "I bring meat and make your fire warm again." She spoke The People's language, but as a child would, with simple words and plain phrases.

"You brought the deer and the rabbit?" he asked.

"Yes."

"Then you are the spirit of this place?"

"I protect the water. The spirits want me to tell you to return across the mountains the way you came. You do not belong here."

"You feed me," Grüdj protested.

"For strength to return. You should go."

Grüdj poked at the fire with a twig. He regarded her carefully. She might be the one who threw his iron stick in the river. She might even be the one who had moved it when he was at the place on the top of the world. It was true that she had brought meat, enough to make jerky for many days of travel. She did it so he would go away. Two Nose was right: nothing comes in the mountains without a price. Well, he wasn't going to do it. But he did need to move on to a better place, a higher place. The instinct was sharp and firm in his mind—somewhere at the source of this river he would find the place where he would find his vision.

He needed to endure a fasting before the vision would be true, a vision that would be complete in its meaning. Sometimes, he knew, seekers after such visions would find the leaves of a certain plant and would eat them on an empty stomach and the vision would come. He did not have these, but when he found the right place, fasting would be enough. He would never be able to enter the dream place so long as he kept eating the meat she brought to him. And now she was saying she would give him more meat, meat for a journey, if he would leave the mountains. Should he go up to the source of the water, or go and find The People while he had the strength?

Grüdj sat motionless with his thoughts. The pale woman sat patiently nearby. At last, Grüdj spoke again.

"I seek a vision," he told her. "I cannot return until the gods speak to me."

"What gods are those?" she said. "Do you see any gods here, in this valley? In this river?"

"The People once knew the old gods who lived in the cold mountains. I went with Standing Hollow Horn when he searched for them. Now I search for them alone. They are somewhere up there where the water begins."

"They will not speak to you," she said in her whispering voice. "Even if they are still there, they will not speak to you. You know this. Return. The only gods you will find are the gods of the water. I tell you to return to your place, to your village."

"You speak truth," Grüdj answered. "The gods of Standing Hollow Horn are not here in this valley place. They will not speak to me here. I must go to where the water begins and be alone in a high place. The last moon of winter is coming," Grüdj went on. "When it is past, I will follow this river to the place where it is born, to where it breaks itself free of the rocks that catch clouds. There I will make my fasting and have my vision."

"No!" she shouted. In her anger she used words from the talk of the white men. "No! No farther! Go back the way you came!"

She leaped to her feet so quickly that it startled him, and in the next instant she had grabbed up her bow and was gone from the windbreak. Grüdj got to his feet in time to see her crossing the meadow with the speed of a deer running. For a moment she was a flash of white moving among the trees before she vanished altogether, leaving him alone with the rumbling of the river and the crackling of the fire.

The next day, Grüdj selected the most pliable of the three deer skins and spent the morning hammering it, first with a stick and then with a rock, trying to get it soft enough to make into a pack. Grüdj felt angry with himself that he could not do a better job of it. Back in the village he made good things, but here he seemed clumsy and uncertain.

"Clever Grüdj," he said, mimicking the way Crows Woman used to encourage him when he was a boy. "You have made a fine carrying pot. Your hands are quick."

He finally made the skin bendable and sewed it with

sinew and gut. It was a very poor excuse for a bag, but it was big enough to hold most of the remaining dried deer meat. Grüdj slung the new bag over one shoulder, put his old parfleche over the other, then picked up his iron bar and started walking upriver. He did not try to hurry. He did not try to talk to the rushing water. He only shambled along, sometimes forcing his way through willow thickets, sometimes climbing over and around boulders, sometimes making a wide detour into the forest to avoid a steep bank. Often he stopped to rest and look up into the mountains that walled in the valley.

On his second day of walking upstream Grüdj saw two things he did not understand. The first of the two things was a cairn made of stone, but not a cairn such as The People used to mark the trail across the mountain. This was no more than a clumsy pile of rocks put there as some kind of marker. The trees around the cairn showed deep cuts made by a sharp axe. It didn't mark a trail. It didn't seem to mark anything.

The other thing Grüdj noticed was across the river. A long, steep side cañon came down from the mountain over there, but it had no water. Yet it came down the side of a giant of a mountain, a huge bulk covered in deep forest. There should be a stream plunging and foaming down over those rocks and logs. The river he was following ran full with spring-melted snow water. There was plenty of water everywhere. On the previous day and on this day, too, he had stepped across small creeks pouring down out of the mountain. But over there on that massive mountain the riverbed had no river in it. Grüdj continued making his way along the rocks, going through willows, sometimes hoisting himself up over ledges. Then he saw it again. Across the river, another dry cañon coming down to join the river.

He could see that the cañon had once held water. The rocks were clean as if scrubbed, the fringe of soil was well back from the cleft in the mountain, and there were small tangles of driftwood where water had jammed them into corners and up against boulders.

Dry driftwood and dry rocks, but no sign of water.

Grüdj went down to the bank of the river. To get the river's attention he reached out and banged on a rock with his bar. The ground heaved and the river moaned but it went on rushing past as if ignoring him.

"River!" Grüdj said loudly. "River! Your children, the small streams, are happy on this side. I have seen them running to meet you. No more does the mountain hold them."

The running water seemed to quiet itself as if it were listening.

"River!" Grüdj said. "Your other-side children. I cannot see them. I see their track where they went. Does the mountain hold them? Tell me. I, Grüdj, can let them free. I have done it on the top of the world place."

Why would a parent stay silent when a child is lost? The river only complained over its rocks and went on pouring down the long flat place to plunge over another chaos of rocks below. Then Grüdj heard a sound as if a mountain cougar had screamed in the distant forest. He heard it again and realized what it was—a hawk was calling from the sky as it soared in a circle over the valley. Grüdj's eye followed its flight as it crossed the river and became a small speck above the heavy mountain. He saw what he was supposed to see. High on this mountain, almost invisible in the trees, a line of freshly dug earth ran straight across the slope.

Grüdj clambered up to a high point above the river to get a better look. Now he could see that this line of fresh earth was above the line where the trees would not grow.

And it looked big, as big as one of the roads where the wagon people went. But why would wagon people build a road away up there? Where would it go?

He went on up the hill to an even higher outcrop of rock and stood there gazing across the valley at the odd sight. It looked like a wagon road, but it went nowhere. He could see how it went around the curving flank of the mountain, vanished into the shade-filled gorge beyond, emerged again to go around the bulge of the next mountain, vanished into the next gorge and did not come out. *It ends in that last cañon,* he decided. Grüdj searched out an angle of stone where the sun was warm where he would be out of the wind and there he plopped down to chew on some jerky and contemplate this thing. Maybe this was what the thin pale girl did not want him to see. He chewed and he studied the far off line of light-colored earth running across the mountains. Maybe this thing was what kept the creeks from reaching the river, somehow.

Somehow.

Grüdj finished his bit of jerky and started down toward the river. The hillside was steep and he often slid, grabbing for bushes to stop his fall. Little landslides of pebbles and dirt went ahead of him. When he finally got to the river and asked it to tell him about the road, the river still only complained and murmured and made crashing noises against the rocks. All he could learn was that the river was angry. He crossed another small creek running into the river and stopped to drink from it and ask it where it had come from. He learned that this little rivulet was happy, that it had been locked in the ice and in the rocks high above on the mountain where the trees could not grow, but now it was on its way into the river. Like the creek he spoke with days before, this one had a dim memory of a vast bitter lake where monsters lived. It knew nothing about any road.

Grüdj wanted to get to the top of the valley where the river ran and see what kind of road it was, but it seemed as if the mountain and the river did not want him to go. The way along the river became steeper and steeper, the footing more precarious. There were no longer any animal trails along the bank. Twice he had to wade into the icy water to get around a rock fall or uprooted tree. Often he shouldered through thick willows only to come to a sheer wall of rock, forcing him to return and seek another way. Late in the afternoon he arrived at a cliff that formed a barricade across the whole valley. The river poured off it in a deafening waterfall. The slope upon which Grüdj stood was far too steep to climb. He would have to turn around, go back down the way he came, and find another way up the mountain. The sun was behind the mountain now and the cold of night was returning. He would need to find a place to sleep.

When morning came, there was no fresh rabbit meat, but Grüdj made himself a small fire, nonetheless. The crackling noise and the warmth cheered him up. The sun slowly rose far enough to shine down into the narrow cañon. Grüdj studied the far-away streak of road, then the torrent of water pouring down the cañon. He had to go on. The farther he struggled, the more certain he became that he would find his vision place at the top of this long mountain.

He left the shelter of the rock overhang and studied the cliff that barricaded the gorge, then made his way down the steep slope to the edge of the water.

"Water!" Grüdj said over the grumbling of the rapids. The water did not reply. "Water!" he said again. "It is Grüdj. I need to cross over."

Still no response. Grüdj grew so exasperated that he resorted to the harsh-sounding tongue of Two Nose.

"Consarn ye, then!" he said. "Dang ye fer a consarn dribblin' crick! Grüdj brings hisself t'help 'ee an' whar's the trade?"

No answer came from the pouring waters.

"*Waugh!* This hos oughta make backtrack, so he should. Pull stakes f'r th' peraira ag'in. Now spread out hyar an' let a Negra pass over!"

"What words are these?" The small whispering voice was suddenly behind him. It was the thin pale woman again. She was carrying her bow and had her quiver of arrows on her back, but she had no rabbit with her.

"The cliff blocks my way," Grüdj said. "I would cross over."

"You are not returning to your people? You still try to go up the river instead?"

"The People would not have me return like this."

"You wish to be a hero to them."

"I must be. It is a thing they need."

"Well," she said. "Then you must cross over the river. Go ahead." Her eyes narrowed into that sly look a fox has.

Grüdj looked out across the river. It was wide where they were standing, wide and fast and dangerous. Downstream it was crowded with jutting boulders and broken trunks of huge trees and the water made deep swirls and whirlpools among them. Upstream a narrow gorge between cliffs made the water white and foaming where it crashed between the rocks.

"With your stick you can cross," she said. "It will give you power. Try it. Once you get to the other side, your way will be easy. It is only another day to where the river is born. Go. Try. Walk out into the water. Your iron stick will balance you."

Grüdj leaned on his iron stick and regarded her suspiciously. Her eyes still held that cunning look.

"*Waugh,*" he mumbled. "Hyar's damp powder, sartain shore."

"What do you say?"

Her confusion pleased him. He did not like it that she knew the talk of The People. She also had the tongue of the whites. But she did not know Two Nose's words and it put her off balance.

"Fust ye'd hev this hos haul freight f'r th' flat country. Then ye'd enjoy t'see 'im walk inta a flood sich as'd make ol' Noah nervous."

Grüdj didn't know who Noah was, but Two Nose often referred to him as a man who had seen a power of water in his day.

"*Waugh!* Somethin' don't shine here, not a-tall."

"Go ahead," she said. "Cross over."

"Mebbe it's *ye* as oughter go ahead," he said. "But this hos has him a better idea. Best ye stand back."

He deliberately turned his back and hiked toward the skirt of the cliff upriver. Wading across that ice cold stretch of thundering water might not "shine", but he had figured out how it might be done. The answer had been in his hands all the while. Reaching the slope where the cliffs met the river, Grüdj struggled up the loose rock by using scrubby bushes for handholds. Sometimes he would stop and plant the iron bar firmly, then haul himself up by it. He was soon perspiring in the cold air, but he shrugged it off and went on climbing. At last he stood atop the rocky pinnacle, a tower of fractured granite overlooking the river. The cliff just upstream was tall and sheer and insurmountable, but it did not matter because he was not going that way. He would cross the river, but not in the way the pale woman expected.

Grüdj stepped out near the edge and selected a crack in the rock, then raised his bar high above his head and drove its point into the rock with all of his strength. The bar rang out and sharp fragments flew like hail. The cloud of rock dust had a smell that reminded him of when lightning strikes. The cliff heaved and shuddered as if it were coming to life. It quivered and swayed, and then the whole cliff face tilted outward and began the long slide toward the river below. Grüdj stepped back and struck again, and again the cliff heaved and twisted under his blow. Huge blocks of granite separated from the cliff, first leaning and leaning, and then shattering and roaring downward. He could not see the river for the dust in the air. It looked as if the avalanche of rock was just sliding down into a brown cloud. He picked out one more place to strike with his iron bar and sent much of the remainder of the cliff sliding down. Grüdj stood on the high shoulder of the mountain and surveyed his handiwork. The newly broken rock at his feet gleamed and dazzled in the sunlight. He leaned on his bar and grinned as he listened to the echoes of crashing rock still bouncing and fading along the cañon.

Sometimes sliding, sometimes almost running, he hurried back down the way he had come. The pale woman was nowhere to be seen. A cloud of dust obscured the sun. When he saw how well his idea had succeeded, he laughed and did an awkward little dance step. With so much rock choking the narrows, the river had stopped running. Its bed was nearly empty. Grüdj picked up his two bags and made his way between the deep puddles, being careful not to slip on the slimy moss. Once safely across, he climbed up to a high spot and ate some of his jerky while he waited for the river to do something to free itself, but nothing happened. A few trickles oozed out from under the rock dam and the dam held.

Too much rock. He smiled. *Next time I'll use less.* He got to his feet and resumed his journey toward the river's source, chuckling to himself. Sometimes he playfully threatened the water with his iron stick.

Grüdj was well upstream when he heard the distant rumble of the dam letting go. The water down there would be angry and loud, but where he stood the river merely sighed like a whipped dog that had crept behind a lodge to lick its bruises. Grüdj saw a small rock in his path, a stone no bigger than a man's head, and, when he used his iron stick like a lance to knock it out of his way, it sailed far out into the river. He repeated this trick with the next such rock he came to, and the next and next until he was tired of the game. The sun was warm. The air was cool. The cañon began to widen and soften as the trees became less numerous. It was starting to resemble the high mountains he remembered from his boyhood, the mountains where Standing Hollow Horn believed he would find the old gods of The People.

With the trees giving way to clumps of willows, which themselves became more and more stunted as he went on, Grüdj could see clearly the line of the wagon road not far above him. And much as he liked taking the easy path along the river where he could often walk in soft grass, when he found another dry watercourse, he knew the time had come for him to climb up to that road and see what it was. The little stream had once run down its own little valley, dropping over ledges, watering patches of grass, forming pools, and washing pebbles. Now its path was dry and bare. The pebbles that had been shiny beneath the water were dull and had a scum on them. The small level grassy places looked brown and dead.

Grüdj found the reason as he scrambled up the last few

feet of the dirt embankment and stood on the road, for it was not just a road. It was a road with a deep, wide ditch running alongside it. The stream came down from the snow fields this far, then had to turn and go along this man-made ditch for some reason. On his last trip with the people of Standing Hollow Horn when he was a boy, Grüdj had seen whites at the soldier town who made ditches for water to run in. They had planted something in the earth and were making the water go to it. But this—this was far, far more water than anyone needed.

He was tempted to take his iron bar and break down the dirt wall and release the mountain stream back to its old course. First, he would see where it was going. Grüdj asked the water, and the reply came in many small voices all mixed together like children playing and talking all at the same time. The voices of these many waters did not know why they were in the ditch. This thing, this ditch, it was catching many small streams and it was taking them somewhere. He stopped listening to the water and listened instead to the light wind that whispered along the slope. He watched the glassy sheet of water flowing down around the far bend of the ditch. He stood alone at this place near the top of the world and realized what it was that was puzzling him.

The river. The river far below in the valley. It was full of water. Yet *this* water did not go down to it.

Grüdj started walking quickly, looking all around as he went. The road along the ditch was open and exposed with only a few short and twisted trees he might hide behind. Anyone on the mountain above or in the meadows and forests below would be able to see him a long way off. Still, the path was smooth and level and he was certain that he was meant to take it.

★ ★ ★ ★ ★

The road along the ditch took him around the jutting angle of the mountain and then back into shadows where it dipped into a steep cañon. It was cold in the shadows and he shivered, hurrying along listening and watching for danger. The ditch emerged onto the steep slope of the next mountain where the ground dropped away so suddenly that it made him dizzy to look down. When Grüdj followed it into the chilly shade of the next valley, he had to stop and sit down because his legs were shaking and his head felt as if he had been breathing smoke from Two Nose's pipe. He had heard that a vision time began with the same kind of swirling in the head and blurred thoughts.

As he walked out into the sunshine once more, Grüdj saw that the road stopped some distance ahead. The mountain was not nearly so steep here, being more of a long slanting meadow hanging above the river's cañon, and the road and ditch ended at the far edge of it. A few trees grew here. The mountain wind whished in the treetops and sighed through the willows and brush. The water flowed, slick-surfaced and silent. No birds sang. Not even a hawk or eagle cried overhead. There was no sound at all. It was not until Grüdj was halfway across the open meadow that he began to hear the sound of water falling fast.

The ditch ended abruptly. The road became a twisting kind of two-rut track that went on down along the mountain and into the forest beyond. Where the ditch ended, there was a stack of logs piled there to stop the water. It had not stopped it, of course. Logs were thrown everywhere, many of them far down the slope, while the water went flowing out of the ditch and over the ledge below to crash and rumble and boom along over rocks and fallen trees on its way to the river. This was why the river had the water,

Grüdj saw. It all came down this ditch and out this opening, and it had carved itself a new way down to the bottom of the cañon. But why would somebody make this ditch and collect all the streams just to let them go into the river again?

He would stay. Here there was a strange thing. It had to do with the water, and it had drawn him here. Here would be his vision. Surely the old gods were somewhere near this place.

Grüdj looked around and was pleased with what he saw. The high meadow stretched far back into a wide valley behind the ditch and road. A little stream ran through this meadow. Grüdj cupped its snow-cold water in his hand and drank, then gently lowered the tip of his bar into it and spoke.

"Are they here, the old gods, the old gods of The People? Do you know?"

The water wriggled and curled about the iron bar. *Gods?*

"What place is this?" Grüdj tried asking.

It is a good place, he heard the water say. *The mountain of this valley catches clouds gently and does not keep them frozen all summer in snow or ice. You see . . . this water can go as it pleases. It is a good place. Gods?*

"Spirit?"

Oh. There is a spirit, yes. This valley is very, very old. Never has it behaved in a rude manner, not toward the water. Even this new thing, the valley spirit leaves it alone.

"What thing do you mean?"

This thing of bare dirt. Water from many valleys comes here in it.

"Who made this thing?"

Men.

"Why?"

It is not known. It seems harmless. Water goes along it and down to the river.

The mountain creek told Grüdj many more things, things he needed to know. It described how the wide flat valley continued back into the mountain a long distance and came to a place where there were cliffs and tree groves. Small fish were in abundance. Small animals, too, could be found back up this wide valley. And deer, especially the large ones that scream through their teeth.

It would do. Even if the old gods were not here, here Grüdj would fast and speak with the spirit of this place. He would think about this ditch and road thing. He would find out if this was the place the pale woman tried to keep him from finding.

Chapter Eight

THE STONE HUT UNDER SPIRIT RIDGE

Two workmen in rough clothes and heavy shoes came down the road, leading two pack burros. They were headed home after four days on the Great North Ditch. And, as usual, they were having their discussion at the top of their lungs.

"And I'll be telling *you,* Finn, ye're out of your mind, that's what!"

"Never the same, I know what I know and know what I saw. And I know I saw what I saw. I'm telling y'again, Paddy, there's somebody that's livin' up there by the headgate."

"In the valley."

"Aye, in the bleedin' valley! I seen moccasin tracks in the road, and smoke risin' 'way back in the trees up there. Injuns, or I'm a Chinaman."

"Well, tell old man O'Byrne if y'will, once we get back. Tell him y'think there's spooks and Injuns hauntin' the ditch. But I know what he'll be sayin'. 'So long as they aren't bothering us, we'll not be bothering them.' But he'll be none too pleased when y'tell him the headgate's all broken again."

"Ah, that damn' thing. I don't know what to do about it, not at all. The spring floodwater comes tearin' down the ditch and it's got nowheres to go except right down that same place. Nothin' seems t'hold it."

"Only thing to do is get up there and get to diggin' again. Soon as the frost is out of the ground, we've got t'get goin' and extend the ditch as far as we can. Maybe in the meantime the old man, he'll figure out something for that gate."

It was late the following day when that selfsame Paddy stood in the doorway of the superintendent's office, twisting his cap in his hands, doing his very best to try and make his report to O'Byrne sound unimportant. Just a visitor squatting up on the high ditch and a broken water gate. He didn't want it to sound too urgent, or else he and Finn would find themselves slogging their way back up to the end of the bloody ditch in the mud and snow to find out who it was and what they were up to.

Neither did Paddy want to make the ruined gate sound too serious, and for much the same reason.

"I'm thinkin' we can wait till the weather warms up and the ground thaws," he said, remembering the misery of digging ditch and hauling logs up there at timberline. Cold mists all morning, freezing winds, terrible cold nights.

Superintendent John O'Byrne listened to Paddy describing the damage to the ditch gate, asked a few questions, then sighed and turned back to his drawing table. It bothered him no end that he could design and build any kind of fine house of stone or engineer any kind of smooth road with perfect drainage, and yet he could not for the life of himself figure any way to divert the ditch water without washing away the whole of the mountain.

"There's another thing," Paddy said. "Besides the ruined gate, I mean."

"Which is . . . ?"

"Like I told Finn, I seen fresh moccasin tracks up in that valley where the gate is, and I saw smoke as well, which was risin' some ways up that creek. Finn, he swears he saw nuthin' at all, but I'm certain there's some fella camped up there."

"Just the one?"

"Seems so. I only saw the one set of tracks, and no horse prints at all."

"You didn't go to see?"

"Well. . . ." Paddy paused. "Us bein' concerned about the ditch gate and all . . . and, besides, he's 'way up that little side valley, a good way from the ditch right of way."

"I see," O'Byrne said. "Probably a wandering Indian or a free trapper. Well, we'll leave him alone and maybe he'll leave us alone."

"And didn't I say the same to Finn?" Paddy said, pulling on his cap.

After Paddy left his office, O'Byrne went back to studying the sketch he had been making, then angrily crossed it out and went stomping down the hallway in search of Fontana.

She and Luned were together. Fontana was at her embroidery frame working on a geometrical design in yellow and blue, while Luned was twisting waxed sinew into a new bowstring. Her bow and arrows lay on the drawing room table. Fontana looked up as John O'Byrne came into the room.

"Trouble?" she asked. "I heard the front door open and close."

"Paddy and that fool Finn are back from the ditch head. The gate washed out. Again. And they say we've a visitor squatting up there."

"A visitor? This time of year?"

"Aye. Naturally your two stout workman had not the

courage between them to investigate, but they saw the tracks of a single man and smoke rising in that broad valley above the gate. So it seems that somebody's come to live there a while."

Fontana happened to glance at Luned and saw her looking at her father with wide-eyed interest.

"Luned? Do you know anything about this?"

"No," Luned said, scowling down at the knot in her bowstring. Her father kept her under his unwavering gaze until she looked up again. "All right," she admitted. "There was one trying to follow the river up, but he was not the one."

"Just one of him?" her father asked. "What happened, Daughter? Why didn't you tell me about him?"

"I gave him meat and told him to go away. He was not the one. He is just a black man, dressed like an Indian. He is fat and has one eye. I told him to go back where he came from."

"Luned!" Fontana said. "It is *not* for you to say who may come, and he must go. I have told you *too* many times. It is not for you to say."

"Ah, let it go," John said. "I know, I know. You assume it's your black man. I wish you two would let me know what you find so important about him. Anyway, I suppose it's up to me to go myself and have a look. Could be some runaway Indian or a fur trapper. Who knows? Either way, he's probably got a perfect right to be there."

"And if he *is* the Guardian?" Fontana asked.

"I suppose I'll know that, then, won't I?" John said. "If he turns out to be this Guardian you say will show up someday, maybe I'll finally find out what it's all about."

"If he is the Guardian, it means it's going to be time for the troubles to start," Luned said, looping the new string over the tip of her bow.

"Daughter, let's have no more of that talk, now." John O'Byrne said. "You've got Paddy and Finn scared of strangers, and you're starting to make me nervous as well. We've only just got the ditch started a ways. Just down to timberline. There's nothing of it to make this trouble of yours begin now. The ditch isn't troubling anyone."

"Not up there, perhaps," Fontana mused. "But something could happen here at Crannog house. If he is the Guardian, he must be brought here. My instinct tells me we need him down here."

"And *my* instincts tell me you need to go up to the ditch and run him off," Luned said. "He just shouldn't be up there, Father."

"No, John," Fontana countered, "what you need to do is go up there and find out who he is and what he is doing. Just you remember, Luned, the prophecy doesn't say what kind of man the Guardian will be. We mustn't take chances." Fontana's voice was quiet but firm.

"Very well," John O'Byrne said. "Very well, I'll see to it. But take care not to put your cart too far ahead of your horse. Just give me a week to figure out this gate problem, and then I'll go up to the ditch and find out who he is. I need to go anyway, just to check on things at the work shack and see what we'll need, come the melt-off."

"And what if he's gone by then?" Fontana persisted.

"So much the better," Luned said, under her breath.

"Luned, you still don't seem to understand . . . ," Fontana began.

"Peace!!" John said. "Peace! I have things to do here, and then I will go. Let that be the final word."

Grüdj surveyed his new home. This valley was the place he would find his vision. In Grüdj's mind there was little doubt of it, and the more he explored, the more certain he became. Following the little creek up all the way to where trees do not grow, he found at its source a peaceful, inviting place even among the rocks and snow. Climbing farther up to the very top of the long mountain, he had the whole region laid out under his eye. He saw the big river flowing down its valley, going south. He saw the flat prairies far, far in the distance to the east. It was a far-seeing place. As if to make him feel even more welcome here, the mountainous country to the north looked like the mountains of Standing Hollow Horn's journeys, so much so that he strained to catch some glimpse of the stone medicine circle on its plateau near the edge of the mountains. Grüdj smiled. One day, if he stayed here long enough, maybe old Standing Hollow Horn and The People would return. Maybe they would find him.

Grüdj looked down at the valley and the ditch. Up here on the summit of this long, long mountain everything took on a broad clarity. Below him was the mountain water, the small creek dancing downhill toward the ditch, then on down to the big river. Far, far out in the haze the prairies stretched away. And there was this ditch following a line like the ones Sanford Thatcher drew on his pieces of paper. At last, everything seemed to belong together like the pictures Who Sees Far had painted on his lodge. The prairie, the rivers, the lines the whites drew, all of it had meaning now, and his vision would tell him what it was.

Perhaps Standing Hollow Horn *would* come here. Grüdj would wait, and, while he waited, he would untangle the puzzle of this man-made ditch. The spirit gods had allowed him to see it. Now it was up to him to learn its meaning for The People. Whoever built it would tell him all about it when they returned.

The next day, Grüdj began to build a shelter, an even better one than the one he and Two Nose Thomas had made. He selected big rocks from the base of the cliff, breaking them into square blocks and shaping them with blows of the iron bar before prying them to the place he had chosen for his hut.

"Sit there," he would say, levering a huge rock into place beside the others.

"You belong next to this one," he would say to another rock.

"I need you for my lodge," he would say as he dug another out of the rubble at the base of the cliff.

His feel for the power of the bar grew with each stone, so that by the end of the second day he could split off the side of a boulder without causing the ground to shake and heave.

Grüdj's lodge was a circular hut of stone with room for a bed of boughs and a fire pit in the center. Inside the wall of big rocks, he fashioned a second rock wall so he could stuff grass between them to keep out the drafts, much as The People had liners inside their skin lodges. He made stone shelves on this wall so he could keep his food off the ground. The rectangular door opening, facing the direction of the rising sun, provided the draft he needed for his fire. Just as in a Crow's Woman's skin lodge, the air came in at the door, met the flames, and went straight up and out the smoke hole in the roof.

The roof was the difficult part. Grüdj searched down in the forest for fallen logs, broke off the limbs with heavy rocks, and dragged them back to his hut to use as beams. He had no way of trimming the ends, so the roof looked much like a pile of brush or a beaver lodge. And being flat, it would not keep out the rain. Grüdj studied it and studied it. The roof needed to be steeply sloped, like the lodges of The People, so rain and snow would slide off. He took six willow sticks the length of his arm and with a piece of sinew he fashioned a framework for a toy lodge like children might make. He could make such poles and stand them up on the wall, but he had no buffalo skins to cover them with.

He tried using flat rocks, but they were too heavy for the sticks of his little toy lodge. But what if he used more poles and wove willow sticks into them until it looked like one of Crows Woman's baskets? There was plenty of willow along the creek. Grüdj hunted until he found three good rocks to chip into axe blades, and then went to the forest again for the tall, slender trees that The People used as lodge poles.

John O'Byrne did not like staying in the work shack on the rough wagon track leading to the ditch. It was better than sleeping in the wagon or on the ground in the deep woods. It was certainly more peaceful than Crannog had been these past few weeks. But the shack was far from being comfortable. It was a mean, dark little cabin to begin with, cramped under the spruce trees that kept sunlight from ever reaching it. Finn and Paddy made it even more stifling by smoking pipes that left a stale stench on everything. The tobacco odor permeated the very walls. Pack rats left their little black droppings on the table and chewed up the edges of the door, the window, and the cupboards. A fire in the sheet metal stove, even a very small fire, would overheat the place until he had to go outside to breathe. When the stove went out after midnight, the freezing mountain air crept through the cracks to leave him shivering in his blankets.

In the morning there were flakes of snow in the air and the sky was gray and overcast. O'Byrne got the stove going, cooked himself sourdough cakes and bacon and coffee, and then sat at the rough wooden table, studying his sketches. He didn't have to go all the way up to the ditch to know what the problem was with the gate. He knew from Paddy's description that the spring run-off had been too much for it. They built it as heavy as they could, using the heaviest logs that three men and two mules could drag, but the water just washed it out again.

He removed a map from the leather tube and unrolled it. It was the dip in the terrain that was the real culprit. They should have surveyed the ditch higher up the slope. The water gathered momentum before hitting the low spot, and the low spot was so low that they couldn't build an earthen wall strong enough to hold the force. Maybe with enough blasting powder they could somehow build a wall of rock. *God knows there's plenty of rock to use, plenty that has to be moved before the ditch goes much farther.* O'Byrne shrugged and took his tin cup to the stove for another cup of coffee, which he drank standing while looking out the window at the snow floating down lightly through the fir trees.

The Great North Ditch Company, he thought. *Jesus, Mary, and Joseph, what in hell are we doin' here?*

The next day the sky cleared and O'Byrne put himself in a better mood by doing chores around the work shack. He replaced a broken corral rail, sharpened tools, gathered a supply of firewood, and fashioned a new wooden seat for the privy to replace the one the porcupines had chewed into slivers. In the evening he sat down at the table and composed a list of other tasks for those two lazy shanty micks to do the next time they were up here.

Morning found O'Byrne in the saddle again, riding along the two-track road through the forest. They had built it simply by following any route that looked like it offered the least resistance, so it twisted one way to avoid a big ponderosa or an old stump, went the other way around a rock outcrop and dipped into sloughs of frozen mud. When the project began, he had fooled himself into thinking that the road would also be the route of the ditch, but it soon became evident that this was not to be the case. The water had to be kept moving at a very gentle speed along a very slight gradient, and if that gradient's path lay through a tangle of tree stumps or a field of boulders, then the stumps and rocks had to be moved.

He was getting close to timberline now, so he watched along the road for a certain axe mark on a tree, a mark that would tell him where to leave the road in order to find the tool cache. And there it was, a double X on a ponderosa. John tied the horses in the road and bushwhacked his way across fallen logs to the low, crude log storage bin. Everything was just as they had left it last fall. The shovels, the picks, and the pry bars all were well protected by the waxed canvas covers they were wrapped in. The two canteens showed some rust, but it was nothing serious.

As he rode out of the trees, the first thing he saw were the remains of their last attempt to barricade the water. The logs were tossed every which way like a game of jackstraws. And as before, all the water the big ditch had collected from the creeks and springs was pouring out through the break, running down the fresh gully it had dug through the tundra to the bottom of the cañon. Last fall they *should* have installed a release gate higher up the ditch, and they *should* have thrown a cofferdam across. But the winter had been closing in and they had to do something in a hurry, so they cobbled together a simple log wall instead, hoping it would stop the water and let the excess seep gently over the top. Except it didn't. Twice before they had built it, and twice before the water had washed it out again. Now the third attempt was no more than a pile of scattered timber.

O'Byrne looked around for any sign of the visitor Paddy had reported. He finally spotted a light wisp of smoke rising at the upper end of the side valley.

"No point in us just standing here," he said to the horse. "Might as well go see who'd be crazy enough to come to this forsaken place. Besides ourselves, I mean."

Grüdj saw him coming, the lone rider, with a pack horse following. Just a single man slowly coming up the little stream. He went ahead and tied the last piece of sinew to hold his door together, then raised the heavy log contraption from the ground and leaned it against the wall. It wouldn't fit the opening as tightly as it might, but, considering that he had done it with nothing more than stone axes and sinew, it was a good job.

John O'Byrne stopped a polite distance away and put his animals on lead ropes to graze. He came toward Grüdj nonchalantly, looking around the valley as if he'd never seen the place and had almost forgotten why he came. A smallish man, he was dressed like the surveyors and his face was that peculiar reddish color white people get from being in the sun. He looked at Grüdj's stone lodge with curiosity.

"G'day to you!" he began.

Grüdj went on trimming the sinew lashings with his knife. " 'Day," he echoed.

"And a fine bright day it is," John added. Grüdj nodded. John came closer and looked at the door. Then he took a close look at the stone wall it leaned against. "You've built 'er hell for stout," he said, touching the wall. "Mind me havin' a peek inside, then?"

Grüdj nodded again and John leaned in the doorway to look around.

"And you've made a liner to it as well!" he exclaimed. "And this is grass you've stuffed it with. Why, this'll be no world of cozy when the cold comes. And you've done it all yourself, I take it?"

Grüdj nodded again. "Grüdj," he said.

"Pardon?"

"Grüdj." He held out his brass medallion for the man to read.

"Ah. That's your name, then. Groodge. John O'Byrne is mine."

"Jonoburn."

"Right. So, Mister Groodge, what brings you to our fair valley, then? Where might you be from?"

He spoke in the tongue of the surveyor Thatcher, and couldn't stop running his hand over the stones and the joints between the stones. Grüdj pointed with his knife toward the east where the wide, flat plains were.

"I see. Well, it's a pretty enough place you've come to, I'll say that. So . . . you've been working on making yourself a door for the hut, I see. Pretty good. Maybe you'd like a hand at puttin' it up now?"

John took a long, careful look at the log rectangle. It was strongly braced and tightly lashed together. He marveled at how the black man had managed to square the top and bottom, probably using only the stone axe heads he saw lying next to the wall. He had a feeling about this young man. Strange-looking as he was, John's instincts said there was no harm in him and no harm in letting him camp in the valley a while. He might even be someone who could be a sort of caretaker of the upper ditch until Fontana's Guardian showed up.

"I see you know how to use Indian tools," he said. "And you dress Indian fashion as well. Lived with Indians,

I expect? Blackfoot, maybe? Crow? Cheyenne?"

"No," Grüdj said. "The People."

He repeated the tribe's name in the tongue of Crows Woman, but the man did not understand.

"Funny," John said. "You're bein' black, I mean. It'd be interesting to learn how you came to be livin' with these 'people' and all. Captured in a raid or something like that? Or just a wanderer they took in?"

"No," Grüdj said. And the subject was dropped.

"So you've got the door to fit your opening there, then," John said. "Hinges might be a problem, the doorway being of stone and all. Anyway, let's set it in place and see what we've got."

The two of them wrestled the heavy door into the hut, where Grüdj set it against the opening. The bottom rested on a flat rock; a second flat rock served as a lintel over the doorway. O'Byrne examined the problem with his expert eye. He saw that the door was larger than the opening, so when it was shut it would seal out most of the draft. But it needed to hinge somehow so it would swing inward.

"The way I see it," he said, "you could drill a hole in the threshold here, over next to the edge of the doorway, and another up there in your lintel. With a couple of good stout sticks for pins set into your door ends, you'd have the thing on a pivot, you see. Holes here and here . . ."—he pointed—"and pins driven in here."

Grüdj saw how the door would swing open and shut that way.

"Then I'll tell you what," John said. "There's a tool cache not far from here, down in the trees. Why don't I go get us a singlejack and sledge, and an augur. Maybe bring an axe and saw just in case. I'll be back directly."

Grüdj stood looking after Jonoburn as the man bounced

away down the creek on one of his horses. Like the surveyor called Robert Green, this sunburned white man seemed to be someone who was always in a hurry. One of The People—or even Two Nose Thomas—would have sat down, smoked a pipe or shared some food, made talk about unimportant things all afternoon before asking a person's name or where he was from. Perhaps not even then. And, of course, a polite person would never look into another person's lodge until they had known each other very well and had been invited in. Still, this Jonoburn was not unpleasant. And he knew about tools and making things. He probably knew about this ditch.

The man came riding back, encumbered with tools. He had a singlejack steel, a one-hand sledge, another hammer, and two augurs in addition to a can of nails and a short pry bar. Behind the saddle he had strapped a one-man cross-cut saw, an axe, and a shovel. Grüdj watched in wonder when he saw Jonoburn coming up the creek, tools clattering and bouncing.

The sun had gone behind the mountain and the evening was getting cold by the time John had returned, so with some reluctance he covered his tools with a scrap of canvas, put the horses on picket ropes, and accepted Grüdj's invitation to spend the night. Supper was roasted rabbit, together with some kind of plant O'Byrne didn't recognize. It was a bit like a carrot, only white and stringy. Groodge said he collected it on the mountain somewhere and would show him where it grew. John's own contribution to the meal consisted of potatoes he had brought from Crannog's storeroom and some sourdough for griddle biscuits.

John lay in his blankets that night looking up at the night sky through the smoke hole. Groodge's fire had warmed the stone walls and the floor of the hut so that the place was cozy as any inglenook. The draft coming in around the door, which they had leaned against the opening for the night, hardly was felt at all. John's bed of boughs was on one side of the fire, Groodge's on the other, and the draft came between them and up out the smoke hole. Taken altogether, this stone hut was about as comfortable a place as he'd ever slept in. Stars for a man to look at while he drifted off to sleep, plenty of fresh air, a good warm bed, and no one to tell him what to do the next day.

"Ever done any singlejacking at all, Groodge?"

The next morning, the two men knelt just inside the door of the hut, where O'Byrne had marked an X on the threshold stone. He showed Grüdj how to figure where to put the pivot pins; after locating the place for the top pin, and, marking it with a stub of chalk, he took out a length of string, tied a pebble to one end, and held the other end against the X. It made a crude plumb bob to show the place where the lower hole should be drilled.

O'Byrne took the drill steel in one hand and the small sledge in the other.

"The reason they call it a star drill is the point, you see," he said, showing the tip of the drill to Grüdj. "Looks like a star. The four points are like havin' four little chisels."

He set the steel on the rock and struck a blow. Immediately there was an X-shaped mark. He turned the steel a little and struck again. Then again. After four blows a round hole began to appear.

"The trick to it," he said, "is to keep twisting the steel so the little chisel points are always cuttin' away the little raised part left by the last blow, y'see. A little twist, then hit it. A little twist, then hit it."

O'Byrne offered the hammer to Grüdj, who took it with

reluctance. What if he struck the rock and everything started to shake and fall around them? He tapped the end of the drill tentatively. Nothing happened. He tapped with more force. Rock dust rose from the shallow hole. He tapped again and again, quickly learning just the right amount of force to use. Too much of a blow and the drill point would wedge in the bottom of the hole. Too little and nothing would happen. He went on twisting and hitting, and the hole grew deeper with surprising speed.

" 'Tis born to the hammer and steel you are!" O'Byrne exclaimed. "Of course I'd say the same to any man who'd do the work instead of myself, for I'm a man who hates singlejacking almost as much as he hates usin' a pick. Awful, tiresome, sweaty work it is."

When the hole was the depth of his finger, O'Byrne blew the dust out of it and pronounced it good. "Now," he said, looking at the stone over their heads, "now things get a bit worse. We've got to drill a hole up here, and without dislodging the rock from its place. T'add to it, the grit is goin' to be falling right in our eyes."

Grüdj put the drill to the X marked on the rock and gave a tap. "This hoss'll do it," he said. And he hit his second blow.

"Never turn down a chance t'walk away from hard work, I say," John said. "While you're doing that, I'll take the axe to the woods and find something for the pins. A length of dry cedar would be good. Shouldn't be too hard to find."

That afternoon, after having opened and closed their door a few dozen times just so they could marvel at their own handiwork, O'Byrne took his surveying telescope, compass, and a map tube from his packs.

"I've got to walk the ditch a ways, just t'see how things are," he explained.

Grüdj said nothing.

"Care t'come along?" O'Byrne said.

"Yes."

As they walked toward the ditch, O'Byrne kept talking about the project, his pride and joy. He explained how it caught the mountain creeks coming down the tributary valleys. He explained the need for gates to divert the water so the laborers could dig the ditch longer. He complained about the floods and how they ruined the gates.

"Where does the water go?" Grüdj asked.

"Go?" O'Byrne said. It wasn't the question that puzzled him as much as the way this black man could switch from speaking in trapper lingo to sounding like an ordinary white man.

"When it's finished, you mean?" O'Byrne asked. "Or right now? When she's finished, the Great North Ditch is goin' to take water to a reservoir in the foothills. From there it goes into various ditches to irrigate the high plains." Seeing puzzlement on Grüdj's dark face, O'Byrne opened the leather tube and took out one of his charts. "This line represents the ditch so far," he said. "We're standin' just about here. This here line, it shows where we hope the ditch will go. It's miserable hard work surveyin' a decent line down through those woods, so we just go forward with the water and try to keep the gradient as slight as we can."

"Resfor?" Grüdj said. "Or gate?"

"Oh, *that's* where we're at, is it? That's the part you haven't caught onto. All right. Follow this pencil line along and you come to where the company plans to build their reservoir." O'Byrne marked a small x on the spot. "That's a lake. To hold the water the ditch brings down out of mountains."

Grüdj understood. A place to keep all the water. Such a thing would be good for The People to have, a place to go when the dry times came. The buffalo would go there.

"Now, as for irrigation," O'Byrne said, "fixin' up your door, y'said you'd been to a soldier fort with big doors. Big gates. Happen t'notice the soldiers grow food as well?"

Grüdj remembered. At the soldier villages there had been a square with a fence around it and plants growing that he had never seen before. The soldiers had a small ditch bringing water from the river to this square place. That was the place where two of the blue coat soldiers had black faces like his and looked at him with great interest. One had started to approach Grüdj to talk, but the other one called him back.

"With enough water for irrigation," O'Byrne said, "people can grow food for themselves and their animals, and hay, and vegetables. Corn, beans, all kind of things."

"The People are hunters," Grüdj explained. "We follow the buffalo. We kill the antelope, the deer."

"Well," O'Byrne said, "my people are farmers. We stay in one place, mostly. We grow our food. Those potatoes we had for supper, my people grew those."

"This water is for you? Jonoburn will grow these things?"

"Not me, no. I'm no farmer. I'd druther singlejack all day long than put my hand to a plow. Farmers will pay for water. Water means they can claim land and live on it."

This was the second time Grüdj had heard talk about people getting land by bringing water to it.

"Sounds a wee daft, sayin' it like this, but we'll buy food from them after they buy water from us."

They stopped at the end of the ditch and stood regarding the ruins of the water gate. Grüdj thought the water seemed happy to be running so fast down the mountain back to the river, but O'Byrne heard the sound of money getting away from him. Not that he cared that much. To him, the real pleasure had always been in doing the thing, in building something that would work.

"See those little stakes we've set out through the forest, where the road is?" Grüdj nodded. "We make the ditch follow those sticks. Right through rocks and roots and all. Someday the ditch, it'll go all the way to the edge of the mountains."

They walked along the ditch again the next day, O'Byrne carrying a shovel and Grüdj carrying his iron bar. O'Byrne was still doing the talking. As they drew near the point where Grüdj had climbed up out of the forest and onto the ditch road, O'Byrne pointed out where he thought he and his crew would try to build a diversion structure to regulate the amount of water coming down.

"In point of fact," he said, mostly to himself, "and purely as hindsight, we should've fixed it so each one of these little mountain streams had a way to jump the ditch and keep on going its natural way until such time as we needed it."

They took turns with the shovel to clear the ditch where silt had washed in during the winter. O'Byrne took out his pocket notebook and wrote down the places that needed fixing.

"Another problem," he said. "By the time the snow is off the ditch and we've got the repairs done to the part we already built, there's precious little summer time remaining to build any more. And the longer the ditch grows, the more time it takes to maintain it."

"May tane?"

"Keep it open. Dig out the silt, like we just done. Clear

out any trees that've fallen into the water, rocks, too. Fix the bank where the water's washed it out. That's how we maintain her."

O'Byrne showed Grüdj some "maintaining" on their way back to his hut. Grüdj showed no hesitation in jumping into the knee-deep water to seize a boulder that had fallen in and heave it down the hill.

" 'Tis a fine strong arm you've got, lad!" O'Byrne exclaimed.

No sooner had Grüdj's buckskins begun to dry out than he waded in again to remove a small tree that was starting to form a trap for other brush and débris, and again O'Byrne marveled at the strength of the squat black man. His instinct had been right: this strange-looking young man could turn out to be a real asset, a real find.

Late afternoon found them at the hut again, where O'Byrne sat himself down to sketch some of the ideas he'd had for the gates. Grüdj built up the fires, the one inside the hut for warmth and the one in the stone windbreak to cook on. Then he went to where O'Byrne was sitting and squatted down to see the drawings. Most of it meant nothing to him, but he began to comprehend what it was the red-faced man was wrestling with. O'Byrne found pleasure in explaining parts of the drawings, for it had been years since he had done this kind of field work with someone who seemed interested. Not that Finn and Paddy weren't interested. It wasn't that, but somehow they were always in a hurry to get on with things. This Groodge character seemed so content to just be there in the mountain valley, with the water and with the loneliness.

"Well, I suppose that's all I can do for now," O'Byrne said as he closed his folio and packed it away. "We'll be back up here in three, four weeks and start diggin' the ditch down through the trees. Need to do that maintainin' as well, and maybe build some gates if I can figure out how." He looked at the silent black man. "But tell me, my friend Groodge. What will you be doin'? Would you be here when we come back?"

"Waugh," Grüdj said after a long moment. "Grüdj stays. The People come, Standing Hollow Horn maybe. Maybe Two Nose Thomas. Grüdj will wait."

"These people, they'll be crossin' over the ridge, then. On their way to summer grounds?"

"Ridge?" Grüdj liked the sound of the word.

"Aye. This long mountain here, the one we're drainin' with our ditch. She's known as a ridge. Just a long mountain without many high points, really. A ridge."

Grüdj looked at him, silently mimicking the word to himself.

"Some men might call it a range, like a range of mountains."

Grüdj liked the sound of ridge better.

"Someday this ditch'll catch all the water from this ridge and take it down to the prairies for people to use. But I've been thinkin', then," O'Byrne continued. "As long as you've nowhere to go and have yourself such a nice hut here an all, how would you like to work for me?"

Grüdj began to think, but said nothing. Two Nose Thomas had described working for other men, many times, and it was something distasteful to him. Those black-face soldiers were working for the white soldiers and Grüdj didn't remember them looking very happy.

"I'm thinkin' you might keep on with cleanin' the ditch out, maybe cut down some trees farther along the survey line. And we always need firewood and logs. In return, I'll send up some food supplies. Oh, and I'll get Luned to bring you some venison and rabbit. Then, twice a year, I hand out the payroll to everybody, cash money, the going wage. What do you say?"

Grüdj said yes, he would stay and do what he could do. He would never turn down food, even if it meant having that strange thin woman come around again. Of "cash money" he had little need, although he could keep it for Two Nose, who always found ways to exchange it for good things. But Grüdj's motives were far more complex than John O'Byrne's philosophy could ever dream, for the dark-skinned exile was already forming his intent to make himself part of this idea of getting land for water. He would obey the vision when it came, and he knew it would come in this lonely place, and he had a strong feeling it would be a vision about bringing this water to The People.

John O'Byrne packed up early the next morning, leaving the tools for Grüdj to use. He had also shown him where the tool cache was. "Hate to leave here," O'Byrne admitted. "A man finds a lot of peace up here. I thank you for all your hospitality, and it's a fine comfortable place you've built. I'd gladly stay, but, if I'm away from Crannog much longer, those women will think I've gone to meet my maker."

"Maker?"

"You know . . . God."

"Up here?" Grüdj asked.

"Sometimes I think He's up here more than He is anywhere else. If it was me that was God, this is where I'd spend my time. Those people down below, though, they'd tell you the only god up here in these mountains is the water itself. Water and land. That's all they want. They figure, if they can get enough water, they can make their own Garden of Eden out of a desert."

"There are gods of the water. Spirits live in it. I have seen them."

"Up here? You've seen your water gods are up here?"

"No. A lake far from here. Here is where the mountains catch the water from the sky. Standing Hollow Horn says the spirits of The People's old gods still live in these mountains. This is the spirit ridge, maybe. Maybe the next ridge."

"Well, if you run into them, you'd better ask them if it's all right to take some of their water."

"Yes," Grüdj said.

"I want to thank you again for your hospitality," O'Byrne said, climbing onto his horse. "And I'll be sending the men up with supplies of food for yourself. You might build yourself a cache for it and for any venison Luned might bring you. Build it strong, 'cause the bears get hungry when they come out of hibernation."

Grüdj nodded, and John O'Byrne rode away slowly.

Spirit Ridge, John said to himself. *Damned if the blessed mountain doesn't finally have a name to it.*

Chapter Nine

DITCH WORK

Day after day the freezing winds of late winter howled around Grüdj's hut. Morning after morning he woke up hoping the wind had stopped. But there were no streaks of sunlight coming through the cracks in the door. It was as if the gray sky had come to stay forever. Braving the cold and the stinging crystals of snow flying on the wind, he would venture out for firewood and hurry back inside. The rest of the day he would sit by the fire, whittling at a piece of wood with his knife or just drifting off into a state of consciousness that was half sleep, half wakefulness. In his states of half dreaming he often thought of the lodge of Crows Woman. In the winters of his boyhood he had spent many comfortable days there by her fire, listening to the soft sound of her talk as she told stories while the meat cooked in the pot.

Grüdj thought about Jonoburn's words, how the ditch would take water from the mountains to the prairie. Much of Jonoburn's talk was of things Grüdj had never heard of.

"Graydent," Grüdj muttered in his empty hut. "Flume. Ree-sur-vore."

Words such as these had no meaning. But some of Jonoburn's teachings were instantly clear. It was like the times when Two Nose explained how to trap beaver or how to load and fire the long rifle—Grüdj had an instant grasp of such things. Singlejacking, the idea of the door hinges, patterns of grain in the rocks, all broke into his mind as understood concepts.

He thought about all the waters he had seen. The river that wanted to take away his iron stick after it took on the power to break the rocks. The ditch water. The small creeks bringing their water to the ditch. And a voice in his head telling him to return to the small, steep ravine near where the ditch began. The water in that ravine would talk to him.

The weather finally broke. One night, Grüdj sat, cross-legged, staring into his water bowl, watching how the fire-light made patterns in it, when the water whispered to him of the coming of sunshine and a time of melting snow. The next morning he emerged from his hut blinking at the brightness of a cloudless blue sky and smiling at the warmth of the sun on his body. He built a fire in the windbreak, the first outdoor fire in many, many days, and stood by it as he ate jerky for breakfast. He liked having the warmth of the sun on his back and the warmth of the fire on his legs and belly. Soon, Grüdj took up his iron bar and hurried to the ditch road. He had work to do.

Slogging his way through snowdrifts, following the ditch path as it wound in and out of the deeply shaded valleys, he finally arrived at the head of the ditch where a little creek came bouncing and bubbling down the narrow ravine. It felt free. It sensed that the ditch was taking it toward the sunrise direction, the direction of the wide buffalo prairies. It remembered a certain summer prairie where tall grass swayed in a gentle breeze and where the earth was dark and warm.

"What about the big river in the valley far below?" Grüdj asked the creek. "That is where the mountain wants you to go." He did not want to tell the creek about the break at the other end of the ditch, where all the water flowed down toward that river.

The creek knew about the big river which went rushing wildly through cañons, cañons so deep the sun could not find the bottom. It ran headlong into huge hard rocks and made many, many turns back and forth. When it came to banks of sandstone, it ate into them until they collapsed into the current. It became full of silt and mud. Finally, it came to a very hot place where some of the water vanished into the dry air; the water that remained in the river eventually flowed into a bitter-tasting lake of enormous size. Yes, the creek knew of this river and wanted no part of it. It wanted to go back to the soft earth and grateful plants of the prairie.

Grüdj squatted next to the place where the creek ran into the ditch and began to explain. He used the language of Crows Woman, but had to use white words as well. It made his talk seem weaker, less effective.

"Here is where the Great Power left a ravine in the mountain ridge," he explained, "so you could come here. You find a ditch here, ditch going toward the sunrise direction. But know that the ditch is new and made by man. By people, but not The People. There was a before-time. In the before-time the water of this ridge always went to the big river. The new ditch turns the water. It carries along the side of the ridge. It catches many other waters this way. All the water together was too heavy. Log walls broke. The water leaves the ditch and goes to the big river. It does not go to the prairie.

"In time," Grüdj said to the water, "all will flow to the prairies. To help The People. It will make the grass grow. Children will play in it. There will be fish to trap. But before that this ditch must be finished. I have said all."

He got up and walked back down the ditch until he came to a high, rocky shoulder of the mountain through which Jonoburn and his helpers had dug the ditch. Grüdj picked his spot and began to tap with his iron bar. The stones cracked as before. He could build a diversion ditch here that no amount of flooding could wash away.

"Water!" he shouted to the water in the ditch. "Water! Here in this place you must go to the big river below. Jonoburn needs to fix the ditch. Grüdj needs to do it. You will leave here. Someday other water will take the ditch 'way to the buffalo prairie."

The peaks began to shake and echo with a sound like faraway mountain thunder. He heard the rumble of rocks rolling down into the forest. And because the late afternoon was becoming chilly, Grüdj trundled back to his hut to rest. Morning found him walking up the ditch road again, this time carrying Jonoburn's axe and cross-cut saw in addition to his bar. Grüdj chuckled as he shambled up the roadway feeling very pleased with himself. He had practiced making a wooden gate, using small sticks from his firewood pile. Afterward, he fell into a deep dream, and the dream showed him what to do.

He needed to build a water gate so heavy that the water could not move it. But he had dreamed a secret way that Grüdj could move it.

Winter's overcast and cold returned, as it always does in the high country, but Grüdj was not unhappy. He sawed logs and fitted them together. He talked to himself as he carved holes and slots into the granite.

"Here the bottom log will slide. Yes. It is good. *Waugh!*"

And he laughed when he said *"Waugh";* Two Nose would laugh if he could see Grüdj carefully picking away at the rock.

"Now," he said at last. "Grüdj will shut this gate and the water will stay in the ditch. It is good."

And it was. The barrier across the opening in the side of the ditch was probably stronger than the ditch bank itself. The next job was to build another gate in the side of the ditch down by the mouth of his own valley.

"It is flat here," he said to the water. "You are not as strong here."

He needed a different idea. And so Grüdj went back to his hut to sit by his fire and experiment with his pile of firewood sticks.

One day, the fire made the hut very warm and Grüdj stretched out and slept. In his sleep he saw how to build the second ditch gate.

"Not as big, these logs," he said as he chipped away at the dirt and rock of the ditch bank.

"You see Grüdj making your gate," he said to the trickle of water, "but you cannot open it. Grüdj can. See?" And putting his iron bar in a certain place, he easily raised the six logs so that water could flow through, when more water came.

As he gathered rocks and tamped them into the holes to fix his log gate in place, Grüdj imagined his reunion with Two Nose Thomas.

"Waugh!" Two Nose would say. *"How be ye, ol' Grüdj? Whar wuz ye, all these moons? What wuz the critters, and what wuz meat?"*

Two Nose would slap his back, the way he used to do.

"Good ol' Grüdj," he'd say. *"Havin' ye back shines some, it does!"*

Crows Woman would also smile to see him once more.

"My son has been away too long," she would say. *"He has grown into a man."*

"Elk Runner and Standing Hollow Horn and Three Eagles will be there," Grüdj said to the rocks and water. "Who Sees Far will tell the village Grüdj has had his vision."

He shouldered his tools and started back up the valley toward his hut.

"Grüdj will tell his vision. The People will feast. Who Sees Far and Standing Hollow Horn will say what Grüdj's dream means."

Grüdj suddenly stopped in his tracks. He had just remembered his earlier dream. Who Sees Far had appeared to him and he knew that the old shaman had gone to the ancestors. It would be sad to see the painted lodge and know Who Sees Far was not there.

While he waited out the winter storms that still visited the high country, Grüdj schemed. He would keep waiting for a powerful vision time, and it would come to him; meanwhile, he would make a friend of the white man Jonoburn.

"Jonoburn will be pleased. Grüdj made good ditch gates." Grüdj chuckled. Two Nose had taught him how to bargain when they bargained with traders who came to the village. He would bargain with Jonoburn. "Something I have for something I want."

And what Jonoburn would want, Grüdj reasoned, was the help of the iron bar. The stick was medicine. The spirits had given him this iron bar at birth. When enemies came, they gave power to the bar. When it was stolen, they let him get it back. The bar showed him the river and led him here to this ditch.

"Jonoburn will have two things to choose."

Either Grüdj could help move rocks with his iron bar, or

Grüdj would use the bar to destroy the ditch walls and let the water free.

He will say: "Grüdj, what do you want?"

Grüdj will say: "Jonoburn must give Grüdj part of the water. Jonoburn must show how to do this claim thing for the lands of the prairie."

The bargain.

It was what fed his slumbering thoughts as he sat by his fire wishing for the winds to cease and the sun to return. Over and over he saw the dream picture—all The People would be moving, the entire village, all the pony drags and dog drags moving, dust rising from the pony's hoofs, children running alongside, men and women talking as they walked together. At the head of the column he would ride beside Three Eagles, with Crows Woman and Two Nose just behind them on ponies. In this dream Grüdj led The People to a place such as the surveyor, Sanford Thatcher, and the red-faced Jonoburn had described to him, a place where water brought the grass and never dried up. A place where the wagon-road people were not allowed to come. The buffalo would come to the grass and The People would have this place and would live in it peacefully. They would keep the buffalo with them. They would grow food the way Jonoburn told him the wagon people and the soldier town people do.

It was a good dream for The People. He knew it was powerful, important, and that was why he needed to be patient waiting for it. He would keep learning from Jonoburn and waiting for his vision. It might be that the vision was waiting for the ditch to be finished so that everything could begin altogether.

John O'Byrne looked down from his window to see Paddy and that fool Finn returning to Crannog. The pack horses' loads were gone, so O'Byrne assumed the two men had successfully delivered the supplies to Groodge up on the ditch. He turned back to reading his book. They'd be in soon enough to tell him how it went.

"All done," Paddy reported. "Everything's shipshape at the ditch camp and the road, she's pretty much open all the way t'timberline. Exceptin' for a few snowdrifts, which we had no trouble breakin' through at all."

"And our new man on the upper ditch, you found him all right?"

"Right as rain," Paddy said. "That's quite the cozy place he's built himself there. *And* he was that glad to see we'd brought him salt pork and sugar."

Finn came into the room and headed for the hearth to warm the seat of his pants. "Cold out," he observed, as if the other two men had failed to notice that particular fact. "Well, Mister O'Byrne, we got your man all set with new supplies. I'm thinkin' he liked the cookin' pot we brought him, and the blankets, but I gather he's not too keen on coffee."

"I'm sure you helped him drink it, then," John O'Byrne said.

"That we did. And can I say it's a fine job you made of the gate there, Mister O'Byrne. A fine job. We'll be able to get right on with the diggin' now."

"The gate?"

"Aye," Paddy said. "The ditch gate. I was about to say the same as Finn. The log gate there at the mouth of the valley where your black lives. You've done a grand job on it. Just enough water t'give us the gradient, and not enough t'wash out the whole concern again."

"But where you found the time!" Finn added. "That new upper gate y'built as well . . . isn't it the key to the whole thing? However y'managed it, I'm sure I don't know. 'Tis brilliant how y'made it run out along that shoulder of rock. It can't never wash out, the way you've put it there. But one thing, Mister O'Byrne . . . how does that upper thing work? We couldn't see any way t'work it, but it's clear that it does. It's art, so it is."

"Finn, you fool, I'm tellin' you I haven't done a thing to the ditch since we left it last autumn."

"Well *somebody* has, and from all the rock they've moved, I'd say they must've used blasting powder galore. If you didn't do it, you'd better get up there and find out who did."

"I've got it!" Paddy exclaimed.

"What?" O'Byrne said.

"I know the answer t'the riddle! 'Tis the workin's of some rival of ours! Somebody workin' for another company has themselves another irrigation scheme goin'. They climbed up there and found our ditch, figured it was abandoned or else they could just jump the claim, and they're pushing ahead with their own improvements. That's got to be it!"

That very evening O'Byrne stuffed a canvas pack with extra warm clothes and food. Early morning found him already on the road up to the ditch. He fretted at having to stop for the night at the work shack, and he hurried on as soon as it was light enough to saddle the horses. He had but one thought in mind, and that was to see for himself exactly what was going on with his project.

As he finally came to timberline and rode out of the trees, he saw that Paddy and Finn had told the truth about the lower gate. It was rebuilt, and it was built solidly. Somebody had dug both sides of the gap back to solid rock, and then had chiseled grooves in the rock to take the ends of the logs. The grooves were capped with heavy stones as well, so that the whole thing seemed as strong as a fortress wall. Whoever did the repair job had also extended the run-off gap another ten or twelve yards beyond the edge of the main ditch and lined it with what looked like quarried stone. Never again would it erode the ditch bank. If they needed to divert the water flow at this point, they could open the gate and send the entire capacity of the ditch down the mountain to the river while all that rock protected it from washout.

But who had come up here in the winter to build such a thing, and why? And how in the name of all that's holy did the thing *work?* How did the gate open?

O'Byrne didn't get down into the ditch because there was still a foot of ice-cold water in it, but he climbed over the side of the gap and peered closely at the logs set into the grooved rock. There was something odd about the way the logs looked, something that wasn't as symmetrical as it should be. He stepped out onto the top log. It held firm under his weight. Well, maybe whoever built it figured they could just lift the logs out to open the gate. But those logs looked powerfully heavy.

One thing was certain. If some claim jumpers had come along and done it, the strange black man would know about it. Odds were good he was in cahoots with them. O'Byrne would have to take great care what he did from this point on, in case they were hanging around somewhere. He rode on up the valley toward the stone hut, half expecting to find more cabins and workmen. He wondered what he would do if challenged by a gang of men with picks and shovels.

But Groodge was all alone and everything around the stone hut seemed as quiet as before. O'Byrne took his horses into the shelter of the trees to tie them and saw no tracks of other horses, nothing to indicate a party of men had been here.

That evening the red-faced Irish mason and the one-eyed black man sat at Grüdj's fire, sharing a stew that Fontana had prepared and that O'Byrne had brought up to the ditch in a kannikin. They put it into the iron pot and set it on Grüdj's fire, and, when it was warm, they each took a spoon and ate from the pot. O'Byrne asked if Grüdj had seen anyone else, maybe somebody working on the ditch.

"Others?" Grüdj replied. "No. All alone."

"Maybe you just didn't see them," O'Byrne said carefully. "Whoever fixed up that ditch gate, I mean."

"No others. Grüdj fixed it up."

"Groodge fixed it?" O'Byrne was incredulous. "You're telling me 'twas *you* and you alone moved all that rock and those logs and all?"

Grüdj nodded. "And the other."

"The other . . . the other what? Oh, the other gate. I remember now. Paddy and that fool Finn did say there was another new gate higher up the ditch. So, who are you workin' for? You need to tell me, you know. Claim jumpin' is a serious offense, and many a man's been shot because of stealing water."

"Grüdj is alone. No others."

"Now, let me get straight on this," O'Byrne said. "You did all this work without anybody tellin' you to?"

Grüdj nodded.

"But I don't see why," O'Byrne said.

"Grüdj would do more. Stay here."

"You did it so I'd *hire* you to do more?"

"Yes."

"I see. Have to take you at your word, at least for the

time being. It's more than I ever expected, you see. So," O'Byrne said, changing the subject, "and did Luned manage to get you some venison for your cache?"

Grüdj nodded.

"That's good," O'Byrne said. "I ought t'be telling you, she doesn't seem to care much for you at all."

"What is she?" Grüdj asked.

"What *is* she? Besides bein' my daughter, you mean. A fair question, I suppose. For openers, you've no doubt seen already that she's fey. That much is for certain. You believe in spirits, you said. Faeries, goblins, leprechauns?"

Grüdj's face was enough to tell O'Byrne that he did not recognize the names.

"People you sometimes can't see, and they live in the trees, in the forests."

Grüdj pronounced the name for "invisible being" in the language of The People. O'Byrne looked blank. Grüdj tried Two Nose's word. "Haunts," he said.

"Well, Luned's kind of a haunt, 'tis true. More like a sprite, maybe. She's the one that brought me here to build that castle down below, the place she calls Crannog. After her mother passed away. Her mother, you see, was more haunt than human, too. Like a faerie. Or a spirit person."

"Spirit being!" Grüdj said. "This Negra saw the same oncet. Vanished into a lake."

"Aye, that's the sort of thing," O'Byrne said. "Me bein' young and foolish, I married one. Luned's the result. Just between you and me"—and here O'Byrne leaned forward to whisper, as if the two of them were not surrounded by miles of empty silence—"it's become very clear to me she's some kind of spirit connected with the water. A water sprite, maybe. You'll find her *very* protective of any sort of water, be it a trickle of a creek or a roarin' river."

"Waugh," Grüdj said, scraping the bottom of the pot for the last bit of gravy and potato.

The next day they walked up the ditch together. John O'Byrne did most of the talking, as usual.

"No need to tell Paddy and that fool Finn anythin' about Luned, or her mother," O'Byrne said. "So far as they're concerned, she's just a strange female. They know she's my offspring, of course."

He chatted about Fontana, the strange woman he'd found wandering in the desert and how she and Luned had led him to come looking for this place in the mountains where the water took its source. Most of the Great North Project had been Fontana's idea, although Luned had also taken a turn at suggesting some things and demanding others. What the house should look like and where the reservoir was to be constructed and so on. But Fontana was really the one who managed it all. She had great plans for her little kingdom there in the high mountains.

They crossed over the ditch on a bridge which Grüdj had fashioned out of two logs, and, less than 100 yards farther along, they came to his massive diversion gate. O'Byrne could only stand and marvel at the thing. Here came the main ditch where they had cut through the high shoulder of the mountain. What Grüdj had done was to cut a new ditch at right angles, somehow blasting it through solid granite; the new ditch led the water out along the shoulder until it could drop in a foaming cascade and then race down to the big river below. Passing through the granite trough that way, it wouldn't erode anything at all.

And the gate itself! The black must have seen something like it somewhere, unless he was some kind of natural genius at engineering. It was made of logs stacked on a central pivot, which was imbedded in the rock right at the corner of where the main ditch met the diversion ditch. If a man swung this barricade outward, it would block the main ditch and send the water down the diversion. Or it could swing the other way, blocking off the diversion channel, and all the water would go down the main ditch. O'Byrne could see how the device used the pressure of the water itself in order to move back and forth. As Paddy and Finn had said: *'Twas brilliant.* But where was the release? What held it open? For that matter, how *would* a man go about shifting all that weight of logs and pressure of water?

"How does it work?" he asked.

"Grüdj knows," Grüdj replied. "Does Jonoburn want water in the ditch now?"

"No! No, this is just grand the way it is. There's just enough seeping through to let me get a gradient figure out down at the bottom end. I'm just sayin' that I don't see how to close the gate."

"Grüdj knows. It will close."

It was a sober and thoughtful John O'Byrne who returned to Crannog days later to begin organizing the digging season on his irrigation project. He thought back to the time when he had a fleeting encounter with a certain voiceless woman of effervescent beauty, and how a few days of reckless abandon had resulted in becoming the sole parent and guardian of Luned. Then there was the finding of the woman in the desert, a regal and imperious woman who called herself Fontana, and whose single-minded ambition it was to create a kingdom out of an irrigation project. And now into his life had come a squat, one-eyed, black creature living on the upper ditch, a man of such strength and cunning as didn't seem altogether natural. *'Twas a good thing whiskey was scarce at Crannog, otherwise a man might be driven to drink.*

"And what does he *want?*" Luned demanded during dinner that evening.

"It's all a bit vague," O'Byrne admitted. "But I think he's saying he'll help finish the ditch for a share of the water."

"A share?" Fontana said. "All workmen will get shares, as soon as we build houses for them and bring them here. Each according to his ability and contribution. That was always my intention. If this Groodge works well and you think he deserves it, then he shall have a share."

"No," Luned said. "It's more than that. He wants more than that."

"And have you spoken with him, then?" O'Byrne challenged.

"I saw what he did with the river. There is great power in that bar he carries, and he will not be content using it only to finish your ditch for you. I think he has been sent to steal the water, all of it."

"How? For who?" Fontana asked.

"I don't *know!*" Luned said. "That's why I tried to send him away. We do not need him. I do not understand him. He does *not* want what we want, and therefore he is dangerous."

"Pardon my Greek, daughter," O'Byrne replied, "but I think he's damn' useful. I've seen what he did, even if I can't figure how he did it, and I'm sayin' right here and now that he's likely to end up saving us months of work. And . . . ," he added, turning to Fontana, "he just might be able to replace three or four other men, thus saving you the cost of their salaries and shares."

"Very well," Fontana said. "That decides it. The

Groodge character will stay so long as he contributes to the building of the ditch. And you, Luned, will see that he has fresh meat."

John O'Byrne saw how fiercely his daughter scowled. *Just like those mountain creeks,* he thought, *she always wants to be goin' merrily along her way with no interference.* "All right," he said. "Then tomorrow I'll get the boys packing for the work shack, and we'll see what ditch building we can do on our own while we wait for these hordes of your workmen to magically appear."

Fontana bristled at O'Byrne's reference to the fact that her plan called for a small village of workmen and their families somehow to materialize just outside the walls of Crannog. The man she had sent to spread the word through the settlements had been gone all winter. She had expected the messenger to return in a month, followed by a wagon train of people eager to have homes and work and a share in her great dream. Here it was nearly time for them to be finishing their houses and planting their gardens, and they had not come. Nor had the Guardian come, the man she had seen in a dream. No Guardian, but another figure she knew nothing about, but who seemed to have some rôle in her plans.

And so it became Fontana's turn to make a trek up through the forests to Spirit Ridge at the edge of timberline to have a look at the strange newcomer who had come to live on her ditch. It was clear from John's description of him that this Groodge would not come to Crannog—she must go to him.

Chapter Ten

FASTING AND FLOOD

The coming-out of the first flowers on Spirit Ridge brought longer and warmer days. Each morning as the sun climbed the eastern sky, Grüdj ate and went to the ditch, where he either broke rocks in the path of the ditch or argued with the water. There was more water now that the ground was getting warmer and the snows were melting high up on the mountains, and it was all impatient to leave the high country before the freezing returned.

"Down on the buffalo prairie it is the Moon Of New Grass," Grüdj told the water. "The freezing time is over for a long time. You do not need to hurry. Be patient."

The small creek in his own valley swelled up and made boggy places for him to step in as it went hurrying to the ditch. The water already in the ditch sometimes reached out and splashed him.

"For now you must go down to the big river," he said to the water as it flowed out through the gate and channel he had built. "To the cañons of red stone and the wide lake with the bitter taste. But only for now."

As if to defy him, water from the creek below the diversion joined water seeping around his upper diversion dam and slammed into the lower gate before turning and racing away down the slope toward the river.

"Soon," Grüdj said, "Jonoburn says men are coming to

make more ditch. Soon you will have another place to go."

And the water went on grumbling and rumbling and causing muddy damp places he would step into when he went from his hut to the ditch.

When the sun gained the middle of the sky, Grüdj made his meal. At first, the supplies that Finn and Paddy had brought were strange to him, but he was learning. He let the Irishmen show him how to take white powder and water and shape it into wet lumps to bake beside the fire. They taught him how to cut open the metal cans to get the stewed tomatoes. And always there was venison. No sooner had he cut the last meat from the deer hanging in his cache than another would be left where he would find it.

This hunter, he thought, *what would The People think of her? A woman who hunted. A woman who ranged far, and always alone. She would not be happy growing things for food.*

After he had eaten, Grüdj went to a high promontory of rock overlooking his hut and the valley. He tied a strip of hide to the end of his iron stick to make a flag, as he had seen Who Sees Far do to indicate a time of vision seeking, and wedged the point of the bar down into a crack. The promontory was flat on top and cushioned with deep moss. From there he could see all the way down his valley to the ditch, and all the way up into the highest ranges of mountains. It was while sitting here one day that his dream of Two Nose Thomas came back to him, more as a memory than as a dream.

"No vision less'n you make yore fast," Two Nose said.

He was right. The man Jonoburn and the strange pale girl Luned made certain he always had food. As long as they were giving him so much food, it was impossible for him to find his vision. But he did not need to eat it.

Grüdj returned to his hut to put on his leather hunting

frock and his best moccasins. He took two water skins and went to the little creek to fill them. He ignored the water's complaining voice.

"Be quiet!" he told the stream, speaking as an elder of The People would speak to noisy children. "Go and do what you are supposed to, and be silent."

He returned to his overlook and sat down to wait. Two days he went without food, and then three days. On the next day he could not remember how many days it had been. The wind soughed through the trees below his promontory and the air seemed as warm as the inside of a lodge. He dreamed of many things but remembered none of it, waking only to fleeting memories of having dreamed.

On the fifth day the clouds began closing in around him. He faced the direction of the buffalo prairies and his vision seemed to penetrate through the mountains one after the other until he could clearly see the great stone medicine circle of The People. Grüdj sat there, staring into the fog, and the vision dream began to happen.

He saw Standing Hollow Horn in the center of the medicine circle, offering a pipe to the six grandfathers, turning solemnly to face one direction after the other. Grüdj's vision flew past the medicine circle and on toward the plains, traveling in a flash past Standing Hollow Horn and the hills on the edge of the mountains. Now he saw deep grass everywhere. He saw vast herds of dark animals, some here, some there, some on one hill and some on another. It was wonderful.

Then he saw the tall lodges of The People, arranged in a circle, smoke drifting gently into a blue sky. He seemed to be flying over them like a hawk, turning in wide circles and seeing all the details below him.

Grüdj looked back toward the medicine circle. Standing

Hollow Horn was standing there with his pipe in one hand and medicine bundle in the other, watching him.

"I come back!" Grüdj called out to him. "I bring water so grass and buffalo will belong to The People forever. I, Grüdj, say this!"

But instead of answering, the elder turned to point toward the valley where Grüdj's lonely hut stood.

Grüdj blinked. He was back again, sitting on his grassy ledge with the mountains and the lowering clouds around him.

He looked down at his hut and saw spirit beings coming up the creek toward it. Two spirit beings on horses. Their images swam and rippled as if they were underwater. Grüdj tried to bring them into focus, but weakness made everything seem blurry and unreal. He sat and swayed, his eye fixed and staring down at the apparition. There were rainbow colors all around the edge of his vision. All he could tell was that they were ghosts or spirits and they were going toward his hut looking for him. It was what Standing Hollow Horn had pointed at. A warning. Grüdj stared harder. There was a glint of light. It came from a shining horn, like metal, sticking out of its forehead. The other ghost had no face at all, just a dark cloak that covered its phantom shape and most of the horse it rode.

Then he heard his name floating up to him. It was an eerie trembling sound that made him close his eye and lift his face to the sky, to the six grandfathers for help.

"Gruuuuuuudge!" it called.

He did not answer.

"Gruuuuuuuudge!" came the call again.

He would climb a little way down the slope and get a better look. The one with the metal horn sticking out of its head had taken the horn away and was the one calling his name.

Grüdj rolled onto his stomach and carefully eased himself, feet first, over the edge of the escarpment, but his foot caught in a tree root and he began to fall. He reached out to stop himself, but his arms had become slow and weak. Something suddenly struck him in the side. His head hit the hard ground and collided with a rock, and, as he lost consciousness, he was aware of his body rolling over and over down the hill. All was dark.

"No bones seem to be broken," the woman's voice said.

" 'Tis a wonder if true," said the voice of Jonoburn. " 'Twas a fearsome long tumble he had. Lift his head up now and see if he'll take a little water from my canteen."

"I'll hold his head on my lap," the woman said, gently arranging herself beneath Grüdj's spinning head. "You fetch the flask of brandy from my saddlebag."

The brandy was bitter-tasting stuff that took his breath away almost as badly as had his fall down the hill. And it did little to clear his thoughts. All Grüdj knew was the touch of kindly hands and the sound of sympathetic voices. Strangely his first words were about the iron bar.

"Iron stick," he mumbled weakly. "Up there. Grüdj must go. . . ."

"You're goin' to your hut, lad," said Jonoburn, "and that's all the farther you'll go for now. What on earth were you doin', rollin' down the hill like that?"

"No food," Grüdj said. "Grüdj must find the iron stick. . . ."

"No food?" the woman asked. "This man is up here with no food?"

"Find the iron stick," he groaned.

"Can't be," O'Byrne said. "Unless somebody robbed him, he ought to have enough for two, three months."

"Well, we'd better get him to his hut and find out. He looks like he needs to eat."

"Stick," Grüdj moaned through the brandy fog.

"Ah for the love of Pete!" O'Byrne said. "Well, then, where in hell . . . 'scuse me, Fontana . . . *where* would y'be leavin' this precious rock bar of yours, then?"

Grüdj weakly pointed toward the promontory from which he had fallen. O'Byrne took out the pocket telescope he used for surveying, and squinted through it. Grüdj recognized it as the metal horn he had seen sticking out of the forehead of the spirit being.

"Yah, there it is," O'Byrne said. "I see it. Safe as can be. Let's be gettin' you over to the hut, and then I'll go back and get your rock bar."

O'Byrne and Fontana got Grüdj onto his feet. She put her riding cloak around his trembling shoulders and the two of them walked him slowly to his hut. When he was on his bed, O'Byrne built up the fire and Fontana brought food from her own saddlebag. She went to the creek to fill his cooking pot and soon had a warm gruel to feed him. His head slowly cleared of its foggy numbness, but a sharp pain came to replace it. The woman heated more water and brought a steaming wet rag to press against his temple.

"Are you feeling better?" she asked.

"Waugh."

"That's a good thing," Jonoburn said. "You're lucky not to have anything broke, the way you came down that hill head over breakfast."

"You said you had no food?" the woman said.

"Nah," O'Byrne said. "That's not right at all. I had a

look at the cache just now, while I was unsaddling the horses. Plenty of supplies in there."

"No food," Grüdj repeated. "Grüdj looks for the spirit talk. Dream time."

"Oh!" Fontana said. "You were fasting so as to have a vision! I understand. Mister O'Byrne here probably doesn't know much about that, but I certainly do. I have been a vision seeker myself. Many years ago. At the edge of the desert."

"Deh-serrtt," Grüdj slowly repeated.

By evening Grüdj was strong enough to help O'Byrne build a couple of sleeping places inside the windbreak. Fontana would have the hut to herself. For supper there were the potatoes O'Byrne had brought along to cook in the coals and a sizable joint of venison from Grüdj's cache.

"I see you've been breakin' more rock," O'Byrne said as they ate.

"So," Grüdj replied.

" 'Tis marvelous. When we got closer to Gate Number Two, didn't I point out to Fontana that somebody had been splittin' the boulders right along the ditch line? You're worth a team of men with a steam hammer, you are!"

Grüdj did not know what a steam hammer was, but he didn't ask. It was good to see Jonoburn so pleased.

"And what's next?" Fontana asked. She, too, was clearly pleased to have Grüdj's help on the upper ditch.

"Well," O'Byrne said, "if you don't mind staying up here another day or two, I'd do a rough survey down along the ditch line a ways, maybe a mile, so's Groodge here can keep on breakin' rock. Might do some figurin' of the gradient, too. Paddy and that fool Finn oughta be here next week, along with as many as four of your new hunkies. We'll make good time, if I can keep the survey a mile or more ahead of them."

"John, I wish you wouldn't call them hunkies. They're going to be settlers, villagers at Crannog."

"Ah," O'Byrne said. "Call 'em what you like, they look to me like hunkies. Gandies, swampers, shanty help, all the same breed o' cat. They'll work good as long as it suits them, but don't be surprised if they pull stakes and leave before you get your precious town built."

In the morning, John O'Byrne wasted little time getting back to the ditch with his transit and telescope. Fontana and Grüdj heard him singing an Irish ditty as he rode off down the creek. She insisted on looking at the bruise on the side of Grüdj's head and bandaging a cut on his leg, then made him sit quietly in the windbreak while she boiled up more gruel and cooked bannock for him. She also made coffee, which made Grüdj's head buzz almost as much as the brandy had done. He didn't care much for it until she laced it with sugar, the way Two Nose Thomas used to.

"Now," she said, settling down on the ground next to the fire and arranging her skirts about her so she could reach the pot and griddle in case Grüdj wanted more, "tell me about this vision questing. Why are you doing it?"

Grüdj thought of when he was a boy and Crows Woman would question him. Why did he like this, why did he go here, what was he looking for, and who did he play with? He knew he was unusual to them, with his one eye and his black skin and especially with his great strength. Always there had been an uneasy feeling among The People when he did something, like talking to the water, because he was different. Everyone seemed curious about him, the way young coyotes come sniffing around new smells.

"Grüdj comes from The People," he began. "Standing Hollow Horn looked for the old gods of the mountains. Who Sees Far told Grüdj about visions, dreams." He went silent, wondering how much he should tell her. He did not look at her directly. That would be rude. But she made him feel good, and there was something about her words that seemed linked with his own. He could not tell what it was. She was not like Crows Woman. She was almost like Who Sees Far, who always knew what a person had in their mind before they put words to it.

"Grüdj is a water dreamer," he said softly.

Fontana was quiet for a long time after that. She took a fork and pushed the remainder of the bannock to the edge of the griddle where he could reach it. Grüdj took it and chewed slowly.

"I see," Fontana said. "I understand. And these people of yours, what do they want you to do?"

He hadn't ever asked himself that question, at least not in those words. "Go," he replied. "Leave."

"You're abandoned, then," she said. "An outcast."

"So. Wagon people buried Grüdj. Crows Woman said wagon people threw Grüdj away. Then Grüdj spoiled a sacred time. The People said to leave."

"And you are an unwanted person anywhere you go. You must believe me, I know how you are feeling. But you told Mister O'Byrne that you wanted to help your people all the same. Wanted water shares for them, he said."

"Water shares," he repeated. "*Waugh*. Jonoburn said Grüdj would have shares."

"So why were you seeking a vision? With so much work to be done, I mean. What do you need with a vision now?"

Grüdj didn't understand.

"Grüdj," she said gently, "I can tell you why. I'm not certain who your adopted people are, but I think they must be Indians of the plains. Are they buffalo people? I know something about such people. How do they get water when they need it? How? Tell me."

"Buffalo people," he repeated. "The People move to find water. Sometimes grass for the ponies gets short, water is better somewhere else, the village takes down their lodges. They go where water is good, grass is good."

"Plains Indians. A hunting tribe. What else?"

Grüdj thought a moment. "What else," he muttered. "Seek the spirits. The shaman cloud dreamer, he calls the six grandfathers to bring rain. If The People are right in their hearts, if they act. . . ."

"Correctly? Respectfully?"

"Yes. Sky spirits bring clouds, rain."

"It is as I thought," Fontana said. "The ones who adopted you are mystical people. Their way is to become one with the sky, the earth, the water. Your people move their lodges knowing the earth always has a place for them, somewhere. Not like the whites who want to stay in one place. You have seen them with their wagons, always looking for one place to be, one place to stay. It is our way."

"Soldier towns," Grüdj said.

"Yes. Like that. Many towns. Towns which always need water. It is the way of the whites to make the water go where we want it to go, do what we want. We do not wait for it or pray for it. We have tools to bring the water to us. Your people are one with the earth and cannot do that. But you are not an Indian. You are Negro, a black man. You should be working with the whites. Many, many blacks work for the white men. We rule the earth. We change it so it will help us."

"Grüdj breaks the rocks and the water goes there," he said.

"Exactly! Exactly!" Fontana said. "You work for us on this great ditch, this Great North Ditch, and together we will all make the mountains give us water for irrigation. For reservoirs. For towns."

"The People?" Grüdj asked.

"I will promise you this much," Fontana replied. "I will ask if the law will allow it. I will find out what your people can have . . . in the way of owning land and water . . . and help you get it for them. *You* can work for shares of water, there's no question of that. What do you say?"

Fontana was excited about this new prospect. She envisioned a whole tribe of Indians farming and raising livestock in her Utopian community, spiritual people in touch with the mountains and forests.

Grüdj managed a crooked bizarre kind of smile. He had this warm lodge. There was work for his iron stick to perform. He had the approval of Jonoburn and this woman whose voice and eyes calmed his thoughts.

There was a booming sound, like faint distant thunder, as John O'Byrne and Fontana were packing up to leave the work shack several days later. They were on their way back to Crannog.

"Did you hear that?" O'Byrne asked. "It sounds as though Groodge couldn't wait to get back to work."

"Is that blasting powder he's using? Wouldn't that be dangerous, blasting all by himself, I mean?"

"Don't know," O'Byrne said. "I've never seen him with any powder at all, and, when I offered to bring some up, he didn't know what it was. He never works on the rock when anyone's watching, I do know that much. 'Tis a mystery what he does, other than to hammer away at it with that steel bar of his."

"He spoke of it as an *iron* bar, not steel."

"Aye, and maybe wherever he grew up anything that was

metal was called iron," O'Byrne said, "but steel it is, and strange steel at that."

"Oh?"

"Aye. I had a good look when I brought it down from that outcrop. For one thing, there's hardly a scratch on it. And for another, the tip has a well-dressed chisel edge to it as though a blacksmith had just finished sharpening it."

"Grüdj must know how to sharpen it," Fontana said.

"Maybe," O'Byrne said. "But hard as that steel is, it'd take a mighty hot forge and a heavy hammer to draw out an edge such as that one. Not to mention a big anvil."

Another faraway booming came down the long valley to them like the sound of a rockslide or small earthquake.

"So long as the ditch is going forward, that's the main thing," Fontana said. "I'm going to look into this question of water shares for him, and for those Indian people who seem to have raised him. We might do well to have a colony out on the plains."

There she goes again, O'Byrne thought. *Her serfs and minions livin' in quaint villages throughout her kingdom. And didn't we leave Ireland because of the same?*

"Tell me, John," Fontana said as they rode together.

"About what?" he said.

"Grüdj. I had several conversations with him, you know. He speaks in broken English like a trapper, and sometimes he drifts into his Indian tongue. He likes to repeat words, like a child does. Is he slow-witted, do you think?"

John O'Byrne laughed. If she had seen how he designed that upper gate, she wouldn't think the man slow-witted at all.

"No," he said. "Bright as new copper is that young man. What he's doin' is learning the English by listenin' to yourself, or to me. Each time I'm here, don't I hear my own words comin' back to me? You're right, about the trapper talk. I'm thinkin' he spent a long time with mountain men, somewhere. He knows their . . . what d'ye call it?"

"Slang? Patois?"

"Aye, the slang. And I gather he stayed with government surveyors a week or two. He can use words he picked up from them, too."

"That's excellent!" Fontana smiled, pausing to listen to the faint echo of another far-off rumble. Again she visualized a community of Indian people living side-by-side with her people at Crannog, with this young man acting as interpreter and teaching them to use English.

Back on the working face of the ditch, Grüdj squinted along the line of sticks Jonoburn had placed. He nodded in agreement. That was the way the water should go. Jonoburn said more men would come to lift the broken rocks and clear away the dirt and sand.

He stepped onto an enormous buried boulder, lined himself up with the stakes, then raised the bar and brought the point down on the rocks just hard enough to split them and make the ground shake a little. There seemed to be no end to his strength, not even a thought of becoming tired as his arms rose and fell over and over again, his iron bar chiseling away at the route the water would take. Standing Hollow Horn had come to him in his vision to let him know that The People were waiting for him, somewhere. Perhaps before the time of freezing came again he would see one of them. Perhaps Two Nose Thomas would find him again, or Standing Hollow Horn's followers would come back to Spirit Ridge and discover Grüdj there. He would hold council with them and let them know about the land they would have.

* * * * *

Peace and quiet had returned to Grüdj's mountainside.

Once more, he got into the daily pattern of eating and talking with the water; instead of going up his hill to meditate, however, he went down where the trees were and resumed shattering rocks for the ditch. Something had happened to change the weather and the skies. Seldom did the warm sun shine down on him. In the mornings, when he spoke to the little creek in his own valley or the seepage in the ditch, the big clouds were rising from behind the peaks. When he began to break rock, the clouds grew thicker, heavier. They slipped down into the cañons and wrapped themselves among the crags. The mountainside became cold and damp. Sometimes the thunder sounded as if the skies were complaining to him.

One day, the cold rain that came slicing down out of the heavy clouds was enough to make Grüdj take shelter under the drooping branches of a spruce tree. It was a very tall, very old spruce tree and its branches made a dry lodge. As he hunched beneath them, watching the rain drip, the wind gusting and whistling, he thought he saw the pale figure moving swiftly through the forest, going up the hill toward where the trees do not grow. Just a trick of the wind, he thought, blowing the rain around. Or it could have been a deer running away from something.

When the storm drifted off to drench some other part of the mountain range, Grüdj went back to his work. He had decided to clear out the rubble himself rather than wait for Jonoburn's other men to come and do it, at least as far as a high hump of ground that lay in the line of the ditch. Grüdj had the idea of building them another gate there, one which would divert the water toward a wooded depression out in the forest. The hump of ground was so high the water would not be able to ruin the gate by digging out around it.

And so he was in the ditch, the walls twice the height of his head on either side, pecking away with his bar. The face of the ditch was a stubborn bit of soft rock that just crumbled when he wanted it to fracture. He heard the voice of sky thunder. Except it did not come from the sky, but came along the ground as fast as a horse running. In an instant, he recognized it as the sound of angry water, rumbling even louder than when the big river broke through his landslide.

Instantly Grüdj knew what it meant—the water in the upper ditch had burst through the gate and was roaring down the slope to the big river. A great rain drowned the high valleys and now a flood was coming down the creeks toward the river.

He was wrong. The water was not racing down the mountainside but down the ditch. The upper gate was open. He had opened the lower gate to the main ditch, so he would have a few inches of water to show him when he had dug the bottom of the ditch to the right level, but it was not enough to let so much water leave the ditch. He was caught in the deepest part, with nothing to divert the water, nothing between himself and the angry flood.

It rose to his knees, and then his waist, then a wave slammed him into the rock face and he dropped his iron bar. The force of the water kept him from turning around, putting his back to it, and so he was pinned against the rock and at the mercy of the flood. It reached over his head like a giant hand, pushing him under. He bobbed up again, gasping for air and struggling to turn and find a handhold on the crumbling rock. The icy water dragged at his legs, his body, twisted him this way and that. It finally had him in its grip and was not about to let go. He bobbed up once more, gasped a lungful of air, went down again and was turned upside down in the swirl.

Grüdj was battered against the rock, sucked down and sent hurtling upward again until the water lost its momentum, and could do nothing more. Hemmed in between high walls at the face of the ditch, all it could do was grumble and threaten. The surface heaved up and down. The water dreamer's battered body was released one last time and floated to the surface.

Overhead, the clouds opened to let the sun look down on the damage.

Chapter Eleven

THE DITCHBREAKERS

The late afternoon clouds rolled away and the long slope above timberline basked in dazzling light. Yellow flowers sprang open as if on command. Somewhere in one of the ancient rockslides a pika stuck its head out of his tiny den and whistled a high, thin note of query. Another pika answered. All was peaceful and quiet. The grass and moss had a glaze of rain water and there was scarcely enough breeze to support the hawk who had risen into the blue sky to search among the peaks for his supper.

The Great North Ditch stretched in a gleaming unbroken strip, a sheet of water curving gracefully along the contour of the long slope. It was full all the way from its upper end in the tundra to its working face down in the trees, but someone was trying to change that. At Gate Number Two, the lower diversion gate just a little uphill of the tree line, a squat, shapeless figure in soggy leather labored to raise the logs. He couldn't find his iron bar under all the water, so he had to lift them using only the force in his arms. But the secret was not in his strength, as Jonoburn had mistakenly supposed. The secret was in the way the gate worked.

Gaining a fraction of an inch with each heave, Grüdj got the top log high enough to release itself on one end. He found a sturdy tree branch to stick down under the water and release one end of the second log. It took only a few minutes for the water level to start dropping. Grüdj waded waist-deep into the chilly water to release the same end of the third log. Now all three remained sticking up like bare animal ribs. Grüdj groped in the water for the wooden pins holding the bottom two logs, then pushed the logs to swing across the width of the ditch. Once again the water ran down the mountain and only a few inches remained at the working face. Grüdj retrieved his iron bar and hoisted himself out of the ditch. He was wet and cold and angry. He wanted to punish the water for nearly drowning him, but instinct told him it was not the water's fault. Not this time.

The following morning Grüdj was on the ditch path by sunrise. His leathers were dry and stiff to walk in. He stopped at each little creek and trickle running into the ditch to study the water and ask about the flood. Yes, the waters told him, a fat-bellied cloud had become trapped against the high part of the ridge. And another one, too, farther along. Two creeks had their rocks stripped bare of moss and many branches of scrubby brush were broken. At one point, a thunderstorm-swollen creek had come into the ditch with such force it had washed a great hole in the opposite side. He would have to fix that with rock. It was clear that his upper gate had broken, the one Jonoburn called Gate Noommerwon. There would not be so much water in the ditch, even with a big rain, unless the gate had washed out and let loose all the upper water as well. He'd have to fix it before he could go ahead with any more digging.

But despite his stiff leathers and damage to the ditch, Grüdj found it a good day to be out walking in the high country where trees did not grow. The rainstorm had cleansed the sky and clarified the air; from the path along the ditch he could look far down into the valley of the big river and even farther to where the river finally vanished among dark forests. He could look up and all around him and see all the mountains and ridges splotched with valleys of snow and ice. New grass and bright flowers grew along the ditch path. Standing Hollow Horn had called this kind of land "the far-seeing-place". The old gods of The People lived in such places, according to Standing Hollow Horn, because they could see the world from there and know what the animals and the people were doing.

But it was not the old gods who had sent the flood to drown Grüdj. As soon as he came to the gate, he sat himself down on a sun-warmed stone and stared at it with his one eye. It was not broken. It was not washed out. It was open. Someone had figured out how to swing it back to close off the diversion. Someone must have been spying on him as he built it, or the few times when he had himself opened it. Otherwise, they wouldn't know how to do it.

Grüdj sat with his eye fixed on the gate and thought some more. This person—someone—had also seen the clouds being stopped against the high ridge and knew the creeks coming down would be flowing full. Someone had been here, or had hurried up here to make certain all the water came down to the face of the ditch where he was working. His suspicion grew and grew. A short time ago he had felt free and alone, glad to be in the high open places; now, as he crossed the ditch on the foot logs, he glowered all around him. He listened for any sound, watched for any movement of anyone spying on him. He moved the big rock that he had carefully placed to cover a certain hole beside the gate's pivot post. He slowly looked around again and, certain he was not being watched, put his iron bar deep into the hole in the rock and pushed.

There was a slight grating noise. He pulled out the bar

and replaced the rock over the hole. The edge of the gate began to swing with the water, the water being forced to move its own barricade into place. As the logs slid back into the groove he had cut into the opening, Grüdj knew there was nothing wrong with the way it worked. Somebody had opened it, but for now the flow from the upper valleys was going down the mountain toward the river again and the water level in the ditch was dropping quickly. Tomorrow he could get back to his work.

After taking one more look around, Grüdj went back across his two-log bridge to the ditch path. Lying just the other side of the logs he found a young doe, freshly killed, the slender white arrow sticking out of its body just where the heart would be.

Several weeks later, John O'Byrne and Paddy were walking the survey line from the shack up toward the working face of the ditch. Finn and four new workmen were down at the shack cutting trees for the new buildings. They had figured on building two additional small cabins for crew quarters, but Fontana added to their labors with a request for yet another cabin. This one was to be larger, with good windows and door and a metal stove, and it was to be built at the edge of a small meadow, nearby, rather than under the perpetual shade of the forest.

Paddy and Finn assumed she intended it for her own personal use. With that premise in mind, they further assumed that the lady would be spending more time at the work site, supervising their labors. It was a prospect neither of them liked. But orders were orders, and so she would have her own special cabin and corral and pole barn and all. When they spoke of it to John O'Byrne, he only shrugged and told them to get about doing it. He would keep his own counsel, suspecting that Fontana was preparing the cabin for the arrival of yet another person, a person probably as strange as herself. He thought he knew who it would be.

"Paddy," he said, "let's be leavin' that to Finn and the boys today. You come with me up the ditch and let's see what's to be done about that diversion gate."

"Mary and Joseph together!" Paddy exclaimed, pointing.

John O'Byrne was speechless.

"What are we dealin' with here, John?" Paddy asked.

"Would that I knew," John replied. "Would that I only knew."

"If the old country wasn't so bleedin' far behind us now, I'd swear 'twas the little people who'd done this."

But some Donnegal crone rising of a morning to find her cow already milked and her stoop already swept was nothing compared with this. Off to one side of the survey line lay a half dozen tall trees which had been uprooted roots and all. Along the line for 100 yards the ground was all plowed up and broken, the rocks shattered. Most amazing of all, the working face of the ditch had been pushed well beyond Gate Number Two. Another 100 yards or more, O'Byrne estimated. Right through a ridge of decomposed granite he himself had been dreading. Awful stuff it was to cut through, too soft for drills and powder and too solid for pick and shovel.

"I'll wager you a month's pay this was done by that Groodge," O'Byrne said.

"Then he's been at the blastin' powder," Paddy said, "and no doubt of it. I didn't think me and Finn left enough in the powder cache to do all *this,* though. 'Tis miraculous, it is. We'll bring up the teams and scrapers. With him doin' this kind of work and your new men and all, we'll have a mile more of ditch cleared before the month is over."

"No doubt of it," O'Byrne said. "The black is earnin' his shares of ditch water, and more. But. . . ."

"Are you thinkin' the same as me, John?"

"That it's too much of the strange? Aye. Let's don't be tellin' the new men too much about this. And tell that fool Finn to keep his cake-hole shut as well. The last thing we need is the word to get around that there's spirit folk up here. Just say we fixed Groodge up with plenty of blastin' powder and he's a wonder at the using of it."

"I'm rememberin' the time, John, when you claimed you'd had yourself a chat with some kind of giant blacksmith! Wine, you said the two o' ye drank. And nobody t'see him but yourself. Weren't *you* wishin' you'd kept quiet?"

"Which you'd do well to do yourself," O'Byrne said.

"Speaking of the rock breaker," Paddy said, pointing at the stodgy figure walking along the ditch path toward them.

"Groodge!" O'Byrne said. "Good to see you!"

Grüdj nodded.

"We're just admiring all this work you've done. It's going to let us make another two, three miles before snow flies again. And Fontana went out to the settlements and found us more workers."

"More people," Grüdj said. "They will have shares?"

"Two of them, yes. They're willing to work for shares. The other two have families and want monthly wages instead."

"Way-jess," Grüdj said. It was another new word. He remembered Two Nose Thomas using it, but in some other way.

"Payment," O'Byrne said. "Money. Like when one of your trappers sells his pelts."

"*Waugh.*" Grüdj understood. "You will dig more ditch now?" Grüdj asked. "Here?"

"That's the plan," O'Byrne replied. "Paddy and I will. We'll start working with a team and scraper. The others are down at the work shack, puttin' up more cabins."

"Grüdj will go." He did not want anyone watching when he used his iron bar. If they knew how he did it, it might take away from the power. Like the spirit lodge beings who visited The People so long ago. They would lose their power if anyone knew where they went, how to find them when they had gone.

His plan was to repair the roof of his hut with new willow branches and to strengthen the food cache. A bear had tried to break it down, and had succeeded in knocking some of the logs loose. Then he would go up to the upper end of the ditch. He had an idea that he could extend it back along the ridge even farther and make it catch one more small creek. More water to give The People when they got their new land.

It was a week later and Grüdj was again walking the ditch path above timberline, up in the bright sunshine and clear air. Everything was peaceful; even the water running a few inches deep down the ditch seemed so placid that he did not want to bother it by stopping to talk. He saw fresh animal tracks on the path and then saw the animals themselves, not deer but shorter, thicker animals with horns that curled down on either side of their heads. Standing Hollow Horn once pointed some out, but at a much greater distance. Grüdj wondered if the meat was good. Maybe Luned would kill one for him, the next time she came. He had not seen her since the time he climbed up to the ditch for the first time, although he often felt her presence. And he never lacked fresh venison. Between the meat and the provisions provided by Fontana and Jonoburn, Grüdj ate very well.

As he came around the last corner, Grüdj saw three strangers at the diversion gate. One was swinging an axe at the logs; another man was hacking at the rock with a pick.

Grüdj hurried as best he could, his short legs giving him an awkward rolling gait.

"No!" he called out. "That is not for you to do!"

The men stopped to look at the thing coming toward them, a barrel-shaped black man with one single eye almost in the center of his forehead, a man in leathers waving a digging bar at them. The man with the axe walked to the end of Grüdj's footbridge and stood there, blocking the way. Grüdj confronted him from the other end of the bridge and there they stood, a black man in the costume of a fur trapper or Indian and a bearded white man in canvas pants and stained flannel shirt. All around them the unpeopled mountains waited in silence.

"Afraid you're wrong there, boy," the bearded stranger said. "This is just what we need to do, just exactly. Unless you know how this damn' water gate works, you just go on along with your business. Whatever that is."

Grüdj advanced a few feet out onto the logs, holding his bar crosswise for balance. "Leave," he commanded. "The water not yours. Jonoburn says where the water goes. Not you. Leave!"

Over by the gate, the one in the faded blue shirt went back to digging at the foundations. The bearded one still stood at the end of the footbridge holding his axe.

"Sorry, boy, but you got no say up here. Get along with you. I'd hate to hurt you, but this here water is ours. Git!"

"Not yours!" Grüdj said, taking two more steps. The bearded man backed up a step.

"Damn right it is," he said. "Your boss . . . assumin' you work for whoever built this ditch . . . your boss is plannin' on stealin' it from us, plain and simple. Why else dig this ditch?"

"No," Grüdj countered.

"Oh, yes. You see those cabins down there? See where that smoke's risin'?"

Grüdj squinted against the sunlight and finally saw what the man was talking about. Faraway down in the valley where the big river was. He saw two little squares in a clearing, smoke rising from one of them.

"That there's the town of Tenpenny now. Me and these boys come up here four, five years ago and staked 'er out. Now we come back t'open a gold mine and we find somebody's dug this here ditch's for stealin' water we need. Water what's legally ours."

"Not there this winter," Grüdj argued. It was two moons, maybe, since he had been to this part of the ditch. But he was sure those tiny little buildings were never there before. He took one more step forward; now he was close enough to hit the bearded man with his iron stick, if he needed to.

"We just finished puttin' 'em up. Your boss . . . did you say you worked for this ditch outfit? . . . he nearly won the first round on us. Right, boys?"

The other two muttered in agreement, but stayed where they were. The only gun they had with them was leaning against a rock away down at the base of the ditch fill and this thick black with the rock bar looked like trouble. The bearded man pressed his case, unwilling to take any more steps back toward the edge and certainly unwilling to remain in range of that steel bar.

"Your boss must've knowed about our claim, boy," he

went on. "Tried t'snooker us. If we'd let this here summer go by without provin' up on it, the rights would revert."

"Vert?" Grüdj said.

"Yeah. Legal talk. Not that it's any of a nigger's business. Just by luck we found out what you was doin' up here."

Grüdj merely stood still, watching the bearded man.

"Yeah," he said again, "lucky thing. We was prospectin' another claim 'way downriver and over a couple of ridges. Along comes this queer kinda, skinny woman carryin' a bow and arrow. 'Ain't you the same as staked out a town site on the big river,' says she. So 'that be us,' says I. 'They're fixin' to steal your water, then,' says she. So here we are. Came back, found it was so. Built our cabins to prove up the claim and now we're protectin' our water."

Luned again. "No," Grüdj said. "Not yours. No shares. You palaver with Jonoburn, he says who has shares."

"Jonoburn? That's your boss man, then? Fine," the bearded man said, shouldering his axe and starting back to the gate. "You go tell him, boy. Meantime, we're bustin' up this gate."

Grüdj was across the log bridge faster than any of the men could believe possible. With the iron stick he tripped the bearded man, grabbing the axe away from him as he fell and tossing it into the ditch. The other two rushed him, one with his arms outstretched to grab at him. The third still had a digging pick in his hands but was uncertain how to use it as a weapon.

The one in the blue shirt was the first to grab Grüdj. Rather, he was the first to grab *at* Grüdj, for he found no way to get a hold on the black's hard, round shoulders or arms. Grüdj's free hand swung in a wild, slow arc that missed the blue shirt completely. The blue shirt got behind him and tried putting an arm around Grüdj's throat while the other man punched at his face. The first punch landed, and was painful, but when he launched a second punch, his fist ran at full speed into the steel bar the Negro had suddenly thrust in front of his face. He stood howling in pain, holding his fist to his mouth. The third man also stood helpless, holding the pick in both hands, unsure whether to push with it, threaten with it, or actually hit the black man with it.

Blue shirt got his arm around Grüdj's throat far enough to lock his wrist with his other hand. But instead of being able to choke him, he found his feet rising from the ground until he was hanging on Grüdj's back. Grüdj dropped his bar long enough to reach the legs of the blue shirt man and drag him off his back. He raised him as easily as he would raise a piece of log or a rock and sent him flying down the embankment, rolling over and over in the sharp débris and gravel until he came to rest in the grass fifty yards below. When he got up, he was limping badly.

The second man stooped to get the iron bar Grüdj had dropped, but found himself looking up at the barrel-like stomach as Grüdj reached down for him. He grabbed Grüdj's legs, wrapped them in his arms like a wrestler, pushed and pulled and shoved with desperate strength. Grüdj tottered and fell to his back, but his fall did not prevent him from getting the other in his hands and tossing him down the embankment. And now it was Grüdj's turn to look up from the ground in fear and surprise, for the man with the pick had finally made his decision. The pick was raised over his head, the sharp point of it aimed at Grüdj's head and about to descend.

Grüdj rolled as nimbly as he could, almost rolling off the edge of the ditch path, causing the first blow to bury the point of the pick in the dirt. Down at the bottom of the embankment the bearded man had limped over to where their rifle was and was aiming it. He hesitated to shoot, but only because he was afraid of hitting his companion.

The eyes of the one with the pick were wide with fear. Once more he raised it high over his head. Grüdj was trapped between the edge and the man with the pick. His iron bar was out of reach, and in a moment the sharp point would come crashing down on his skull.

Then the blue-sky quiet of the mountains was split asunder by the thunder of a gunshot.

It came from up the ditch, and it went echoing out across the treeless tundra and down into the forest. At the same time he heard the explosion, Grüdj saw a puff of dust fly out from the man's shirt, and then a blotch of red blood spread across his chest. The man began to frown, as if he was puzzled, and his body jerked. His arms came down and he dropped the pick and stretched out on the ditch path, as if he meant to sleep a while. The two men down below the ditch bank forgot about Grüdj. They were frozen in place, pointing up the mountain toward a small cloud of white smoke drifting lazily skyward. The man who had picked up the rifle said: "There! There he is!" And he took aim at the figure standing there, farther up the ditch.

It was not the best idea the miner ever had, but it was certainly his final idea.

"Wham!" went the repeating rifle. The bearded figure folded like a ruptured bag of grain. Up the ditch, another puff of smoke went rising into the blue sky. Grüdj looked toward the shooter, then back down the mountain to see the third miner hurrying away into the trees.

Grüdj stood up and retrieved his iron bar. How could anyone be there on the upper ditch? Where had he come from? No one had come past him. He hadn't seen anyone for days. No one could get to the upper ditch unless he made a hard climb up from the big river valley, or unless he scaled the far side of the ridge and dropped down over impossible cliffs. But there he was, on the ditch path upstream of the gate.

The gunman was walking toward him, emerging from the glare of the sun and the dust like a spirit. He was a tall figure in dark clothing, wearing a broad, flat-brim hat and carrying a revolver in a holster at his belt. He had a long rifle in one hand and was leading his saddle horse by the reins. There was no way for him to be there. Nor was there any way for the horse to be there—Grüdj would have seen the tracks.

The new stranger did not speak. He made no sign of greeting or recognition; he only stopped on the ditch path a good distance from Grüdj and stood there, silent, watchful, as if he had always belonged there.

The Guardian had come.

Chapter Twelve

THE WATER SPIRIT

During the weeks that followed, the Guardian became just another part of the routine, silently eating his meals with the workmen and occasionally bringing elk and deer to hang in the food cache at the work shack.

It was a new frontier and a new land for the Europeans. The Industrial Revolution gave them the tools to push civilization across the plains and deserts, while the Great Experiment in democracy gave them freedom. And yet for all the progress humankind had wrought, the Great North Ditch camp was in almost all respects identical to any gathering of laborers anywhere in Europe, at any time in history. They wore the same thick shoes, the same heavy trousers, and the same shapeless homemade shirts of their predecessors. And like their predecessors, they would light a fire of the evening in order to keep the dark at bay while they mended leather and sharpened tools. Somewhere in the dim past, a worker sat in the light of burning peat, pushing holes in a piece of hide with a stone awl. Now his descendant sat in the light of burning pine knots, auguring buckle notches into a bit of mule harness.

They now had an overseer as well. Not a Roman soldier standing guard with a spear over a camp of men building a great wall across Britain. Not a knight in armor posted to protect construction workers rebuilding coastal fortifications in Wales. Not even a British redcoat with his musket, assigned to watch over workers on some obscure fishing port in New England. The spiritual descendant of these sentinels was the man in black, the tall, silent figure who wore his revolver tied down and carried a repeating rifle. In the evenings, when the workers lit a fire to keep off the mosquitoes and sat around smoking their pipes and mending harness, the Guardian kept to himself, usually grooming his horse and cleaning his weapons. By day, they would see him standing on some outcrop or pinnacle like a statue, or someone would catch a glimpse of him riding across the tundra on some mission beyond their imagining. Sometimes, he would vanish for a few days, and it was understood he had gone down to Crannog to speak with Fontana and John O'Byrne. He always returned with fresh tobacco or a small keg of liquor for the men, saying that O'Byrne had sent it, but he never accepted their offer to stay and share. Instead, he would go to his own cabin, give his horse its rubdown, clean his saddle, and go to bed.

Before dawn he would be up again, riding up the ditch or taking his post somewhere above the working face of the ditch. When he and Grüdj encountered one another, the Guardian acknowledged Grüdj with an almost imperceptible nod of his head. If Grüdj saw the Guardian coming, he would sit down among the rocks and stare at the ground as if deep in thought.

The men digging away at the ditch face would sometime hear his rifle, the sound of the shots fading into echoes caroming from one side of the valley to the other. Each time he made the trip to the upper end of the ditch, he stopped and dismounted at Gate Number One to fire his rifle down toward the miner's "town" site. A few workmen who had seen him do this, while they were up there cleaning the ditch, assumed he was doing it to frighten the miners. In point of fact, he had selected a particular white rock at the edge of the trees and used it as a target so he would know the range when the miners came back. They would not soon return, however; the miner who had survived his encounter with the Guardian buried his partners and retreated to a mining camp many miles downriver. He vowed to return, someday, with more men and guns, but none of his acquaintances was eager to test the marksmanship of whoever was watching over the ditch.

Just as their ancient European predecessors had a keen curiosity about the doings of the noblemen and knights and ladies up at the castle, the Great North workers liked to talk among themselves about the Guardian's eerie silence and cool indifference to shooting people. There was also a good deal of fireside gossip about the behavior of the lady, Fontana. She came up to the work site three separate times that spring, supposedly to see how the work was going, but also to check on Grüdj's welfare. She took what the men believed to be an unnatural interest in the squat black man. The two of them were often seen talking together; one evening Paddy started out for Grüdj's hut with provisions and turned back, embarrassed, when he saw them sitting, side-by-side, in Grüdj's stone windbreak, their heads almost touching as they stared into the fire and had their conversation. Paddy was pretty sure she had stayed all night, too.

Worse, perhaps, was that Fontana spent other nights at the work site in the cabin of the Guardian. What went on during those nights no one dared speculate, except for the fool Finn who got a resounding punch from Paddy for doing so. She was a lady, with a lady's poise and carriage and manners; he was a gunfighter with a cold heart. Any man who made loose talk simply because the lady chose to take shelter in the Guardian's cabin was asking for more trouble than he could possibly imagine.

It was during one of her long evening conversations with Grüdj that Fontana shared part of her secret mind for the first time. No one else knew anything about her thoughts, with the possible exception of Luned, who always seemed to understand much more than people wanted her to know. John O'Byrne, of course, was told no more than was necessary.

"Just as you have your visions," she confided to Grüdj, "just as you speak with the water, I know things and see things others cannot. My care is that the water is used by those who need it. Not for washing gold from the rocks, not to run wild down desert cañons to some sea, but to nourish and feed."

Grüdj poked a stick into the fire and stirred the coals. "*Waugh,*" he said. "The water. It likes to be wild. It likes to go everywhere. It likes the buffalo prairie, too. It does not know about The People, but it will help them."

"Yes," Fontana said. "That is the right destiny of the water. That is what we want for it. But others do not. More miners will come to break the ditch and use the water and spoil it. The Guardian will stop them. Men might come to steal tools, steal food, cause trouble. When the ditch finally reaches the lower hills to be used for farming, men will try to take the water without paying. The Guardian will not allow this. *I* am the one from whom this water comes. *My* task is to make certain the water keeps flowing and send it in the direction that is right for it. I am the source. The Guardian protects the source."

Grüdj pondered on it a while. She was trying to say something else, but he could not think what it was. It was like listening to a shaman talk in stories meant to be lessons.

"We will marry," she said at last. "The Guardian and I."

"Marry?"

"Yes. Like your Two Nose Thomas and Crows Woman. Man and wife. Not now, but before this time next year the Guardian will be my husband. It is the way it must be. I have seen it in my own dream visions. I know it will be."

"He will take shares?"

"Shares? Oh, of the water, you mean? No! Oh, Grüdj. You are so worried about your shares, aren't you? I understand. No, he will not have any of your shares, Grüdj. He is here to protect your interests, not take them away. I will make you a promise . . . one day . . . not long from now . . . I will go to the territorial government and ask them if your people can have land for your shares of water. There will be papers to sign and legal records to register."

"Terra-tor . . . ?"

"The government. The men who say what will be. They send soldiers, tell settlers where to build houses. The surveyors you met, they work for the government. The government is the law."

"Like the elders of The People when they go into counsel to say how things will be."

"Yes. I am going to speak with *our* elders on your behalf. I will ask them to allow The People to make a village. It will be like a town I have heard of in Kansas, a town where all the people are black, like you. They built a whole town for themselves. But there is another thing for you to know. Something the workers do not need to know, not yet. Next summer the Guardian will move to Crannog, where I live, and *you* will have his cabin near the work shack. The ditch face is getting farther and farther away from here. Soon it will be a very long walk. The cabin will be better for you."

"Yes," Grüdj said. He liked the idea of living at the

cabin. It would be warm and comfortable. He had seen it, although he had never been inside, and knew it was a good place. It would be nearer to where the other workers lived. Maybe he would eat with them and join their talk around the fire. He wished Two Nose could see him living in a tight, warm, log house just like a white man. And talking and laughing and telling stories beside a fire with white men, like the trapper gatherings Two Nose had told him of. Two Nose would laugh.

"Groodge!"

It was Paddy, calling from the slope above the ditch. Earlier in the day Grüdj had started to break rocks for another diversion ditch, but now he was just squatting beside the excavation as if he were asleep. Grüdj heard the call, and looked up.

"Groodge," Paddy repeated. "I can use a hand up here! Seein' as you're the only one in sight, I'm wondering could you help me out a bit?"

Grüdj rose and made his way up the hill to the granite outcropping where Paddy was trying to drill a hole.

"Mister O'Byrne wants a few buildin' blocks cut outta this fine granite here," Paddy said. "And I'm findin' it devilish hard drillin'. Maybe you could hold the star drill for me and give it a turn now and again."

"Doublejack," Grüdj said, taking hold of the steel.

"Aye! That's the name of this game," Paddy said, smacking the drill with his sledge. For a few minutes they worked together, Grüdj sitting next to the hole turning the star drill every time Paddy hit it, but between the altitude and the exertion the Irishman soon found he had to stop to get his breath.

"Give it to Grüdj," Grüdj said, holding out his hand for

the sledge. Paddy relinquished it eagerly—and immediately realized he may have made a mistake. It would now be himself holding the drill while a one-eyed man swung an eight-pound sledge at it. Too late to say he had changed his mind.

Paddy discovered that being the "jack" could be just as much work as swinging the hammer if a man of Grüdj's strength was doing the pounding. To Grüdj, the teamwork was like a tonic giving his muscles fresh strength. The drill cut so deep with each blow that Paddy had to pull up on it in order to give it the next quarter turn, and pulling it up was not easy. In two hours' time both of them were sweating. The rock dust clinging to their damp faces gave them the look of ghosts, and both were grinning at the progress they had made. Where Paddy alone had managed to make a single shallow dent, there was now a half dozen deep holes in a line along the granite.

"It's enough," he said. "Just one more thing to do." Paddy fetched his water bucket and a canvas bag holding a number of thick round wedges cut from juniper wood. One wedge went into each hole, Grüdj pounding them down hard, and then Paddy gave each one a good soaking.

"Now all we'll be needing to do is come up here every other day or so and pound them again. In a little while Mister O'Byrne, he'll have his granite block. You're a good fellow t'be workin' with, Mister Groodge, surely you are."

Paddy grinned and Grüdj grinned back.

"Yes, sir, good t'work with. So tell me then, what will y'be doin' when the work's all done?"

Grüdj looked at Paddy without understanding what he meant.

"When the job's finished. Me and the fool Finn, we'll doubtless be lookin' t'hire out on the railroad, unless there's another ditch bein' built somewheres. Hard t'find good work, as y'probably know."

"Hah?"

"Well . . . ," Paddy drawled, "surely it's even harder for a free Negro to find a decent job of work. Hell, in most any town you'll see them signs in windows, Help Wanted, No Irish Need Apply. Worse for a black man."

Grüdj shrugged, and Paddy took it as a sign the conversation was over. He picked up the sledge and steel and started for the work shack.

Grüdj went back to the diversion ditch where he resumed his moody contemplation of how to begin building the third diversion gate. Thinking about ways to do it gave him a sense of contentment the likes of which he had not experienced since he had helped Two Nose Thomas build the winter trapping cabin. It had been his practice to go down to the ditch face to shatter rocks in the very late evening or even in the very early morning, so it would be done without anyone seeing. It was an unspoken arrangement between himself and Paddy, who bossed the workmen. But after this day of doublejacking, Grüdj saw no harm in doing his rock breaking right alongside the other men.

The problem right now was to make another water gate. The first one swung with the water's own strength. The second rose on one end. What could he make this one do?

No gate was needed for the time being, but Grüdj went ahead and cut wide vertical grooves in the rock so logs could be slipped into them to make a barricade. The work crew needed the main ditch to be dry, maybe the rest of the summer, so as to get the bottom scraped and leveled. Finn brought up mules and a slip, and he and Grüdj moved dirt, thick, rich, and black, until the water from the high snow fields went flowing along the new channel and into a natural basin in the trees. Jonoburn was of the opinion that the basin had once been a lake, many years ago, but its source had dried up somehow and the water had drained away. Grüdj remembered how he had drained the tiny lake far above where the trees did not grow because he did not want the mountain to hold the water. Now *he* was trapping the water in a lake of his own making.

When Fontana saw the basin, she pronounced it a "very romantic and private place," and indeed it was. The secluded pond nestled in the midst of the slender fir trees and towering white aspen like a jewel. Because it had been a meadow, the bottom of Grüdj's new pond was all in grass rather than mud; the shores, too, were meadow grass and flowers. The water twinkled and sparkled under the blue mountain sky as if it belonged there and nowhere else and had been there since the beginning of time.

When Paddy or Jonoburn did not need him to break the rocks, he liked to go to that place to be alone. He enjoyed how he could follow the diversion ditch out through the trees and find the meadow suddenly opening in front of him to reveal the little lake. It did not occur to him to go there for his fasting or to meditate. In fact, he had not felt drawn to seek his vision or dreams for—*when was the last time? When Fontana came? When the Guardian came?* From time to time he thought vaguely of returning to his promontory above his hut or even going up to the top of Spirit Ridge to see if he could invoke the spirits of The People, but these thoughts were always pushed aside. Sometimes Paddy and Finn needed him to help them with a big rock or log. Sometimes he just sat and doodled in the dirt, thinking of ways to make another water gate. Grüdj was beginning to believe they could not do without him. He was needed nearly every day. This was his new world and he had a place in it. He could work beside these men, and, when the ditch was finished, The People would have shares in the water and land of their own. Then Grüdj would be content. He was at peace with what he was doing.

"Waugh!" Two Nose Thomas had once told him. " 'Tain't fancies and fooferaws thet makes a man *satisfier*. Nossir, 'tis findin' whar his stick oughta float, who he oughta make meat with. Nuthin' shines like bein' with yore good companyeros."

The next time Grüdj saw Luned, his peace of mind would be shattered again.

Grüdj had not seen the strange pale woman for a long time. Not many days after the Guardian arrived, it was he who brought venison for Grüdj. The deer were always shot cleanly through the neck or the heart; sometimes the Guardian rode up to Grüdj's hut in broad daylight, a fresh deer draped over the pack horse's saddle.

"For you," he would say, taking it from the horse and laying it on the ground.

"Waugh," Grüdj would answer.

Grüdj had not seen Luned in so long he had nearly forgotten about her. She did not matter. He just went about his work, cracking rocks where needed and using his strength to help clear trees from the right of way. Whenever he was around the other workers and used his bar, they stopped what they were doing to watch and wonder at how a simple downward thrust of the rock bar would lay the stone wide open. Sometimes they felt the ground rise under their boots like an earthquake was happening far beneath the surface. Around their evening fire they talked about it, some saying " 'twas magic" and some saying "the Negro is just much stronger than he looks." Most of them had heard folk legends, stories from the old country, about men of super strength.

"Wasn't it your granny as told th' story of that knight who haunted Ben Bulben, him in all his rusty chain mail, and could lift ten men at once?"

"Aye," said another, "but next to the giant Cuchulain, he had no more strength than a baby. I mind how 'twas told me. . . ."

And each day, they marveled at how Grüdj moved a massive rock, tossed a thick log aside like a twig, or shattered a whole hill of granite with his iron bar. But one day Grüdj found the rocks harder to break, more resistant to the power of the iron bar. He labored hard at it, and by mid-afternoon he was more tired than he had ever been. Puzzled by this strange weakness, he went in search of a quiet place in which to rest. He walked along the ditch until he came to the second gate, and then followed the diversion channel down through the trees. There was no breeze. The warm sun on his leathers acted like a sleeping drug; he lay down in the grass by the lake in the forest and before long he was drowsing in half-awake immobility like a fat marmot sunning itself. He heard the water rippling in the lake, then heard the water whisper a warning to him. A dream, he thought, for there was no breeze to disturb the lake's surface. But the water spoke again.

He opened his eye and raised his head in time to see a woman rising from the middle of the lake, a naked woman as white as the aspen trees. She had come from beneath the water, her hair streaming wet, her skin glistening in the sun, her arms stretched upward as if to embrace the sunlight. It was not until Grüdj sat up that he realized who she was. A thought flashed instantly into his mind that it was the woman of the spirit lodge and she had come to take away his dream power. But it was not she.

It was Luned.

She moved toward him, more and more of her body revealing itself as she came out of the water. When she was near enough that the water only reached her knees, she stopped and laughed at him.

"Does Grüdj sleep beside the water while other men build his ditch for him?" she taunted.

Grüdj only sat and stared, still not quite believing that this was not a dream of some kind.

"Go dig in the dirt, water dreamer!" she said. "Go break your rocks! You are one of them now, one like my father who thinks only of taking the water away for money. Go! Work!"

"Grüdj rests," he finally managed.

"Oh," she laughed. "Grüdj rests! He dreams no more? Can you still hear when the water speaks to you, old Grüdj?"

"Grüdj hears the water."

Luned pivoted slowly and he saw her naked back and buttocks. She lifted her arms and made a mocking supplication to the water spirits.

"Do you hear, oh, mountain lake! This black one, this ugly one, he *hears* your voice! He is fat with eating the Guardian's meat! He is fat from my father's beans and bread, yet still he hears all that you say to him! What do you say, water?"

The naked woman stood there, pretending to be listening to the water's answer, then she turned back to Grüdj to confront him.

"Did you hear, black?" she said. "Do I have to tell fat Grüdj the news this water brings to him? Or does he hear it?"

Grüdj scowled. "This water told me nothing," he said.

"Ah!" she said. "Ah! Grüdj's power is dying. He works for the whites and loses his Indian power. I will tell you. This water was snow when it was caught by the ridge, very high up. It came a great distance and saw something on the other side, far north of Spirit Ridge."

"What?"

"People. The People. Your shaman, your elders. Your mother. Does Grüdj remember the great stone medicine circle, far north?"

"Waugh."

"They are there, Grüdj. They wait for the water dreamer. They thirst. The water from the high ridge told me so."

No more words. She turned and waded back into the small lake, sinking deeper and deeper until she vanished beneath. Grüdj watched without blinking. In a few moments he saw just her head above the surface as she swam back to the far side, and then there was a white gleam as she walked out of the water and into the trees, and she was gone.

He stood up, supporting himself on his iron bar. He looked toward the top of the mountain. He must go and begin fasting. He must invoke a vision. He had forgotten the ancient gods of The People. For the first time since he had been attacked by the angry miners and the Guardian had come, Grüdj felt fear. But it was not fear of men who might come to break the ditch, nor was it fear that after all his work he would not have a share in the land. He feared losing his power before discovering its real meaning.

In the morning, the workmen uncovered a large boulder in the way of their scraper. "Go find that black and his steel," one said, but they looked for him in vain. Finn unhitched one of the mules and rode to Grüdj's hut, but he wasn't there.

"Just as well," Paddy said. "With this cold fog rollin' in like it is, I say we take the day off and stay inside where it's dry. A man could die of chill, workin' in such weather. Tommora we'll use the blastin' powder."

Grüdj was soaked to the skin by the chilling mist, but he labored up the ridge in spite of it. One hand was torn and bleeding from slipping on the rocks and his knee had suffered badly in the same tumble. At first, he tried to avoid fighting his way through the wind-twisted brush by clambering up a series of steep rockslides, but, after taking a fall and then having his toes nearly crushed by loose rocks, he went back to the crooked willows and stunted pines. His ascent became a matter of pulling himself up, bush by bush and limb by limb, making so many zigzags that he was going 100 yards back and forth in order to gain ten yards upward. The cold fog clung to the trees and dripped down the branches in rivulets.

Grüdj had just entered a small clearing when the bushes immediately ahead of him seemed to heave up off the ground. At first he saw a shapeless hump in the fog, then it took the form of an animal. When it caught his scent, it rose on hind legs and raised enormous forepaws as if scooping the intruder's scent toward its nose.

"Waugh!" it roared, and *"Waugh!"* again and again until the echoes made it sound as if there were bears roaring all around the clearing. The beast slashed the air with its long claws. It showed its teeth and began to move toward Grüdj like an awkward dancer. To Grüdj it was more than a bear surprised in its foraging; it seemed the embodiment of the mountain itself, an ancient god who had materialized in the shape of a bear to protect the home of all the other gods. It

was so tall its giant head seemed about to disappear into the fog. The black claws gleamed like long obsidian knives, the roaring mouth like a dark red cave. Nothing could harm this apparition, nothing could stop it. Luned's slender arrows would have no effect. Not even the heavy bullets from the Guardian's rifle would kill it.

Grüdj retreated to the brush, but the bear came after him, lunging on its hind legs and ripping the air with claws and hideous roaring. Grüdj moved as fast as he could, stumbling from thicket to rock, trying to hide, looking desperately for a hole to climb into. His moccasins slipped and slid in the wet tundra. He fell. He rose again, only to fall again. Crawling now, dragging the iron bar like a useless weight, he scurried uphill toward an outcrop of rock.

The bear had dropped to all fours to follow the scent. Grüdj could hear the beast breaking through the limbs and crushing bushes as it came, roaring *"Waugh!"* with its muzzle close to the ground. When he got to the outcrop, he had to cradle his iron bar in his arms so he could use his hands to climb. His feet skidded and slid, frantic to find any kind of purchase on the slippery granite. How he finally gained the top of the rocks he never knew, but, before the bear got there, Grüdj was out of its reach. It moved around the rock, rearing up and clawing, looking for a way up. The sound of the great claws scraping and screeching against the stone was as terrifying as the growl coming from its throat.

Grüdj stood in the center of his small sanctuary holding the point of the bar toward the animal to jab at it if it managed to get its head over the edge of the rock. Gusts of mist whipped his soaking wet leathers. Water ran down his wide black forehead and into his eye. He thought of the small bag strapped to his back and the jerky and hard bread in it. His knife was also in it. But the food—maybe if he threw it some food the bear god would follow it and leave him alone. Or it would come back for more.

Frustrated by his quarry, the bear ceased roaring and growling and paced around beneath the rock. It looked up now and then and sniffed the air to make sure its prey had not escaped. A few times it tried to climb the rock, but failed. Grüdj shivered in the cold. Gradually the first heart-racing sense of fear left him. What would Two Nose Thomas do if he were chased by a bear? What if he were here, now? Run away? Hit the bear and run away? Make an offering to it? What do warriors do when *they* fight bears?

Grüdj remembered the day he faced the enemy at that place far away where stone piles showed the way across the mountain to Spirit Lake. He remembered the boys playing at being dog soldiers and staking their sashes to the ground. That is what a dog soldier would do here with this bear. He would die with his lance and bow beside him.

"Ho, bear!" Grüdj said suddenly. "I am going over your mountain. Go and eat your berries and leave me. The People wait for me."

The bear stopped and listened, growling under its breath.

"Bear!" Grüdj said. "I am going higher, where the trees do not grow. The gods want me to make a fast. They have a vision for me. I am Grüdj. *Grüdj!*"

The bear reared onto its hind legs and wrinkled its great snout to show Grüdj its teeth.

"Go eat berries!" Grüdj repeated. "I am not for you."

The bear hesitated. It stood there as if considering what Grüdj had said. It was time for Grüdj to act, for he could not stay there shivering in the cold mist much longer. He raised the iron bar as he had done when he faced the enemy on the Spirit Lake path. He brought it downward and drove its point into the rock at his feet.

The ground around the stone outcrop heaved and rolled. Trees swayed, dry limbs falling. Sharp shards of the granite flew out to strike the bear, who first stood amazed, then dropped to all fours again as the rising and falling of the ground made him lose his balance. Then the beast, or god, went hurrying away in his clumsy half-galloping, half-running manner.

Grüdj thought the rock would split in half. As he raised his bar to strike, he was expecting the rock to shatter into many pieces beneath him. But it had not. The blow had caused the ground to bounce. It had broken off a big piece of the rock, enough to frighten off the bear, but it was less than should have happened. His iron bar was losing its power; he must find his vision place soon.

He warily climbed down and resumed toiling up the ridge. The misty rain diminished as he climbed, and by the time he reached timberline the valley fog was below him. The sky was empty of clouds, not so much as a speck of an eagle or hawk marking its deep and endless blue. The sun dried his leathers and took away the forest's trembling chill. Walking became easier with thin grass and little hummocks of flowers to walk on rather than wet rocks and moss. When he topped the ridge, Grüdj looked down the other side expecting to see the medicine circle far away in the distance at the edge of the mountains, but there was only the same dense fog filling the valley. No People, no Standing Hollow Horn, no sign or sound of anyone. Once again, he was alone on the top of the world.

The mist and fog floating below his ridge top hid the valleys, but far, far out in the distance he could see the long line of the horizon. Just below the horizon of the buffalo plains, a column of smoke was rising. At first the idea that it must be coming from some village made his heart feel good. There were people out there, and life. But even at so great a distance, Grüdj knew it was too much smoke to be the cooking fires of a village. Even the white soldier forts did not make so much smoke. It was the grass. The grass was on fire. The summer had been too dry, and the prairie was burning. Once before, when he was a little boy, he had seen the sky turn black with smoke. Crows Woman took him to a hill and pointed out the line of red flame running beneath the clouds of smoke.

"The grass burns," she told him. "It burns when the rains do not come."

Chapter Thirteen

BETWEEN TWO WORLDS

"*Hiiii-yeeee!*" the reedy voice cried. "Go it, Moreau!"

"Give it over, Frenchman! Let this Munsterman show y'that step!"

LeFevre's fiddle and O'Donnell's mouth harp scratched and twanged away at a mad pace while heavy boots beat out the rhythm. Moreau kicked his legs in what he imagined to be an Irish reel, while Paddy waved his arms and stomped his feet in a kind of dimly remembered hornpipe. The four other ditch workers watched and grinned, passing the jug and clapping out the fiddler's rhythm as best they could.

"Let's see y'do this one, then!" Paddy shouted, putting his hands alongside his legs and attempting an Irish kick dance which landed him on his tail-side in the dirt.

"Hah!" Moreau returned, pointing at the prostrate man from Munster, "I think I cannot do that, no!"

LeFevre's fiddle stopped. The others were all drinking, while his own throat was dry. He wanted to take a turn at the jug before it was all gone. It was handed over to him and he drank, wiped his mouth, handed the jug on to O'Donnell. As they passed it back and forth, slaking their terrible thirst, the two musicians agreed with each other that they were providing outstanding entertainment.

Not to be overlooked in all the fun, the fool Finn took it upon himself to fill the intermission with entertainment of his own. He wrapped his stained bandanna around his head so it covered one of his eyes, then he blackened his face with charcoal from the fire and took up a broken shovel handle to use as his iron bar.

"Call me Groodge!" Finn slurred. "*Waugh! Waugh!* Whar's some rocks what need breakin', anyway?" He pounded the ground with his stick and made his audience laugh. He smacked a small rock and yelled—"Ow!"—as he put his hands to his mouth, pretending he had injured himself. He hit the rock again, then picked it up and peered at it in amazement, uncovering his other eye. "It didn't break at all, the damn thing! *Waugh?*" He waddled around with his knees bent and legs apart, stumbling over things. More laughter. Finn squatted down like a frog, stood up again, and looked behind him, then gave the other men a wide-eyed look.

Paddy roared. O'Donnell shook so hard it seemed he would fall off his log.

Finn the fool began hurrying around in a circle, looking for rocks to smash, tripping and lurching and mumbling until he ran into a tree. At this the workmen applauded outrageously and cheered for more.

"*Waugh!*" he laughed. " 'Tis tough t'see where ye're at when y'got one eye gone!"

But there was no audience response to this last quip. The audience had gone quite silent, their holiday revels interrupted by two figures who had entered the proceedings. One was the Guardian, dark and serious. The other was the lady Fontana herself. The Irish whipped their caps from their heads while the Frenchmen bowed their heads slightly in her direction. Finn crept to a log and sat down.

"Paddy," Fontana said, "where is Grüdj?"

"I don't think we've seen him these two days at all,"

Paddy replied. "Any of you boys seen the black?"

There was no answer.

"I could go to his hut and find out if he's there," Paddy volunteered.

"*Do* that," she said. "When you find him, tell him I am going to the settlements and that I will speak to the government about his people."

"Yes, ma'am."

"I'm also going to order winter supplies and recruit more families for Crannog. If you are in need of anything, I want you to make out a list and give it to him." She indicated the Guardian standing next to her.

"Yes, ma'am."

"One more thing. No more of these cruel pantomimes. Of *anyone*."

"Yes, ma'am."

Paddy would not find Grüdj at the stone hut, for Grüdj had been climbing the ridge and was far above the ditch valley, on the very highest point of the ridge. While the ditch workers celebrated their day off, he had begun building a shelter in which to begin fasting and await his vision. There were wide, flat rocks all over the windswept ridge, ideal for making the walls of his fasting place. Grüdj made the wall curve in a circle enclosing a piece of tundra, just large enough to lie down in. The narrow opening faced in the direction of the sun's rising. When the wall was high enough, he searched out some longer stones to make a kind of roof, a little protection from rain and sun. That done, he dug a place in the ground to hide his pouch of food from animals. Another rock would cover it.

When Grüdj had his fasting place prepared, he took his iron bar and wiggled and wedged the point of it deeply into a crack in the rocks a few feet from the entrance to his shelter. It would be safe there. It was unlikely anyone else could pull it out again, he had jammed it in so hard. And then it was time to see if the vision would come.

Grüdj did not know what prayers to say. He had no offerings to make. He simply went into the shelter and sat down. He fixed his eye upon on the iron bar and waited.

Far away from the mountains, far out on the eastern plains, the smoke of the burning grass went on rising until it bent over in a streak across the blue sky. The mountain plateau to the north where the great medicine circle lay was wholly obscured by fog. Fog also hid the long slope of tundra to the south where the ditch ran. Invisible, too, was the big river of the mountains as it wound its way toward the red stone country and the bitter sea. The sun warmed the rocks of Grüdj's little shelter a while before slipping down the sky. For a time it left long shadows, then there was no sunlight but only a strange luminescence surrounding the ridge, and at last the darkness returned, and the cold, and Grüdj slept.

When the sun came up the eastern side of the sky, it peered in the door of Grüdj's shelter to awaken him. He stretched his limbs carefully and crawled out to stand upright. He drank water from his water skin and looked around him. The ridges and valleys on either side of the ridge were still hidden from sight, and a thick haze kept him from seeing the eastern horizon. Behind him, to the west, high clouds had begun to gather ominously over the peaks. Grüdj shivered and crept back into his circle of rocks. The afternoon passed, then the evening, and a wet mist came over the ridge during the night, driving its chill deeply into his body. At one point, he wanted to go search for fuel and make a fire, but since he could not force himself to leave what little comfort there was in the shelter, he only curled up and drowsed and shivered.

The second day brought the hungry rumblings in his stomach. He dozed or sat staring into space, sometimes watching the eagle circling the ridge, sometimes watching the tops of the clouds below him as they changed and drifted. By evening, he was tempted to eat something, just a little bite of jerky perhaps, but he fought off the desire and forced himself to think of other things. The night was not as cold and wet as the night before had been. More dreams came to fill his sleep, dreams of sitting in a warm lodge where a kettle of meat steamed over the fire, and dreams of walking the prairie. Grüdj even dreamed that he had long legs that carried him swiftly across the grass.

And then he dreamed that he had awakened and found a freshly killed fat rabbit at his feet, a gift from Luned.

The morning came at last, bringing bright sunshine to awaken and warm him. Grüdj unfolded his stiff legs and crawled from the shelter, limping his way to where the iron bar stood wedged in the rocks. Holding on to it as he looked into the morning sunlight, he spoke in the tongue of Crows Woman.

"Spirit of the sun, it is Grüdj. Spirit of Who Sees Far, it is Grüdj. Let me see the great medicine circle. I have come for a sign!"

He faced north.

"Mountains of the bear, show me a sign."

He faced west.

"Mountains where the sun sleeps, show me a sign."

He faced south.

"Direction of the buffalo, place where the water goes, I seek."

All that morning the thick dark figure stood alone on the summit of the long ridge, turning in one direction and then another. He muttered phrases he remembered from watching The People's rituals as a boy. Sometimes he spoke aloud or shouted, explaining the need of The People, and, as nightfall came and he went back into his rock shelter, Grüdj had a feeling of accomplishment. To his dreams that night came the faces of those he had known, the wise old face of Two Nose Thomas, the concerned face of Crows Woman, the anxious and questioning face of Standing Hollow Horn. Spirits of buffalo ran across his night dreams. Three Eagles led young men on a hunt. Grüdj dreamed that *he* was an eagle soaring over a big village of many fine lodges where women laughed and gossiped as they scraped hides and watched the children playing games in deep grass. He tried to see the lodge of Crows Woman but could not find it among the other lodges.

The following morning, something strange took place. The first light of dawn woke him just as it had before and he was glad to straighten his cold, cramped muscles and limp out to greet the sun. But on this morning, as soon as he was out of the shelter, his feet seemed weightless and detached. He wobbled back and forth as if he would fall down, yet his body seemed to have no substance. The whole world around him swam in a strange shimmering light, and, when he recovered his balance, he found that he could move across the rocks without effort.

Maybe in another day Grüdj will fly as in his dream, Grüdj thought.

His floating steps carried him toward the iron stick, but when he put out his hand to grasp it and steady himself, it was not there. He could see it, but it was not where his hand was. Grüdj corrected his position, took steps this way and that, feeling with his hand like a blind man until he touched the familiar cold metal. Clinging to it to keep from falling, he tried to think what to say to the sun. He felt dissolved, more spirit than flesh. He could see all the water everywhere, the small trickles flowing down from the ridge where they had been locked in snow and ice, the great river of the valley winding through cañons of red stone and spreading out at the edge of a lake that seemed to have no banks, the tiny threads of sluggish water that had once been wide, gentle streams flowing across the buffalo prairie. He saw Spirit Lake and saw a camp of The Enemy there beside it. He saw the smaller lake where the medicine lodge had gone, but he saw nothing of the warriors or the spirit woman. All the waters, even the waters he had released at the top of the world, were going along doing what they always did. He knew there was almost no water on the plains because the rains had not come. But in the mountains and on the other side of the mountains there was plenty. If he could speak to The People, he could tell them where to find it.

The thought of The People roused Grüdj from his trance. A dim boyhood memory told him he needed to address the sun before it went any higher up the sky. He would ask the sun to show him where the old gods were.

Before he could speak, however, he saw something even stranger than the iron stick seeming to be where it was not. Its shadow lay on the wrong side of it, stretching out along the rocks toward the south. Grüdj blinked his eye and looked around for his own shadow, which was behind him where it should be. It wavered and shimmered and was hard to keep in focus, but it was where it ought to be. And the shadows of the rocks were also where they should be. But the shadow of the stick pointed another direction. South and east. He sighted along the path of it, squinting to see farther in the morning glare. The shadow pointed toward the buffalo plains beyond the foot of the mountains.

He had not seen water in that direction. Had The People gone that way?

Grüdj began to lose the feeling of being weightless. He became heavier and heavier until all strength left his legs and he collapsed beside the iron stick, unable to rise. He was dizzy, helpless. Just before losing consciousness, he looked up into the sky and saw an eagle circling. Weakly he tried to call out to it.

"The old gods," he said. "Standing Hollow Horn's gods . . . go ask the sun where to look."

In his stupor there came once more the dream of the big village, of many lodges. As he floated above the center of the village, Grüdj saw hunters returning with antelope slung across their ponies' backs and old people slumbering in the warm sunshine. There were high stacks of good firewood and much meat hanging on the drying racks.

Then he saw the wagon people coming. The wagons wanted to go through the camp. A bluecoat soldier in a big hat went ahead of the wagons, and Grüdj heard him giving orders that The People were not to be permitted to touch the wagons. He threatened them with great harm, but, because he spoke in the language of the whites, The People could not understand him.

In the next instant, Grüdj saw a great wide road where the camp had been. The circle at the center of the village was pounded into dust. Many lodges lay trampled into the ground and others were burned so that only charred, smoldering poles remained.

A white man raised his rifle and pointed it at the eagle.

"Crack!" came the noise.

"Crack!" it came again. Grüdj felt the jolt in his chest and he was falling.

"Crack!"

With great effort, he turned his face toward the west, the direction of the loud noise. The sky over the high mountains was black. Dark, angry clouds rolled over each other like stampeding buffalo, or like the pouring rapids of a flooding river. Other clouds, long like tall trees, reached out from the boiling ones. To Grüdj, they were like the outstretched arms of a great bear and the thunder coming from deep within the mass was the bear's voice.

"Crack!"

Lightning flashed inside the bear-cloud's mouth. Lightning streaks traveled along the bear-cloud's arms and the beast walked on feet of lightning. Its breath was a freezing wind carrying hard hailstones.

"Crack!"

Grüdj rose, but stumbled in his weakness. He fell. Hail battered his shoulders. Jolts of lightning twitched at his flesh. He crawled and pushed himself across the rocks, now on his feet, now on his belly. As he folded himself into the deepest corner of his rock shelter, the lightning was so near he could smell it. With deafening explosions of thunder, it raked the ridge like many warriors shooting arrows of fire. Waves of hail pounded down around him until he clapped his hands over his ears in terror.

And outside the shelter, through the curtain of hail, he saw the glow of a faint light.

It was his iron bar, pulsing strangely yellow in the middle of the storm.

The storm continued for what seemed like days. Rain poured down. Thunder shook the valleys and peaks. There was mist all around him and then the rain would hit again.

Water ran from all the rocks. Water came in sheets across the flat tundra. Stinging hard rain washed the hail away until deep piles of it could be seen wherever there were crevices. Grüdj lowered his head and folded his arms tightly about himself to endure it. Sometimes he almost fell asleep only to be awakened by another bolt of lightning crackling across the ridge. Once he imagined the iron bar glowing red-hot and hissing as the rain struck it.

Night brought a steady, drenching rain that went on far into the morning. When the rain lessened, the wind rose up to blow clouds of mist across the barren tundra. A deep calm finally returned to the summit of the ridge before nightfall. Grüdj shivered and trembled in his sleep, dreaming of bears and roaring floods. The night sky cleared and the stars came out, and in his dreams he returned again to the buffalo plains, except now he was on foot and it was winter. He dreamed he walked and walked until he stood on a hill from which he could see many buffalo. The buffalo were walking south. Some hunters of The People followed after them, calling to them.

"Buffalo!" the hunters shouted. "Come back! Our children are hungry. Old people freeze because they have no robes. There are no hides for lodges, for moccasins. Come back!"

Grüdj tried to shout, too, but his voice was too weak to be heard.

"Buffalo! Follow me. Follow me in the other direction. I will bring water for you."

But the buffalo kept walking south.

Grüdj dreamed that he turned and saw The People milling about in confusion, going here and there without purpose, without hope. They tried to go where there would be no more wagon roads or soldier towns, wandering ever farther south where tall dry grass no longer stuck up above the snow. Where the snow had blown away, the ground was only sand. He looked for some sign of Crows Woman and Two Nose, but he saw none. They were not with the tribe. He saw The People leading a horse so thin its ribs stuck out, and the horse was dragging a travois on which there was a tightly wrapped bundle. In a wide, dry creekbed, they found a dead cottonwood tree, and in its branches they left the bundle. They went away, the long poles of the travois trailing in the sand.

When Grüdj woke, the sun was already high in the sky. Most of the piles of hail had melted away. Some of the rocks had dried. The eagle was gone, although a small hawk came up over the ridge, hovered on the air a while, and disappeared down the other side. Grüdj felt weak and sick. He needed food in his stomach. But when he saw the water skin hanging next to the shelter, he fought back the desire to eat. He would drink water instead. He was a water dreamer. Who Sees Far had said it. He would go without food for one more day. One more afternoon. At sunset he would eat.

So the water dreamer sat quietly, watching new clouds forming in the valley to the north. They rose quickly, swirling up into domes and cliffs of gray and white. Sometimes they turned into a vast range of floating mountains shimmering with different colors; sometimes the whole sky looked green or red and the clouds shimmered like magical rainbows. And as he sat and stared into the hypnotizing mass, Grüdj began to see the faces. A high, rounded cloud mass boiled up into the sky until it resembled a human head, and then it had a face. The face was that of Who Sees Far, pointing downward toward where the mountains leveled off before sloping down to the plains.

"Black One," Who Sees Far's face whispered to him. "Black One. Here is what you seek. Come, come this way. The great medicine circle is here."

Grüdj stared hard, but he saw nothing except mist and trees far below. Yet, the human head made of clouds hovered above the place where he had always thought the medicine circle would be.

"Black One, Grüdj," the face of Who Sees Far whispered. "You must come."

More faces, larger faces, materialized in the clouds behind Who Sees Far. It was a council. Grüdj recognized faces he had seen when he was a small boy, faces of men who had long ago gone to be with the gods.

"No," the oldest voice said. "No. This one did not respect the spirit lodge. This one, this black, he is not of The People. He is some other."

"No," agreed another voice. "He is some other. The power of the medicine circle is not for him. He cannot know the secret of the circle."

"No," said another. "He uses his strength for the white wagon road people to make this ditch."

Grüdj struggled to his feet and stood swaying weakly as if the earth were heaving beneath him.

"Hear me," he pleaded. "You know me. It is true I have seen where the spirit lodge goes. I know why the warriors and the water woman return to their lake. I will tell The People. It is true . . . I have helped the whites make their ditch. But I will bring water shares to The People."

"Come to the medicine circle," the face of Who Sees Far urged. But his voice was a faint hissing whisper from the clouds.

"No," said the eldest of the other faces. "It is not for

him. He is not of The People. Soon The People will come to the ancestors, and he will not be with them. I have said it. This one, this black, will follow the straight path of the whites. They will die and he will live."

"I would see the medicine circle," Grüdj insisted. "I would speak with the old gods of Who Sees Far and Three Eagles."

The cloud faces lingered a while, watching Grüdj in silence, then melted back down into the shapeless heaps of mist that were moving slowly down the valley. Grüdj stumbled along the ridge to seize his iron bar and pull it from the crevice. In his frustration, in his resentment of the powers that had led him here and then denied him, Grüdj raised his bar high above his head and brought it down on the earth with all his strength. He did not care if it split the whole ridge in half.

Nothing happened. The ringing noise of steel against granite echoed a moment along the empty tundra, and nothing else.

Chapter Fourteen

AFTER THE STORM

So this was the end of it.

After the terror of the angry bear, after the storms of lightning and thunder, after the rain and the starving, this was his message from the old gods of Standing Hollow Horn. He was never to stand in the medicine circle. He was never to take the prayers of The People to the old gods, nor would he carry any words from the gods back to The People.

He did not understand. The elder said The People would go under, but not Grüdj. The People would go to their ancestors, but he would not be with them. How could it be? Why would he go on living, when all the rest were with the dead?

The only thing he had learned from his fasting was that Grüdj, the water dreamer, was only a water dreamer. Nothing more.

He went slowly down the mountain, taking a long way around the place where he had been attacked by the bear and avoiding the steep slopes of loose rock. When night came, he sheltered beneath some tall trees and in the afternoon of the second day he came again to his little stone hut in the valley leading down to the water ditch.

A day later John O'Byrne came riding up Grüdj's creek and was glad to see the familiar toad-like shape sitting outside the hut. Grüdj was eating a rabbit he had roasted slowly over a small fire after catching it in one of his snares. O'Byrne raised his hand in greeting and got a nod in return, but no words passed between the two men until he had tied up his mule and sat down on the log next to Grüdj.

"It's good to see you back," he said.

"Umm," said Grüdj, savoring the mouthful of rabbit meat.

"Had some awful storms while you were gone, Groodge. See any of it, did you?"

"Umm," Grüdj answered. "Cold rain. Thunder. Up there." He gestured toward the ridge.

"Is *that* where you were, then? Up on the *ridge?*"

"Waugh."

"My God and the prophet Moses! Man, you could have been killed up there! The boys and me were working like devils to save the ditch and every time we looked to the mountain there was nothing but lightning and clouds boiling like the devil's own cauldron!"

Praw-phet. Cawl-drun. Grüdj did not know these words, but he was not interested. He used his teeth to strip the last bit of meat from a leg bone and tossed the bone into the fire.

"So you were up on that ridge all the week long," O'Byrne continued, marveling at the idea. " 'Tis a miracle you didn't meet your maker. It *is*."

Grüdj looked at O'Byrne, and the Irishman thought his eye looked older and wiser than it ever had before. There was sadness in that eye, too.

Grüdj studied Jonoburn's face while he searched for some words with which to empty his heart. But the words were not to be found, not in the language of the surveyor Thatcher, not in the talk of Two Nose Thomas, not even in the language of The People.

"You went all the way up there looking for your magic again, I guess," O'Byrne said. "I figured it might be the case. Well, never mind all that, old Groodge. Never mind all that. Let's you and me go on down to the ditch together, for the storms left us with a power of work to be done. We need that strong back of yours, and no doubt about it. You never saw such silt as washed down. And logs! Didn't whole trees come right down the creeks into the ditch? Come along now."

When they reached the ditch path and walked upstream looking for the work crew, Grüdj saw that Jonoburn had not stretched the truth at all. Just around the first bend a heavy dead snag jutted up out of the ditch. It was a weathered old log, polished to a pewter color and made hard and dry by decades of tundra winds. Grüdj took hold of a thick branch and pulled with all his strength, but the snag did not move.

"Can't shift it," said Jonoburn. "Didn't figure you could. It's going to take two men and a good whipsaw. Cutting her into chunks is the only way we'll get it out. Come on."

They next came to a place where there was another tree, one that had been green and living when the flash flood tore the earth and rocks from around its roots and carried it down to the ditch.

"Would you look at that silt," Jonoburn said. The evergreen's branches had blocked up enough silt to fill a couple of wagons.

"And I don't think the scraper can shift it, either," the Irishman said. "Thick, wet stuff it is. Men with shovels, that's what's needed."

And so they went, finding spot after spot where there was silt to remove or logs to cut and haul out of the ditch. Once they held their noses because of the stink of a rotting bighorn carcass caught in a tangle of driftwood. In places the banks had eroded and would have to be shored up with rock. The work crew was already doing just that, repairing a part of the ditch bank upstream of Gate Number One. Grüdj saw that his log gate was still halfway open, as he had left it, and it had held firm—although it might have been better if it had broken and released all the flood water down the valley.

"Paddy! Finn!" Jonoburn called out. "Look who I found!"

Glad for any reason to stop wrestling with blocks of stone, Paddy and Finn and the other men climbed up out of the ditch to greet Grüdj. A couple of them took advantage of the work break to pack their stubby briar pipes with shreds of foul-smelling black tobacco and light up.

"So"—Paddy grinned—"not drowned, are ye? Where in blazes did ye get to?"

Grüdj pointed toward the distant ridgeline.

"Ah?" Paddy nodded. "On top o' the ridge, is it? Well, count your lucky stars none of that lightnin' struck 'ee. It cracked and tore 'round our cabin like the banshee herself. An' didn't it hit that big ol' spruce tree? Why, slivers flew as big's my leg, just like ye'd blown 'er up with blastin' powder."

"True," Finn added. "Miracle that none of the animules was hit. And weren't we praying like all get-out, Paddy?"

" 'Tis true. Some of the boys here hadn't been on their knees since they was confirmed, but they were doin' their genuflecktin' that night!"

"The ditch," Grüdj said. "All broken? Done for?"

"Done for?" O'Byrne asked. "What makes you think that? No, Groodge, it isn't done for, not at all. We just need to spend the rest of this season putting things right is all. A little delay. No need of you looking so worried."

Finn winked at Paddy. "Ol' Groodge, he's worried for his shares he is."

Paddy grinned broadly. He and Finn had long since lost any faith or hope in this scheme of getting shares of water and land for their work. As long as they were paid in food and hard cash, they kept working. Being shanty Irish and having first-hand experience with the prejudices of the Christian world, they found it supremely amusing for a black man to think he could claim farm land and hand it over to a bunch of Indians.

"I'm thinkin' you'll be too old t'farm your land by the time ye get it, Groodge." Finn laughed. "Miles to go, this ditch has. Miles to go. And us able t'work it but three months of th' twelve."

"And if you don't all get back to work, we'll be *another* season just repairing this section here above timberline," O'Byrne said. "All right, boys. Stir your shanks. I want this bank fixed by afternoon, and I'll see you getting started on shoveling the muck out of it by nightfall. Grüdj, let's you and I look over the rest of the ditch and see where we might best use you."

Grüdj and O'Byrne returned down the ditch the way they had come, O'Byrne stopping from time to time to write things in his pocket notebook. The spruce at the cabins was not the only tree struck by lightning; as they approached timberline, Grüdj saw one tree broken in half and another that looked as if it had exploded. Gate Number Two was intact, although the water had forced it part way open.

"Can you fix it?" Jonoburn asked.

"Yes," Grüdj said. "Tomorrow."

O'Byrne caught up his mule, which he had left to graze in Grüdj's valley, and he led it by the reins as they went on with their inspection. The next diversion ditch looked unharmed, mostly because Grüdj had not yet figured out a gate to put there. It was clear to see, however, that most of the flood water had gone out the opening and off through the trees, heading toward the new lake. Grüdj climbed down into the ditch, waded across the thick silt that sucked and pulled at his feet, and hauled himself up the other side.

"Grüdj goes to see what the water did," he said.

On the ditch path O'Byrne put his foot in the stirrup and swung into the saddle. "Sounds good," he said, waving across the ditch to Grüdj. "I'll see you down at the work cabins, then. I brought the fixings for a proper supper. You're welcome to share."

"Thank 'ee," Grüdj said.

Silt clogged the whole diversion channel. Silt and mud. Wherever driftwood had jammed among the trees or hung up on the rocks, there was silt so deep it filled the channel up to the rim. The water still ran, but it ran through a meandering trench it had dug in the silt for itself. And when Grüdj saw the little lake in the meadow, he felt his heart go cold, for what had been a shining pool of crystal water mirroring white aspen trunks and dark green spruce trees was now a basin of sodden mud, mud that smelled like rotting things. He remembered how Luned had emerged from it and had submerged herself in it again, a sight that now seemed ages ago.

The ditch water went sluggishly across the muck and vanished down into the trees on the other side of the basin. Grüdj walked around to the place where the water flowed out and tried to see where it was going. It was not going to the big river. Instead, it went down into some other dark, steep valley. He touched his iron bar to it.

"Water!" he said in the tongue of The People. "It is

Grüdj. I have been to where the mountain catches you. I know why you are angry. Soon you will have the ditch to take you to the buffalo prairie. I have said it."

The water went on slipping over the edge of the meadow and running down into the woods, indifferent and silent.

"Water!" Grüdj said again. "Speak to me. Where are you going? Is it to the prairie of the buffalo? They need you. I have seen the smoke of grass burning. Take the rain to the prairie."

But the water had no words to say to Grüdj, the water dreamer. It went its way in mystery, following whatever course it could, answering to no one. Grüdj thought of Luned and wondered where she was, half expecting to see the white shape moving in the forest. If she was anywhere near, he could not see her. He took his bar and turned his steps back toward the ditch and toward the work cabins. Maybe Jonoburn was already cooking supper. Maybe he had brought potatoes and some of the butter from Crannog, the kind with the grains of salt in it. A good supper, then a tight warm cabin in which to sleep—if the Guardian had gone to Crannog. Grüdj hurried along the ditch path through the forest, using his iron bar as a walking staff, still watching for some sign of Luned among the trees.

Either John O'Byrne's assessment of the ditch damage had been far too pessimistic, or the repair crew had worked overtime just to get back to the comforts of cabins and decent meals. Whichever the case, it was just over two weeks later when they returned to the work site down in the trees at the ditch face. They found Grüdj making some progress along the survey line, but it was obvious that he was now working harder at it. In places they found he had drilled holes in the rock for blasting powder rather than splitting the rocks with his magic steel. In other places the rocks were broken in half but still lying in the way of the scrapers as if he had been unable to shift them to one side.

Paddy went in search of the strange black man and found him more than a mile down the survey line, hammering away at a rock. It split just as Paddy walked up, but Paddy could see that Grüdj was sweating and breathing hard with exertion.

"There y'be, ol' Groodge!" he called out amiably.

Grüdj leaned on his steel bar and looked at him.

"Ye're a good way from th' diggin's, ye are," Paddy said. "Workin' all alone down here?"

"Jonoburn has gone to Crannog," Grüdj said. "The man who came to make food is at the cabins."

"Ah! That'd be the Frenchy the old man hired, would it? O'Byrne said he'd have us a decent cook, time we got quit with th' fixin' of the ditch. So how's his food?"

"Bad," Grüdj said. "All bad. What is the place Jonoburn makes food come?"

"Y'mean the garden? Down at Crannog?"

"Garden," Grüdj said. "This one you call Frenchy, he brings strange food from there. Plants. White and fat. Round things, too." Grüdj made gestures with his hands as if he were shaping a large globe.

Paddy mimicked him. "Cabbage?" Paddy exclaimed. "Honest to God cabbage, you're sayin'?"

"Bad," Grüdj said. "He spoils all meat. Boils plants too soft. Bad."

"Didn't ye tell 'im ye're a ol' mountain man and likes your meat tough and half cooked then?"

"*Waugh!*" Grüdj said, and almost smiled. "Thet don't shine, no! Thet coon kain't palaver mountain talk a-tall. Two Nose, he'd say 'hyars pore bull fer certain sure.' "

Paddy laid a sympathetic hand on Grüdj's shoulder. "So the food ain't t'your likin'. I'll be lookin' into it for ye," he said. "I'll be gettin' back t'the boys now and we'll see what the Frenchy has in mind for supper. Will y'be there?"

"Waugh," Grüdj said. "One more rock and Grüdj will come."

The early evening light was upon the forest by the time Grüdj gave up trying to break another boulder with his iron stick and began walking back toward the work camp, dragging the bar behind him. In among the trees, there was a soft dampness to the pine-scented air and the deepening shadows seemed welcoming and serene. From time to time, a bird flicked into sight and vanished again; small squirrels saw the strange figure lumbering toward them and scurried up the nearest tree.

A tiny stream flowed over the two-track road, scarcely enough water to wet the feet. Indeed, some of the men leaped across it without stepping in it at all. Grüdj always looked forward to seeing it again as he went back to the camp, particularly the small pool it made back in the shadows above the road. Twice before this, by leaving his iron stick standing against a tree and approaching the water carefully, he had been able to listen to what it was saying. Now he once more paused for a drink, placing his stick by the tree while he bent down to cup the water to his mouth. It was cold and pure.

"Come," the tiny stream said to him as he bent for a second palmful of water.

"Someone is here," it murmured. "Come."

Grüdj looked back at his iron stick. He didn't feel right leaving it behind. But instinct told him the water would be afraid of his iron stick and would not speak to him if he carried it.

"Come," the water whispered again.

Grüdj stepped through the willows that screened the small pool. And there was Luned.

She stood in the middle of the pool. The water was scarcely deep enough to come above her ankles, yet she held her white dress clear up around her hips. It had also slipped from one shoulder to expose a pale breast. Grüdj had not seen her since his journey to the top of Spirit Ridge and even now, in the twilight gloom of the forest, he was not completely certain she was real.

"Grüdj has dreamed of me?" she taunted. He did not answer. "Perhaps Grüdj remembers seeing me at the lake? Remembers many times, every day? How I looked?"

"No," he said. "Grüdj minds how Luned made meat come. Deer, rabbits. Good meat."

Luned laughed with glee, her white teeth gleaming as she pulled the shoulder of her dress up to cover herself. "You want fresh meat! Is *that* why your work goes so slowly, so badly? Is that why you grow tired? Because you want more meat? Sometimes I watch you when you do not know it."

"Where is the meat?" Grüdj asked.

"Where is Fontana?" Luned laughed again. "*She* is the one who tells me to kill deer for you. She is the precious source of everything. She decides. Now she has gone away, I cannot trouble myself about Grüdj being hungry. Father has hired someone to cook for you and the others at the work camp. You are a workman now, and you must eat like one."

Grüdj reached down and cupped another handful of water to drink. The water wriggled between his fingers as if afraid, anxious to be on its way. *"Waugh!!"* Grüdj shouted at Luned, or her apparition. "Then be done wi' ye!"

Her only reply was to turn her back on him and begin

walking up the stream among the willows, until the white of her skin and dress melted into the gloom of the forest. In an instant, she was gone.

Grüdj stomped down the creekbed, his feet raising swirls of sand. He grabbed up his bar and hurried on down the road. The damp tracks left by his moccasins lingered only a few minutes before being absorbed by the dust and evaporating into the air.

Several days later, Grüdj was once again returning to camp for the night when he saw four animals in the corral that had not been there that morning. He recognized one as the tall, well-groomed riding horse of the Guardian. One was a pack mule and the other two were just nondescript horses. The Guardian himself was standing outside the new cabin. When he saw Grüdj approaching, he stuck his head in the door and said something Grüdj could not hear.

Fontana stepped out. "Grüdj!" she said. "I am back! It's so good to see you again!"

Grüdj only made his *"Ummph"* reply, but the woman thought he looked glad to see her, too.

"I'm afraid we must put you out of the cabin for a few days," she said. "John says there are some extra bunks among the crew? I hope you won't mind sleeping with them."

Grüdj said nothing.

"And, we have a guest with us," Fontana continued. "I met him as I was traveling back to Crannog . . . you might say our paths literally crossed . . . and he agreed to pay a visit to my workmen and their families. He's a priest, you see. We met, and we were talking, and then John happened to mention *you*. As soon as he heard John's description of you, he was anxious to come and talk to you."

A moment later, a tall, spare figure dressed all in black emerged from the trees behind the cabin.

"Oh, here he is now!" Fontana said. "Father Janson, this is the man John told you about. This is Grüdj."

Grüdj looked at the stranger, and knew him immediately. He was suddenly a youth again, standing among the lodges of The People. Children laughed and played. Old men gossiped. Warriors painted shields, braided bridles. There was the smell of wood smoke and meat cooking. Two Nose was there, and so was Crows Woman.

Grüdj reached into his shirt and drew out the tarnished brass medallion. He held it up on its cord for visitor to see. "Black Robe," Grüdj said.

"Holy Jesus!" the stranger said, pressing his hands together as if in prayer. "It's true! *This* is the boy! I remember the very day I made that medallion for him."

And then his voice grew quiet, somber. He and Fontana looked at each other as if they shared some secret and awful knowledge.

"I remember the day," he repeated. "They were such happy people then. They went out and killed buffalo, and then there was feasting and joy. I remember seeing old people sitting in the sunshine with bowls of boiled meat in their laps, smiling as if they'd been blessed by God. There was a beautiful little stream running beside the village, and I baptized some of the youth. Everyone was happy."

Grüdj knew the day.

"Grüdj, tell me," Fontana said, "when did you last see your people? Can you remember how many years it is? Do you remember where they were, or where they might have gone?"

Grüdj closed his eye. He sent his mind images traveling back through the days of his long journey. His lips moved as if he were recounting the story to himself. He traveled through two freezing times? No. Three winters? His stubby fingers moved one by one as he counted with them, remembering building the log hut with Two Nose, making a crude medicine lodge by the river, the time with Thatcher at the place on top of the world, on The Enemy trail. He finally had all four of his fingers extended. He opened his eye and looked at Fontana.

"Four?" she said. "Four years?"

Grüdj knew the word *year.* Two Nose had told it to him. Twelve moons. But it had little real meaning.

"No," he said, meaning he did not know.

Grüdj felt the empty stomach feeling again, like when he was making his fasting. Thinking about the village, thinking about The People, he felt as lonely as when he had camped alone beside the big river. These people standing around the work camp meant nothing; they might as well have been trees, or rocks. Grüdj wanted to see the village again, *his* village, his place. Seeing Black Robe brought it all back to him; he did not belong here, making a water road for the whites. He must return to The People, make peace for offending the spirit lodge, and live in the lodge of Crows Woman and Two Nose Thomas. And, if the elder who spoke from clouds was speaking the truth, and The People were going to "go under" and join the ancestors, Grüdj would be with them.

It was the only life he could imagine. It was the only life that made any sense.

Fontana interrupted his thoughts. "Grüdj," she said very softly, reaching out to touch his arm. "Do you know how the whites call your people? What tribe they say you are?"

Grüdj looked blank.

"Did the whites call them Kiowa? Pawnee? Crow?"

"Not Crow!" he said sharply. "Not Crow! No!" The Crow were enemies. Two Nose Thomas always had to spit upon the ground whenever he said the word.

"What, then?"

Grüdj looked off into the trees, where the fading light was making the forest into a wall of darkness. This talk was over. He would eat, and sleep, and in the morning he would begin his journey to find The People.

"Grüdj!" She pulled hard at his sleeve. "Grüdj! This is important! You must know what they were called, the people you used to live with!"

He looked at her. He wanted to show her his impatience, but her face wore a concerned look that softened him. He remembered the evenings with her outside his stone hut, when she had spoken of many things. And he had spoken of many things, too.

"White Buffalo People?" he said at last. "A boy came once, a runner, a Shea-e-ahla, and called us Travelers-After-Buffalo."

"Not Arapaho?" Fontana asked the question with her heart in her throat.

Grüdj stared straight ahead, thinking. *Ah-rah-pah-ho. Arapaho.* There was some kind of memory of that word, but he could not get hold of it.

Fontana waited for him to answer, her hand clutched at her bosom. Grüdj saw Black Robe put his hand on her shoulder as if to comfort her.

"Maybe," Grüdj said at last.

"One hunter man came for Two Nose. Trapper, him. Trader. This one who came said . . . 'Two Nose, y'old coon, thar's *compañeros* what say ye'd druther cache with th' 'Rapho than make tracks fer white man rendezvous. Thet don't shine with some.' "

"You remembered all that?"

"Yes. He was a red hair."

"And he said Arapaho?"

"No. 'Rapho.' "

Fontana looked at Black Robe, who looked softly back again and gently squeezed her shoulder. Neither of them spoke, and after a long silence Grüdj asked his question. He had been waiting many days to find out if The People were to have shares of the water. Now that he had made up his mind to go and find them, the shares did not seem to matter. But, if water meant a place he could take them to, it would be good. Water made deep grass, fat buffalo. The village would be happy again.

"Did Fontana . . . ?" he began awkwardly, for among The People it was not considered polite to ask direct questions.

"Yes?" she said. Her voice sounded as though she were choking back some tears.

"Did Fontana speak for The People?" Grüdj asked. "About shares, water? Will the council of the wagon people allow shares for The People?"

"Grüdj, I did ask. I found out that the territorial government *can* set aside land for Indians, provided they are sponsored."

"Spawn-soar-d?"

"You and I can talk about it later," she said. "First, you must speak with Reverend Janson. What did your people call him?"

"Black Robe. He who brought the buffalo to The People."

"You and Black Robe speak. Then we will have supper. Then you and I will talk. Will you talk to him, Grüdj? For me?"

Puzzled, Grüdj only nodded.

He and the priest went apart from the workmen and the camp until they found a log where they could sit alone together. Black Robe again put his hands together and looked up into the sky and did not speak for several minutes. It was Grüdj who finally broke the silence, although he still knew he was being rude.

"Has Black Robe been to The People?"

"What? Oh. You want to know if I've seen them. A while ago. Last summer."

"Crows Woman? Two Nose Thomas?"

"No," the minister said sadly. "I am afraid they have gone."

"To the ancestors?" Grüdj asked. "To the spirits?"

It was inconceivable to Grüdj that his parents might be dead. He could not envision them wrapped in death bundles.

"I can't tell you that," the priest said. "All I know is that they left The People and went off on their own. While I was in your village, She Who Hides told me Crows Woman and Two Nose Thomas went away to find something to do. Hunting was very bad. She Who Hides thought Two Nose might return to trapping. No one knows where they went."

"*Waugh,*" Grüdj muttered.

This was like Two Nose, to go off wandering again. Grüdj could not imagine him dead, but he could imagine him sitting with other mountain men, doing the palaver, trading skins for gunpowder, trading moccasins made by Crows Woman.

"It was Two Nose who gave you your name," Black Robe said. "Before I made that medallion for you."

Having said that, the priest changed from white talk to using the tongue of The People. His grasp of the language had matured and he no longer sounded like a little child when he spoke.

"Tell me, Grüdj, when the one called Two Nose gave you your name, did he also speak of your father, of your mother?"

"It is the way of The People," Grüdj said, "that a good friend of a child's father should be the one to give the child a name. A warrior or shaman is best. Two Nose has strong powers. He makes the beaver come even if he is not of The People, but white like the wagon road people."

"But when you were named, did Two Nose tell where you came from?" asked Black Robe.

"Waugh," Grüdj said in trapper talk, so as to sound like Two Nose. "On the peraira. By the wagon road. Grüdj's father was gone under. His mother was gone under."

"Did Two Nose say Grüdj was a child of the wagon people?"

"Yes. But Grüdj's father went under. His mother, gone under. The wagon people threw Grüdj away. Now he belongs to The People."

The priest looked at him sadly. Grüdj went on talking.

"Grüdj knows why Black Robe has come here," he said. "Black Robe comes to bring Grüdj to The People, as Black Robe brought the buffalo to the village. Black Robe will rest here, eat meat, talk to the Irish. Make medals for the Irish to wear. Then Grüdj and Black Robe will go to The People and bring them for shares of this water. And land."

"Shares," Black Robe said. "Fontana has told me about your plan to get land and farms for The People. But Black Robe needs to know one thing more."

Grüdj listened politely. The priest made one more effort to determine who the black man had lived with. Maybe, through a miracle of God, it was a small group wandering apart from the rest. He had heard, somewhere, that a man named Standing Hollow Horn led such a group.

"What did . . . ?" Black Robe began. "That is, does the word clan mean anything to you? Do you know about the blue stone people?"

Grüdj actually smiled.

"Blue stone, me!" he said excitedly. "Other villages call The People that name. People of the blue stones. Grüdj's people. Where did Black Robe see them? How many days from where we are?"

"It is too many days, Grüdj," Black Robe replied. "I will tell you the story now."

And he told how The People gradually drifted south, just as Grüdj had seen in his dream, hoping again to find the vast earth-shaking herds of buffalo, always trying to put a greater distance between themselves and the wagon roads, and the soldier villages. The People moved this way and that, now living near the mountains, now living far out on the plains. But always their pony tracks led south. Finally they came to where the rivers were made of dry sand and the grass was meager. Their lodges were wearing out. New lodge poles were needed, but no one knew how to go to the mountains without starting a fight with white men.

Hunger walked among the lodges, making the babies cry and the old ones sad.

Grüdj nodded. He had seen the same things in his dream. "It will be many days," Grüdj said. "We will find them again. We will go to them. We will bring The People here and they will have water, and the buffalo will come where the water is. Water makes the grass grow, grass brings the buffalo."

"No, Grüdj. No." Once more the sad-eyed priest raised his hands toward heaven for guidance. "There was a place where the river was all sand," he said. "The People came there. The soldiers came there. There was a fight. All wiped out."

Grüdj looked into the face of Black Robe without comprehending. He did not understand what the priest was saying to him.

"The People are with their ancestors," Black Robe said. "Soldiers killed them all. Children, women, old people, all. Soldiers hunted them all down and killed them in the sand."

Fontana saw Father Janson coming toward the fire circle alone. The workers were chatting and laughing as they ate, but Fontana and John O'Byrne sat alone, speaking in hushed voices. She had finished telling him her fears, and what she knew about the massacre on that dry sand creek out on the plains. She looked behind Father Janson to see if Grüdj would be following. She saw only the shadow of a thick, squat figure disappearing into the darkening forest.

Minutes passed, and then they heard the sound of the iron bar, banging on the rocks.

About the Author

James C. Work was born in Colorado where his family had lived for three generations. His mother's grandparents were in Leadville and Cripple Creek during the gold rush days, while his father's forebears were pioneer farmers on Colorado's eastern plains. He grew up in Estes Park and attended Colorado State University and the University of New Mexico, and holds degrees from both. He taught literature at Colorado State University. Work has received awards from the Western Literature Association, the Colorado Seminars in Literature, the Charles Redd Center for Western Studies, and the Frank Waters Association for Southwest Writing. He is the editor of the classic textbook, *Prose and Poetry of the American West*, and, in addition to writing Western fiction and editing Western literature, he has published a collection of essays titled *Windmills, The River and Dust: One Man's West.* His expertise in English and American literature merged with his interest in Western history to produce the Keystone Ranch series of novels, beginning with *Ride South to Purgatory* (Five Star Westerns, 1999). Here history mingles with allegory, myth finds foundation in fact, and the ancient tales of King Arthur's knights find new life as Work shapes them into chronicles of the Keystone Ranch. Each novel in the series takes a unique approach to the West of the later 1800s, yet every novel is grounded in historical research and flavored with archetype and myth. For fans of the mystery genre there is Work's other series in which a professor at a Western university solves murder cases through his knowledge of literature, and include *The Tobermory Manuscript* (Five Star Westerns, 2000) and *A Title to Murder* (Five Star Westerns, 2004). Work lives in Fort Collins, Colorado. Additional information concerning his works may be found on his website: jameswork.com. His next Five Star Western will be *Grubline Rider*.